CARRION SAFARI

JONAH BUCK

SEVERED PRESS
HOBART TASMANIA

CARRION SAFARI

In Xanadu did Kubla Khan
A stately pleasure-dome decree:
Where Alph, the sacred river, ran
Through caverns measureless to man
Down to a sunless sea.
So twice five miles of fertile ground
With walls and towers were girdled round;
And there were gardens bright with sinuous rills,
Where blossomed many an incense-bearing tree;
And here were forests ancient as the hills,
Enfolding sunny spots of greenery.

But oh! that deep romantic chasm which slanted
Down the green hill athwart a cedarn cover!
A savage place! as holy and enchanted
As e'er beneath a waning moon was haunted
By woman wailing for her demon-lover!

"Kubla Khan"
-Samuel Taylor Coleridge

ONE
DENIAL, ANGER, BARGAINING, & ACCEPTANCE: STAGES OF CONTRACTS

June 6, 1925

Denise DeMarco woke up to the sound of pounding on her office door. She sat up in the chair she'd fallen asleep in, her back creaking in protest as she did so. An empty bottle of whiskey sat on the desk, right next to a small puddle of drool where her head had rested during the night.

The sun sent creepers of light around the edges of her office curtains, indicating that it was well into morning and probably closer to noon. She squinted against the feeble tendrils of sunlight, wishing for something to blot out the sun. A cloud. A plague of locusts. Anything would do.

"Go away. We're closed," she called to whoever was rapping at her door. Her head felt like a swarm of centipedes wearing steel-toed boots were trying to kick her skull apart from the inside. While the sound of her own voice was enough to make her wince a little, the knocking on her door sounded like it was coming from a battering ram. Right now, she just wanted to curl up somewhere and let the world carry on without her for a decade or two, just so long as it did so quietly.

The pounding stopped, as if whoever was out there was surprised they'd finally gotten a response. Then it started right back up again.

"Ms. DeMarco? I'd like to speak with you," a voice called through the door.

"We're closed, pal. If you're looking for a safari tour or big game hunt, there's plenty of other places in Cape Town."

DeMarco & Company Hunting Tours had been closed for months now, in fact. Before that, it had been one of the most successful safari companies in South Africa.

But that was months ago. Now, Denise had shuttered the place, and she was so deep in debt she couldn't see the surface anymore. She'd been living in the upstairs room since she stopped paying rent at her house and was kicked out by the landlord.

She was the "& Company" part of DeMarco & Company. Her father, Cedric DeMarco, was the original man behind the company. He'd come down to South Africa from England during the Second Boer War to administer a military refugee camp and never returned to the United Kingdom.

Instead, he took his experience in the bush and started a safari business for tourists who wanted to hunt African big game. Denise was his only child, and she'd taken over the business when he disappeared on a hunt a few years ago.

"Ms. DeMarco, I would very much like to speak with you. I've been told you're the best hunter in Cape Town."

"I *was* the best hunter in Cape Town. *Was.* Now go away." Even if her head still felt like it had been kicked down the street by an entire marching band and then run over by a float, the black haze of sleep was starting to recede from her brain. She tried to hang onto it and go back into her hibernation, but the voice outside kept talking.

"I've been instructed to deal only with you."

Denise wiped away the puddle of drool on her desk with her sleeve and opened up a drawer. She stuffed the dead bottle of whiskey inside, where it clinked against a couple more empties. Grimacing at the kink in her back from sleeping stooped over last night, she dragged herself to her feet. Her spine crackled like a string of wet firecrackers as she lurched upright.

The voice outside was American. Denise heard plenty of accents when she worked as a hunter, guiding the rich and famous through the veldt to find the perfect trophy. She spoke English as well as Afrikaans, the form of Dutch the Boer settlers in the country's interior used. In addition, she had a working knowledge of the Bantu languages, mostly Zulu and Xhosa, which was often useful in the field.

This voice had the trimmed, nasally quality that was the calling card of the American Northeast. A hint of something else flavored the words, maybe some vestigial Bronx or Boston that even prep schools couldn't quite scrub out of the palette.

That accent was only going to get more nasally if she broke the nose of whoever was refusing to leave her alone. She plodded across the room, stomping in the boots she'd never bothered to take off last night. *Stomp stomp stomp.* Quite frankly, she was not a happy camper, and she didn't want to deal with some rich twerp who wanted a stuffed lion's head above his mantle.

She threw open the door and leveled a glare that was meant to punch straight out of the back of the interloper's head. Her glare shriveled into a squint as soon as she opened the door, and the bright African sunlight shoved daggers into her eyes.

Her scowl wouldn't have blown out the back of her visitor's skull anyway. He was quite tall, and she found herself glowering at the knot in his tie before adjusting her sight upward.

He didn't even do her the courtesy of allowing her dirty look to scour the flesh off his face. Instead, he simply reached into a pocket and produced a business card. She took it without looking at it. If she just kept her focus, maybe her mental powers would kick in, and she could at least boil his eyeballs out of his head.

If her visitor noticed she was trying to explode his skull with her mind, he gave no heed to the fact. "Ah, Ms. DeMarco. It's a pleasure to meet you. I'd like to discuss a certain business matter with you."

"I'm not open for business. Now scram."

"Maybe not, but I have it on good authority that you're in arrears on your payments for your office here, and I also understand you've been removed from your residence for failure to tender rent payments as well. Your bank says they'll be taking this place within a week."

That took some of the wind out of her sails. She calculated the date in her head and realized the man was right. Over the last few weeks, she'd lost track of time. She'd be on the street no later than Friday.

However, that still didn't mean she would go on a hunt with this schmuck. The few hundred dollars just wasn't worth it to her.

Obviously, this fellow heard she was out of the business but thought he could wrangle her into a deal with a bit of hardball.

She looked down at the business card in her hand. The name of a company she'd never heard of, Yersinia Bioresearch, was printed in big bold letters on the top of the card. Beneath that was the man's name, Roger Pick.

"My finances are my business, and I don't do hunts anymore," she said.

Pick raised his hands, and for the first time, Denise noticed he was carrying a small briefcase. A chain led from the handle of the case to Pick's wrist, and Denise realized he was handcuffed to the briefcase.

Casting a brief glance over his shoulder to make sure no one was watching, Pick opened up the briefcase an inch and tilted it toward Denise. She caught sight of neat, crisp bills stacked on top of each other.

"There's ten thousand dollars in this case, and there could be a lot more if you're willing to help my organization with something." Pick flashed a winning smile that showcased a set of perfectly white teeth.

Denise reached out and grabbed something propped next to the doorframe. She leveled the shotgun at Pick's chest.

"Listen, I don't know what sort of shady business you're into, but I know trouble when I see it. People don't just walk up to your door with ten thousand dollars unless they're up to something, and I don't want any part in it. I didn't want any part of it when I thought you just wanted to go on a hunt, but now I just want you out of my sight. Go." She gestured with the shotgun to emphasize her point. Pick didn't need to know the weapon wasn't loaded.

"Wait," Pick threw up his hands, his eyes staring down both barrels. "This…this isn't what you seem to think it is. I just want to hire you for an expedition. Have you ever heard of Yersinia?"

"Not before you handed me your card."

Pick spoke quickly. "We're a medical research firm. Based in New York. We develop medicines and pharmaceuticals. They sent me out here to talk to you. Herschel Hobhouse wants to hire you for an expedition. I'm just supposed to get you to sign on." Pick's voice dropped most of the clipped, upper-class polish and reverted to pure Bronx.

"Ten thousand dollars for a single expedition? I don't believe you," Denise said. But a part of her did believe him. That was real fear in the man's eyes.

However, that still didn't mean what he was saying made any sense. The only people who ever approached her with that kind of money before were smugglers and poachers, and they'd scampered away when she put the business end of a shotgun in front of their noses. Even when she was the most in demand hunter in Cape Town, she didn't receive anywhere near that amount of money for a single hunt.

Now she didn't hunt at all. She lowered the shotgun but didn't put it away.

"Mr. Hobhouse had heard of you, and he specifically requested you for this excursion."

"Who is Herschel Hobhouse?"

"He's Yersinia's new head of research and development. He very specifically asked for you. All this money comes from Yersinia, and it can all be yours if you come with us for this project." Now that he didn't have a gun practically stuck up his nostrils, Pick had reverted to some of his salesman pitch. Denise almost preferred him when he thought he was about to die.

"I already told you. I don't do hunts anymore," she said. She started to shut the door on Pick, but she took one last glance down at the stacks of cash still visible inside his briefcase.

Sensing his opening, Pick pounced. "But this isn't a hunt," he said, placing his foot in the door to prevent her from shutting him out. "You don't even have to fire a gun, and you can still get the ten thousand."

"Uh huh. You don't come to the office of the best hunter in Cape Town and offer her ten thousand dollars for something that isn't a hunt. Don't piss in my lap and tell me it's raining."

"The best hunter in Cape Town? I thought you *were* the best hunter in Cape Town, Ms. DeMarco." Pick grinned as if he'd just scored a point.

Denise internally debated taking the shotgun and loading it. There was some ammo in a cabinet nearby. She'd had about enough of this joker and his benefactor, Mr. Hobhouse.

"You have five seconds to tell me what you really want, or I'm going to shoot you, stuff you, and use you as a piece of office décor," she said.

The smile fell off Pick's face like the wind tearing a cheap sign off a building. "I can't. Not right away."

"Five."

"It's more complicated than that. That's the reason there's so much money involved."

"Four."

"Hobhouse instituted a policy. This is top secret stuff for Yersinia. No one else can know. Absolutely no one."

"Three."

"Look, please. Just hold on a second. Wait." Pick reached into his jacket and pulled out an envelope.

"Two."

"You have to sign this non-disclosure agreement. Then I can tell you what this is about. You have to trust me. This is completely on the level. I just need your legally binding agreement to keep this a secret first. That's all. Please. Just give me a chance."

Denise sighed. Despite her better judgment, she was curious. She was very curious indeed. More than that, she was about to be kicked onto the street.

She glanced down at the briefcase full of money again and bit her lip. Pick smiled again. This time, he actually had scored a point, much as Denise hated to admit it to herself.

That briefcase had its hooks in her. Frankly, she was pretty sure she didn't want anything to do with Yersinia or Herschel Hobhouse or non-disclosure agreements or anything else that the man at her front door was promising. On the other hand, she knew damn well that she was slowly sinking into the quicksands of oblivion here. She barely had enough money left to feed herself, let alone keep herself from being tossed out on the street in the next few days.

In theory, she could do something else. She didn't want to hunt anymore, but she could become a seamstress. She could work as a hostess at one of the glitzy restaurants and hotels that served the British bureaucrats that administered South Africa or its tourist hunters. She could meet a nice man who didn't fuss at her too much and pop out a couple of children and live comfortably.

But she couldn't do any of those things without also pulling out her hair in great fistfuls and going completely out of her mind. She'd grown up at her father's knee out on the savanna. She wanted to roam and ramble and rove across the tip of the continent.

And she used to be able to do that, but that was before she gave up hunting. She'd tried a few times since that one fateful incident a few months ago, but she just couldn't do it. Denise DeMarco was born and bred to hunt, and yet she couldn't anymore. She was like a hunting dog kept in an apartment all the time, growing more and more neurotic by the day as the wildlands outside beckoned.

Maybe that's why she opened the door wider for Roger Pick to come inside with his confidentiality agreement. Or maybe it was the briefcase full of money chained to his wrist. Or maybe it was just plain old curiosity, that famous serial killer of cats. Over the next few days, she would wonder to herself just which one of those incentives made her open that door.

Even if there was no way to know it at the time, it didn't take her very long to realize what a horrible mistake she'd made in opening that door.

Pick nodded his appreciation and stepped through the doorway, unsealing his envelope as he did so. She walked over to her desk, and Pick set the confidentiality agreement down in front of her. Good thing she'd sopped up that drool earlier. A little housekeeping came in handy sometimes.

She glanced over the agreement, just enough to make sure that she wasn't contracting herself to do anything odious by signing it. True to Pick's word, the various clauses swore her to secrecy about any details between herself and Yersinia. It also promised eye-popping litigation if she ever blabbed and the details leaked out to the wrong people. Her curiosity only grew stronger.

Fishing out a pen, Denise slashed her signature across the bottom line. Pick smiled again. She was really beginning to dislike that smile.

Pick was sitting directly beneath a blown-up black and white picture hanging from the wall. The wall used to be covered in mounted animal heads and trophies, but Denise sold all of those months ago for some quick money. The picture was the only decoration left in the whole office.

Right in the center of the frame stood Teddy Roosevelt, America's most prominent big game hunter, and its former president. Roosevelt stood with a long rifle in his arms, smiling like a man who's fought the whole world and licked all challengers.

He stood with one knee propped up on a downed rhinoceros, the huge beast laying where it fell mid-charge. There was a furrow in the grass behind Roosevelt where the rhino went down and slid.

Denise hadn't kept the picture for Roosevelt's grinning presence, though. Standing next to the former president was a figure smoking a pipe wearing a satisfied smile of his own. That was Cedric DeMarco, looking every inch the greatest huntsman in the Cape.

He had his arm wrapped around the shoulder of a gawky teenage girl with pigtails and a rifle of her own. Teenage Denise smiled for the camera, but her eyes were tilted away to catch a better glimpse of Roosevelt and his prize.

Since that picture was taken, Denise had lost the awkward coltishness of her teenage years and developed into an excellent hunter in her own right. Also, since that picture was taken, Cedric DeMarco had disappeared on an expedition into the Namib Desert, presumed dead, and Denise had taken over the business where the picture now hung.

"Alright, I'll carry Yersinia's business secrets with me to the grave or Herschel Hobhouse gets my first born child, three arms, a leg, most of the money in South Africa, and a partridge in a pear tree. Now, what in the world is this all about?"

Pick leaned forward and took the non-disclosure agreement. It disappeared back inside its envelope and found its way into his jacket.

"There's an island," he finally said.

"Whoop-de-doo."

"It's a few hundred miles off the coast of Sumatra, deep in the Indian Ocean. It's not exactly uncharted. A good map will include a little speck to indicate where it is, but it's never been fully explored. There have been a few scattered stories, though. Mr. Hobhouse is under the impression that isolation has allowed some unusual organisms to thrive there. Possibly even...prehistoric organisms."

Denise snorted. "And your boss wants to pay me ten thousand dollars to go hunt dinosaurs with him? First of all, that's crazy, and I don't do crazy on my hunts. Second of all, I don't hunt anymore. Full stop. End of the line. Do not pass go. Do not collect ten thousand dollars."

"No, nothing so absurd as that. And as I already mentioned, this isn't a hunt. This island has attracted Mr. Hobhouse's attention because Yersinia believes some of the organisms there might have some medicinal or scientific value. Mr. Hobhouse wants to assemble a team of elite hunters and trackers to catalogue and procure samples from the island. If this venture proves fruitful, Yersinia would turn the island into a private preserve for scientific study."

"And probably sole access to extremely lucrative and patentable resources."

Pick shrugged in a *that's the way it goes* gesture.

"So let me get this straight. Yersinia and Herschel Hobhouse are willing to pay me ten thousand dollars just to toss some critters and plant samples from this island in a terrarium and bring them back to you?"

"Well, yes and no," Pick said.

Aha! Denise thought. *Here's where they try to take all the money away.*

"You do get ten thousand dollars more or less just for traveling to the island inspecting its flora and fauna; however, if you're able to capture some specific specimens alive, the ones we're not entirely sure exist, you'll receive one hundred thousand dollars."

Denise blinked. "One hund—How much was that again? I think I misheard you."

"No, you heard me correctly. One hundred thousand dollars. That's a one followed by five zeros. But that's only if you're able to capture a specimen alive, just to be clear. We're not expecting that to be easy. You're guaranteed the ten thousand. There's just a ninety thousand dollar bonus if certain conditions are met."

"Alright, you have my attention."

"Good. We've already signed on nine other hunters. You'll be the tenth. Mr. Hobhouse would like nothing better than to give each of you one hundred grand, but we don't even know for sure what we're expecting on the island."

Denise had never done live captures before. This was similar to hunting, but maybe she could actually do this. Plus, if there was ten thousand dollars just for showing up, that was almost too good to be true.

"So, I'm not expected to kill anything?" She wanted to make that perfectly clear to herself.

"No. It's more like a biological scavenger hunt, assuming you don't have anything against that. You don't have to fire a gun at all the whole time you're on the island, if you don't want to. If you like the sound of that, I can show you the contract you'd be signing with Yersinia and Mr. Hobhouse. The ship sets out tomorrow."

"There must be a catch," Denise said.

"There is one thing in the contract I'll point out to you. You might call it a catch of sorts."

"Oh, really. And what's that?"

"You'll be staying on the island for an entire month."

"That's not bad."

"But we only pay you if you survive."

TWO

THE SHIELD OF MITHRIDATES

Denise held the tray of food in front of her. Hot pancakes. Scrambled eggs. Crispy-looking bacon. An apple. It had been a long time since she'd woken up this early in the morning, and it had been almost as long since she took a solid breakfast.

Her stomach did a little loop de loop as the cabin boy pointed her in the direction of the ship's dining room. Not only was her body adjusting back to trying to eat real food, but the gentle swaying of the ship was just enough to keep her perpetually off balance.

The *Shield of Mithridates* was a small cargo ship that had been retrofitted into a sort of floating hospital and luxury yacht. The ship belonged to Yersinia, and it had already picked up the other hunters from various points around the globe, and now it was steaming north up the coast of Africa, toward the Dutch East Indies.

Denise hadn't met any of the other hunters yet. She'd forgotten to ask Pick about them. All she knew was that a few of them were Americans, some were Europeans, and at least one other was from South Africa.

She moved down the short hallway from her bunkroom and entered a wide open space. Light from a dozen huge windows swept into the dining room, leaving a panoramic view of the ocean and the distant shore. Tasteful art pieces hung on the wall that blocked off the kitchen. And sweet Jiminy Christmas, there was even a grand piano in one corner of the room. Denise felt like she'd stepped into some seaborne version of the Stork Club.

Several long, stately tables ran down the length of the room, but only one of them was occupied. Six men sat at the table, laughing and telling stories. They weren't dressed like the ship's crew, so these must be her hunting companions.

Denise debated turning around and going back to eat in her cabin, but she forced herself forward. Even if she didn't want to discuss why she'd quit her hunting career with a group of strangers, she'd agreed to live for a month on a relatively tiny island with these people. She might as well introduce herself and get to know them.

Three of them had their backs to her and hadn't noticed her yet. As she walked closer, the three who were facing her dead on grew quiet and watched her approach.

She set her tray down next to one of the men turned away from her and forced a smile onto her face. Better to be friendly, even if she didn't really want to be.

"Hi, I'm Denise. You all must be the rest of the hunt team," she said.

The man she'd set her tray closest to looked down at it. "Hey, more food. Perfect. Just what I was hoping for." He reached over with a fork and scooped Denise's pancakes onto his own plate. Slicing at them, he popped a syrupy morsel into his mouth.

"Whoa. Hey, those are mine. I'm not part of the kitchen staff. I'm another one of the hunters Yersinia hired."

"Oh, I know you're not part of the kitchen crew, love," the pancake thief said between another big mouthful. "I just don't care."

"Gentlemen, really now. Let's just hold on a moment here," the hunter across from Denise said. He had dark eyes and long hair, and he looked just a tad like Oscar Wilde.

"Ooh, eggs. Don't mind if I do," the man next to Oscar Wilde said, shoveling some of Denise's scrambled eggs onto his own plate. She slapped his spoon away, sending quivering egg gobbets down the length of the table. Someone else managed to spear her bacon and cart it off like a hyena stealing part of a lion's kill while the big cat was distracted.

Mr. Pancake Thief tried to grab her apple as well, and she slammed her fist down on his hand, smashing it against the table. He yelped and dropped the apple. Oscar Wilde's neighbor made a grab for it, but Denise snatched it up before he could.

"You assholes!" she shouted.

The man at the far end of the table pounded a calloused fist on the table. Plates and silverware jumped and rattled as if the ship had just grazed a reef. The raucousness at the table died away. A few stray lumps of scrambled eggs wobbled where they'd landed.

"That is enough," the man said, his voice rumbling out of his thick chest in a growl.

Denise hadn't paid the man any attention during the scrum for her food because she'd come up behind him. She didn't need to see his face to recognize that voice, though. She'd heard it plenty over the years.

"Balthazar van Rensburg," she said. The huge Boer hunter must be the other South African hunter hired for this expedition. Balthazar was a big man. Denise could combine any two of the other hunters at the table, and Balthazar van Rensburg could still eat them for dinner and then rip the arm off a third for dessert.

Even though Balthazar was probably the age of her father, almost none of the big Boer's mass was fat. His arms were thick with slabs of muscle and scar tissue. His chest was as thick around as a steam engine bellows, and the chair he sat in looked like it was under visible strain not to splinter apart under his mass. He was almost as big as the game he hunted.

Since the last time Denise had seen him, his hairline had retreated further, and what hairs were up there were increasingly silver-grey. His face was still the same though, as craggy and wind-beaten as a catcher's mitt that had been used too much and then left out in the sun.

He owned his own hunting business operating out of Pretoria. As some of the best hunters in the land that perfected the safari adventure, their paths crossed often. Far more often than either of them would like.

"Denise DeMarco. They told me that this was a trip for real hunters. What are you doing here?"

"And they told me that I wouldn't get to see any big, dumb animals until we actually got to the island. They releasing you and your monkey troupe back into the wild for scientific study? Maybe putting a tag in your ear so they can track you later?"

Balthazar van Rensburg had never liked her. Not since the very first moment they'd met. He'd already had a great reputation as a hunter, and she'd been eager to meet him. Her father had never introduced the two of them, so she'd expected to have a polite exchange of professional courtesies. Instead, he'd shouted at her and said some truly reprehensible things until she left. Every time they'd met after that had gone about the same. This was quite tame by their personal standards.

Frankly, she didn't know why Balthazar was such a brute. Just as frankly, she didn't care. Assholes were assholes were assholes. There was no point in studying them, trying to tease out why they were the way they were.

She'd made a few enemies since breaking into the hunting field and subsequently breaking out of it. Lately, it was because she'd burned some bridges, but sometimes some hulk of testosterone just couldn't accept that *a girl* was a better hunter than him. Some fellow hunters took it as a personal affront that she'd dared to steal the secret of firearms from the hunting gods, and now they wanted her chained to a boulder at Mount Asshole so a vulture could tear out her liver every day.

Assholes all the way down. And Balthazar van Rensburg was their philosopher-king as far as she was concerned.

"No one wants you here, Denise," Balthazar said.

"For the record, I don't have a problem with her here," Oscar Wilde said.

"Noted and overruled, Silas," Balthazar said, shooting the dark-eyed man a dirty look.

"I'd rather not eat at the slop trough with the pigs anyway," Denise said.

"Go find somewhere else to enjoy that apple of yours. Or better yet, just throw yourself overboard and head for shore. I want you out of my sight."

Denise bounced her apple up and down in her hands, debating whether or not to throw it at Balthazar's head. Instead, she leaned over and spat into the remaining eggs on her plate. She slid the tray to the center of the table, knocking over a glass of water in the process. "Eat up. My compliments," she said.

Storming away from the table, she didn't look back as she stomped onto the ship's deck. Her heart thundered in her chest, and her teeth ground together hard enough to make her entire jaw ache. She just wanted to grab every one of the other hunters by the scruff of the neck and slam their faces against the table. She felt bile and rage churn in her stomach, an acidic maelstrom.

Part of her just wanted to retreat back to her cabin and give up. There must be some booze secreted away on this ship. She could just hole up and leave the cretins to their fun. They could turn around and drop her off back at the nearest port. She didn't want to share an island, no matter the size, with those imbeciles. Her fingers were clenched so hard against her palms that her nails were in danger of gouging into her skin.

"Ahoy there," a voice called. "You must be one of the new hunters that we picked up. Want to join us for breakfast?"

She looked up in surprise. There was another table out on the open deck, apparently for anyone who preferred to eat under the sun and stars. A sun umbrella kept the light off the two people sitting there, plates of food in front of them. A third figure, an Asian man, stood by the railing apart from the other two people.

One of the people at the table, a woman with her hair tied back in a long braid waved at Denise. The other figure, a black man, lifted a fork in her direction by way of greeting.

"Ahoy there," he said again. He turned to the woman. "Wait, is 'ahoy' the right word? Avast? Eh, screw it; it's fun to say. Ahoy there. Welcome to Scalawags' Cove, home to miserable wretches and scurvy dogs. Looks like you met some of your new colleagues. Want to join us at the cool kids' table instead?"

"Sure." Denise smiled at them. "You three are part of the expedition, too? Did you get kicked out by Balthazar and his cronies as well?"

"Yes. I'm Gail Darrow," the woman said, offering her hand. Denise shook it. "I've only barely met Mr. van Rensburg, but he's not the reason I prefer to eat out here. I take my meals out on the deck to get away from Jubal Hayes. He's a sack of badger crap but without the charm."

"I didn't catch anyone's names in there," Denise said. She felt a pang of annoyance that Balthazar was apparently only unpleasant to her.

Gail described the man who had first started stealing Denise's pancakes. "That's Jubal Hayes."

"Oh. Him. We met. It didn't go over well."

"And I'm Harrison Quint, New Orleans native, wild hog hunter by trade, and handsome devil by nature. Pleased to meet you. I'm sure you're charmed already." The black man offered his hand, and Denise shook with him as well.

"Denise DeMarco. I run a safari company in Cape Town. Did you say you're a hog hunter?"

"That's right. Big wild boars. They get huge in the South. Coarse, thick bristles. Tusks like razors. Tempers like nitroglycerine. They're mean sonsofbitches. I once saw one, I swear to God, it was fifteen feet from snout to tail, and it killed an adult gator. Gored it to death. They get onto peoples' farms, uproot all the crops, knock down the fences, and people hire me to exterminate them.

"Well, technically, they hire my assistant, Clark. He's a big white boy that looks like some Italian master chiseled his features out of marble. He drives the truck up to the front door of any given plantation that gives us a call. Then he introduces himself as Mr. Harrison Quint, owner of a fine small business, upstanding citizen, and hirer of poor, illiterate jigaboo assistants like myself. Pretty soon, Mr. Imperial Grand Dragon is giving Clark a mint julip and is halfway to offering him his third daughter for marriage. Trust me, folks down there react a lot better to an eloquent white boy than they do seeing a black man with a fearsome big rifle marching straight up their driveway. Once we get out in the forest or the bayou, I take the gun and Clark spots for me. Works like a charm." Harrison smiled wide.

Denise had to admit that Harrison had a clever system in place, given that America and South Africa both got their undies in a bunch about blacks. She was thinking more about the fact that he was a hog hunter, though.

Even with the non-disclosure agreement and the contract signed, Roger Pick hadn't offered many details about exactly what she could expect on this expedition. She'd expected most of the other hunters to have safari experience like herself.

"Gail, what do you hunt?" Denise asked.

"I have a hunting and fur trading business in Montana. Nothing big, but it's been a modest success since I opened it. If somebody wants to hunt bears, elk, bison, wolves, deer, or anything else in the region, I can take care of them."

"What do you hunt, Denise?"

"These days, nothing. I got out of the business a little while ago, but it used to be African big game." She didn't bother to explain why she refused to hunt anymore. "They made it hard to turn this offer down, though."

A hand grasped her shoulder. "Oh, that's by design. We wanted the absolute best for this expedition, so I made sure we got them."

Denise turned around to find herself face to face with a man she'd never met before. He had eyes the color of rich honey and hair that ruffled in the sea breeze. Even though he wore a dress shirt unbuttoned at the top, he also had a well-groomed little beard that would have looked at home on a Bohemian painter.

"Hello, Denise. We haven't formally met, but I'm Herschel Hobhouse. I work with Yersinia's research and development department to explore new avenues for researching medicine and biological sciences. I see you've already met Harrison and Gail. Has Shinzo introduced himself yet?"

"That might take a while. That guy likes to keep to himself," Harrison whispered in Denise's direction.

At that moment, an absolutely gigantic golden eagle swept over the ship. Its wings flared open, spreading over seven feet wide. Fluttering and screeching, the fearsome-looking bird swooped down at them.

Shinzo held up an arm clad in a long leather glove. The eagle landed on his forearm, its talons sinking into the leather sheath. He reached into a pouch and fed a little tidbit of something to the eagle. The bird gobbled the hunk of meat down and then stared at the assembled onlookers with keen, intelligent eyes.

"Mr. Takagari is joining us all the way from Japan," Hobhouse said. "He's a master falconer."

Shinzo merely nodded in her direction. Then, his bird flapped its wings and lifted itself into the air. With another screech, it took off over the ocean, sailing above the rolling blue waters. Denise might have put money on the golden eagle versus an older model biplane fighter.

"Have you met the other hunters yet? Silas Horne, Creighton Montgomery, Jubal Hayes, Andris Razan, Dr. Grant Marlow, and Balthazar van Rensburg should all be finishing breakfast inside."

"I've met them," Denise said, trying not to sound too sour.

"How are you enjoying the *Shield of Mithridates* so far? Are your quarters to your liking?" After meeting Balthazar and company, Denise was afraid this entire voyage would be absolutely miserable.

"It's an impressive ship," she said, unsure what else to say. The vessel was obvious top of the line, but she knew the savanna, not boats.

"Indeed it is. Officially, it belongs to Yersinia. Sometimes it's taken out and used to wine and dine various executives or company benefactors. Yersinia does a lot of charity work, so we like to throw a black tie event every once in a while for some of our more generous donors. We get some of the best chefs in New York on board, and we sail down the coast for a night. It's amazing.

"Usually, though, we temporarily lease out the ship to governments that have seen a major disaster or ongoing strife, and she serves as a floating hospital. We keep some Yersinia staff and doctors on board, and we treat everything we can. The cargo hold can be swapped out into a bay of triage suites and emergency rooms in a matter of hours. We treat everything from endemic diseases to gunshot wounds here. It's really fantastic work."

"Kind of a shame to take it away on company business then, don't you think?" Gail asked.

"Oh, don't get me wrong. We do some wonderful things here, but Yersinia has taken a major interest in this project. We need this ship. Hopefully, you'll be able to help us fill up the cargo hold with live specimens. There's no guarantee obviously, but we really think that we can derive some new treatments from what you're going to find. In the end, taking the *Shield of Mithridates* out here for a short while will do more good in the long run than any single place it might be in the short term. That's the hope anyway."

Denise tried to ask something, but Harrison spoke up first. "Interesting choice to name the ship," he said.

"Do you like it? It's named after an ancient king of Pontus, a region that's now northern Turkey. Mithridates was one of the great experimenters in early medicine."

"I know about Mithridates," Harrison said. "He would feed various poisons to flocks of ducks. If any of the ducks survived, he knew for sure that they'd eaten a nonlethal dose, so he'd slit their throats and drink their blood. That way, he could build up a tolerance and immunity to most ancient poisons."

"Yes, exactly," Hobhouse said. "That's the vision we want the *Shield of Mithridates* to project. Through bold experimentation, Yersinia wants to protect humanity from all ailments and sicknesses, albeit we're more focused on natural diseases than poisons."

"And if the pulp magazines are right, he probably gained all the super powers of a duck, too," Harrison said.

Hobhouse gave him an odd look.

"Then again, I mostly remember Mithridates from my history books because he launched a series of rebellions against the Romans," Harrison continued. "Pontus didn't like that the Romans had the bad habit of enslaving everyone they came into contact with. Mithridates coordinated a massive uprising that killed eighty thousand Romans in a single day when it began."

"Today, he would probably be labeled a terrorist, yes. But we think his legendary immunity to poison was too good a symbol to pass up."

"I was going to congratulate you on naming the ship after a freedom fighter but, hey, whatever." Harrison shrugged.

Denise jumped in before the conversation could turn into a history debate. "You said you were hoping we could collect live specimens. However, our contracts never said exactly what we're supposed to collect. It just referred to 'unique botanical and zoological organisms.' I've brought dart guns, nets, and everything else I could think of, but I still don't know exactly what we're looking for when we get there. I'm not a zoologist or a botanist or a biologist. What exactly are you sending us out to collect?"

"Dr. Grant Marlow actually is a zoologist as well as an expert hunter. I'm sure he'll be able to identify species that diverge from their mainland counterparts."

"That's not an answer."

"I know. Believe me; I'm dying to tell you. However, I don't want to go into details until we get closer to the island. Right now, we're still close enough to land that someone could get a message ashore. Passenger pigeon. Radio. Even a note in a bottle.

"Yersinia has many competitors. BioSyn. Wormwood Enterprises. Some of them would be happy to pay a huge sum of money just to learn more details about what we're doing out here. It's not that I don't trust you. Any one of you." Hobhouse smiled at them.

"I just don't want to let this little secret out of the bag too early. Trusting you four is easy. Trusting everyone on the ship, from captain to cook, is much harder. Rest assured, though. You'll get plenty more information from me by the time we get closer to the island."

"Your man Roger Pick told me that the island might harbor some downright prehistoric life. I just want to know what I should be looking for. Will it be obvious, or do you want samples of each species of moss that grows under every rock on the island?" she asked.

Herschel's smile collapsed in on itself. "Mr. Pick shouldn't have mentioned that."

"Admittedly, I might have been pointing a shotgun in his general direction at the time. Just a small one."

"I'll tell you this. What you're looking for should be pretty obvious. Plenty of people have sailed to this island and not seen anything out of the usual. However, no one who's stayed there for over a month has ever come back alive. We think whatever you're looking for is just as likely to find you first."

THREE
OVERBOARD

Denise had learned to adapt to life aboard the ship as it chuffed northward toward whatever lay off the coast of Sumatra. Every day, she ate with Gail and Harrison, sometimes playing cards with them late into the night as the stars crawled across the sky.

Silas Horne, the English Oscar Wilde lookalike, sometimes ate with them as well. He was always perfectly friendly, though he usually ate with the other hunters inside the ship's dining room. Usually, he stayed with the expedition's other Englishman, Creighton Montgomery. Whenever the two groups needed to communicate for some reason, Silas was usually sent as a sort of emissary. He always seemed slightly embarrassed by the behavior of his colleagues, but he wasn't willing to split from them completely. Meanwhile, Shinzo Takagari and his golden eagle kept to themselves.

Herschel Hobhouse refused to say another word about what they could expect to find at their destination. Denise had asked several more times, and he'd said he would address everyone when they finally drew close enough. Now, they were only about a day out from the island, but he still hadn't said anything new.

Denise had thought about what he'd said, though. Mostly, she'd decided it was probably a bunch of bologna. She'd heard plenty of hokum before. All sorts of stories developed about far off and isolated places.

Ghost tribes. Forty-foot-long river crocodiles. Impossible monsters. She'd heard it all at some point. Usually, there was a kernel of truth wrapped in an exaggeration inside a hazy memory based on a mistranslation. If everyone who tried to stay on this island really died, it was more likely to be from disease and malnutrition than some horrible predator. She was almost surprised the stories didn't also say that the island had a hollowed-out mountain shaped like a human skull.

At the moment, though, she had something much more important to think about than whatever goofy myths surrounded the island. She and Harrison were both losing their shirts to Gail in a poker game.

"Fold," Denise said, putting her cards down in disgust. The highest card in her hand was the ten of hearts. Gail and Harrison raised each other a couple of times, throwing pennies and nickels into the pot.

"So, Denise," Harrison said, picking over his cards.

"Yeah?"

"Do you know what '*kaffir*' means?" he asked.

"Did Balthazar call you that?"

"No. It was Creighton Montgomery, the other Brit that hangs out with Silas sometimes. He said he learned it on a hunting trip to South Africa. He called it a term of great respect. I asked van Rensburg about it, but he just shook his head. Given that Creighton thinks being able to trace your ancestry back to a bunch of inbred medieval royals makes him the hottest snot around, I don't really trust him calling me words I don't know."

"He didn't get the word from van Rensburg?" Denise felt another stab of annoyance that Balthazar seemed to have a grudge against her alone. It would have been less obnoxious somehow if he didn't like her friends as well. "I hate to break it to you, but '*kaffir*' is basically the Afrikaans equivalent to 'nigger.'"

"Oh. Well, that's a relief," Harrison said, still studying his cards as if he could will them to match up into a full house.

"A relief?" Gail asked.

"Yeah, well, I managed to convince him that 'peckerwood' was a term of great endearment back in the South. Creighton's family tree probably looks like a wreath when you look at all the great family intermarriages, so maybe that explains why he's such a dipshit. It would have been embarrassing if *kaffir* actually did mean something nice."

"Not bad at all," Gail said. "Now, are you done stalling before I win this pot, too?"

Finally, Harrison laid his cards down. Two of a kind with sevens.

Gail flipped her cards over. Two of a kind with queens.

"Dammit," Harrison said. "Where do you keep getting these cards?"

"Wanna play again? If I win, I get all your bacon at breakfast tomorrow, though."

"You got all my bacon at breakfast this morning," Harrison said.

"And mine," Denise added.

"I don't even like bacon anymore after so many hog hunts, but can't you at least leave a man with some shred of dignity here?"

"Whiners," Gail said, smiling as she shuffled the battered deck of cards.

Denise was only half paying attention, though. She kept looking up, waiting to finally see the tiny speck on the horizon that indicated they had reached their destination. They were still supposed to be a good day's travel away from the island, but she couldn't help herself. She felt like a little kid, constantly checking if they were there yet.

The ship's crew had been bustling all over the ship since dawn. They kept checking all the rooms and crawlspaces. One of the ship's officers would come inspect a supply closet, and five minutes later, a different officer would go check it.

She assumed that this was related to the imminent end of their journey in some way, but she couldn't make sense of what anyone was doing. It almost looked like they had lost something and the entire crew, from captain to cabin boy, had gone in search of it. If this was an inspection of the equipment, it was a very thorough one.

Denise spotted Herschel Hobhouse coming toward them as Gail started to deal cards out. He had the captain of the *Shield of Mithridates* with him. Gail had just picked up her cards, perfectly stone-faced as always, when he stopped in front of their table.

"I have some bad news," Hobhouse said. Everyone put down their cards to look up at him. "One of the crew has gone missing."

"Missing?" Harrison asked.

"Who?" Denise said.

"Our dishwasher. The chef last saw him while they were cleaning up after dinner last night. He says the dishwasher went up onto the decks to have a cigarette before going to bed, and that's the last anyone saw of him. He didn't show up to help with breakfast this morning, and we've checked his bunk. We've checked everywhere, as a matter of fact," Captain Englehorn said.

"What happened?" Gail asked.

"He must have gone overboard," Hobhouse said. "Probably shortly after he went up to have a cigarette."

"That seems odd. We didn't have any rough seas last night," Denise said. "No big waves to knock a man over the railing."

"It could have been something else. Maybe he tripped on a wet patch and went over. Maybe it was intentional."

"Intentional? Surely you're not saying he was murdered?" Gail asked.

"No, no. Of course not. Nothing of the sort. He might have chosen to...take matters into his own hands," Hobhouse said, trying to discretely find a way to bring up suicide. "Right now, we just don't know. All we can say is that he's not on the *Shield of Mithridates* anymore, so he must have gone into the water."

"Are we circling back to look for him?" Denise asked. She looked up to see if she could tell that the ship had changed direction at all, but there was nothing but blue ocean and sky all around them.

"No," Captain Englehorn said. "If he's been in the water that long, he's most likely dead already. By the time we get back to where he probably fell over, that will certainly be the case. For that matter, we don't even know exactly where he went over, and the currents will have moved him around a bit since then."

"You're just going to leave it at that then?" Gail asked.

"No. We radioed it out to every ship we could contact. We also managed to get on the horn with the British Navy, and they'll divert a couple of ships to investigate. If anyone finds him, it'll be one of the ships that's already a lot closer," the Yersinia executive said.

"That still seems rather callous," Gail said.

"The man is almost certainly dead already," Captain Englehorn replied.

Denise was still searching the horizon toward the prow of the *Shield of Mithridates*. She squinted against the light on the water. "Is that another ship out there?" She asked.

"It shouldn't be. We're way out of the shipping lanes," Hobhouse said.

"Where?" Englehorn asked. She pointed, and he raised a set of binoculars dangling around his neck. He adjusted the focus and gazed out over the water. "It's a pleasure yacht. Looks like it might be in trouble. The main mast is collapsed."

"Are we going to help them?" Harrison asked.

"We'll see if there's anyone to help," Englehorn said. "The boat could have broken free of a pier in a storm months ago with no one on board." He marched away toward the ship's bridge, ordering the first crewmen he saw to find the first aid kits and bring and ready a dinghy.

A few minutes later, the *Shield of Mithridates* changed course and lowered its speed. The engines chuffed toward the stricken boat like tired but wary horses.

Denise watched the boat grow closer and closer. Soon, she could see with her own eyes what Englehorn spied through the binoculars.

The boat was some sort of sailing yacht, the kind wealthy adventurers sometimes used to sail around the globe. However, it had seen far better days.

The main mast had splintered close to the deck. It lay across the side of the boat. Shredded sails trailed from the mast in the water like the top of some gigantic jellyfish cruising the surface. Not only were the sails ripped to pieces, but they were discolored and crusted with clusters of small barnacles, as if they'd been dragging in the water for a long time.

She could just make out the name of the boat painted on the side, the *Venture*. The *Venture* had clearly ventured too far. Denise didn't see anyone on the decks. No one came out from the yacht's quarters to wave them down.

Maybe that was a good thing. Maybe Captain Englehorn was right, and the *Venture* had been swept out to sea in a monsoon with nobody aboard. Maybe whoever was piloting it had engine troubles and was rescued by a passing freighter a long time ago but had to abandon the boat.

Those were the best case scenarios. Any other scenario was almost guaranteed to be bad. Very bad indeed.

As they approached, the other hunters and the crew came out to the decks to watch. Captain Englehorn and his first mate helped prepare one of the ship's dinghies.

Englehorn and three of his crew hopped aboard as the lifeboat dangled from its ropes. He cupped his hands and yelled to the assemblage of gawkers. "Alright, I don't know what we're going to find out here. Who knows first aid?"

Denise and a scattering of others raised their hands. Her father had served with the British military and taught her all the basic field medic techniques. Once or twice, she'd seen people injured during her safaris, mostly twisted ankles and the occasional broken bone. Once a client disobeyed her and bumbled too close a wounded water buffalo, and the animal managed to break most of his ribs and fracture his jaw before someone else put it down for good. Another time, someone lost a hand to a river crocodile. Her father's medical skills were plenty useful on those days.

"You, you, and you. Get aboard." Englehorn pointed to Denise, Dr. Grant Marlow, and Herschel Hobhouse. They all clambered onto the dinghy.

Marlow was older than Denise, maybe about Balthazar's age. A bushy white mustache perched on his lip. Even though he was part of Balthazar's clique, he didn't seem actively interested in making her life unpleasant. Jubal Hayes and Creighton Montgomery were the main instigators, though van Rensburg took particular interest in making sure Denise didn't feel welcome. Marlow was perfectly pleasant on his own, but he seemed to enjoy the grade school antics of the others too much to associate with Denise, Gail, and Harrison.

"I thought you were a doctor of zoology, not medicine," Denise said as they stepped onto the small, motorized craft.

"I am," Marlow said. "But I can suture a wound or stuff guts back inside a body with the best of them." He paused for a moment. "I'm sorry for the way some of the others have treated you on this trip. I know it must be hard."

She glanced away from the crippled yacht to look at Marlow. The sympathy wasn't nearly enough to counter some of the open hostility she'd received from Balthazar, Creighton, and Jubal, but it was appreciated nonetheless. Denise smiled at him.

"Thank you. I genuinely appreciate that."

"I mean, a ship is no place for a woman, let alone a hunting expedition. This is a place for men. You're already outside of your natural sphere of homemaking and child rearing. Adding this additional stress on you could do irreparable harm to your fragile feminine psyche."

The smile withered on Denise's face. "I think my fragile feminine psyche will be just fine, thank you very much. And I think I can handle some duties in addition to homemaking and brat taming."

"The greatest thinkers in the social sciences could easily tell you that having you here is against the natural order of things. It's simply scientific fact."

"Yeah, well, the greatest thinkers in the social sciences haven't met me, which is why they aren't eating all their meals through a straw right now."

Marlow made a little sound deep in his throat. "Very well. I just hope you know what you're doing if we find anyone in need of help on that vessel. You don't faint at the sight of blood, do you?"

Denise decided to count slowly to ten while the crew lowered the dinghy down into the sea rather than knock Marlow over and drown him. After a moment, they touched down into the sparkling water. The dinghy swayed under them as Englehorn started the engine and steered it toward the stricken yacht.

When they pulled up beside the *Venture*, Englehorn tossed a rope up onto the yacht and threw the ends into a knot. Part of the boat's side railing had been torn off, and a couple of windows were smashed in on the sides, but Denise couldn't see up onto the deck yet.

No one came out to greet them. No voices cheered for rescue. The only greeting they received was a surprisingly cold ocean breeze that cut right through Denise's jacket.

"Hello?" Captain Englehorn shouted. There was no response. "Hello?" He tried again. They all waited for a moment, but the only sound was the hush of the wind.

"Check it out, Captain," Hobhouse said.

Grabbing a length of railing overhead, Englehorn used a busted-out porthole to boost himself up onto the deck. He looked back down at them for a moment before slipping out of view.

Nothing happened.

Englehorn didn't say anything. The *Venture* creaked and groaned as it bobbed in the waves, but there was no other sound. Denise strained her ears, wondering if she could at least hear the man walking along the deck in his boots, but there was nothing.

"Englehorn?" Hobhouse called. "Captain?"

There was no response.

"I'm going up," Hobhouse said. He grabbed the railing and clambered up the side of the yacht.

Denise waited a moment, but Hobhouse didn't stick his head over the side of the railing to wave them up either. Almost a full minute passed. The crew fidgeted in their seats. They didn't like this any more than Denise did.

Finally, they heard a voice, surprisingly quiet. It was from Hobhouse. "You guys should see this."

Everyone followed Englehorn and Hobhouse up onto the deck. Denise went last, hauling herself up until her face was level with the deck.

At first, all she could see were the backs of everyone's shoes and legs. She pulled herself all the way over the railing and found herself staring at everyone's backs.

Pushing her way through the group, she finally saw what had captured everyone's attention. The wooden deck was marred by dozens of sets of deep gouges. Some of them chewed all the way through the surface of the wood and opened up ragged slits to the areas below decks.

A number of the gouges also featured dark stains nearby. Sometimes, the stains were small, no more than a few spattered droplets. In other places, they were big, where some dark liquid had been splashed and smeared across the whole deck. The sun had washed some of the color out of the stains, but they were still a visible maroon.

As if to remove any doubt about where the stains came from, a few bones lay scattered across the deck. A jawbone, cracked roughly in half, lay near the feet of Captain Englehorn.

Obviously, the *Venture* had not merely blown out to sea during a storm. There had been a crew aboard when this happened. How big of a crew, Denise couldn't say. The bones scattered around could have come from multiple people of just one very thoroughly dismembered individual. A stump grinder would have a harder town reducing a person down to less.

Denise bent down on her knees and put her hand up against one set of gouges. The four deep scratches were set significantly further apart than her own fingers. They looked like claw marks, but Denise didn't know of anything big enough to make such huge scores in the wood. Perhaps a truly monstrous bear could do something like this, but there was no place for such an animal on a boat this size.

"I think I've seen enough," Captain Englehorn said at last. The rest of the crew nodded along with him. "We're not going to find anyone to help here."

"Right," Hobhouse said. He bit his lip. "Alright, let's head back to the ship. Englehorn, make note of our coordinates. Then, I want you to scuttle this boat. We'll tell the authorities later that we confirmed it sank. All hands lost."

"Wait. Scuttle it? Why?" Denise asked. "Maybe a bigger ship can tow it into a port and find out what happened."

"No, we'll sink it. What happened here is pretty self-evident, and the family of whoever this is would probably be best off not know the full truth. Something clearly attacked this boat and devoured everyone on board. That's both good and bad news."

"How in the world is that good news?" Denise asked.

"It means that the stories I followed out here are true. This is what we came out here to find. This is the whole purpose of the expedition."

"If that's the good news, I'm afraid to ask what the bad news is."

"You'll be stuck on the island with whatever did this."

"Peachy."

FOUR
CHIROPTIARY

Night had fallen over the *Shield of Mithridates* as it continued north into the very heart of the Indian Ocean. They were hundreds of miles from anything but their destination.

Whereas before Denise had been excited to finally get off this ship and find some space away from Balthazar and the other hunters, now she was a lot less enthusiastic. She'd told Gail and Harrison what she'd seen aboard the *Venture* before Englehorn holed the ship and it sank beneath the waves.

Right now, the entire hunting team was seated in the dining room, albeit spread out into the groups they'd settled into. Denise sat with Gail and Harrison. Shinzo Takagari sat by himself, his eagle asleep in its cage now that it was dark. Balthazar, Silas, Creighton, Dr. Marlow, Andris, and Jubal all sat in a tight little cluster.

Silas looked bored to tears by his present company. He caught Denise looking in his direction and nodded politely.

Normally, all ten hunters wouldn't sit in the same room at once. However, Herschel Hobhouse had requested they all meet here tonight after dinner. Supposedly, now that they were as far away from prying eyes as they could get, he felt Yersinia's corporate secrets were being adequately protected.

They were all finally about to learn what the hell they were supposed to be doing and why it might be worth one hundred thousand dollars. The room buzzed with murmured conversation, part anticipation, part bravado meant to paper over fear after discovering the fate of the *Venture*.

"Maybe it's just because I didn't see it with my own eyes, but I'm still not convinced. A giant animal? On a boat that size? How does that even happen? Some sort of sea monster? Because let me tell you right now, I do not have the sort of equipment to hunt the Loch Ness Monster," Harrison said.

"All I'm telling you is what I saw," Denise said. "The deck was scratched all to hell by enormous claw marks, and something had torn apart at least one person aboard that boat. I can't rule out other possibilities, but it looked like an animal attack. A bad one."

"There's other possibilities. Maybe whoever died on that yacht was trying to fix a piece of faulty equipment, like a motor with a big propeller. Something goes wrong, the propeller chews them apart, slices up the deck, and falls overboard. Seabirds take care of the rest of the body, so it looks like the accident was even worse than it already was."

Denise actually liked that possibility a lot more than what her own mind pointed to. A freak boating accident was a lot easier to accept than some sort of beast doing that and then vanishing without a trace.

There were problems with Harrison's idea, though. "I dunno. The scratch marks were all over the place, but they were consistent. Four big cuts, every time. Like a big claw. I don't think a piece of mechanical equipment would do that."

"Let's just suppose for a moment that it was a creature," Gail said. "I'm not saying it was. I'm not saying it wasn't. But let's just think like it was for a minute or two here. Do you think that's what could have gotten the dishwasher who disappeared last night?"

"I don't know," Denise said. "I mean, unless it came out of the water, I don't know how it would attack anyone on a boat, and the deck of this ship rides a lot higher off the surface than that little yacht. Plus, nobody has found any huge claw marks anywhere on the *Shield of Mithridates*. Given the way that yacht was torn up, I'd expect at least a little damage around here."

"A little damage and a lot of screaming. People don't get eaten alive quietly," Harrison added.

"That too," Denise said. She still didn't like the coincidence, though. So far, they were missing a member of the crew, and they'd also found another vessel where everyone aboard had been massacred. Any enthusiasm she might have had for this excursion was going straight down the crapper.

At that moment, Herschel Hobhouse entered the dining room and found his way to a table at the front of the room. The murmuring swirling through the room died down and then faded to nothing. Even looking tired from a long day, Hobhouse's enthusiasm was evident. It shone through his dark eyes, grabbed the audience by the shoulders and said, *listen up because I've got something to say.* His presence immediately commanded the room.

"Ladies and gentlemen. Thank you so much for your patience with me over this long journey. I know I haven't been completely open with you, but that's by design. This has been my pet project since I joined Yersinia, and at first, no one at the company believed in it. Since then, I've slowly convinced enough of the right people to authorize this. This project has been my baby from day one, and I didn't want it being jeopardized by sending a trail of whispers to rival companies. However, we've reached the point where it's necessary to inform everyone just what their roles are in this scheme of mine. Thank you for being intentionally strung along. Here's what I haven't told you. Here's what only a handful of people not on this ship know. We'll reach Malheur Island tomorrow."

"And what can we expect to find there?" Balthazar rumbled at him.

"Frankly, I don't know. At least, not exactly. What I can tell you is the evidence I have for what I'm hoping to find on that island. Or rather, what I'm hoping you'll find. They say that good management often just involves finding a collection of skilled team members and getting out of their way, that's why I wanted the very best and brought all of you along on this expedition."

Harrison raised his hand. "Sure. Great. I don't want to stop you from stroking my ego here, but what was the name of the island again?"

Herschel looked annoyed at being interrupted. "Malheur Island."

"Could you spell that?" Harrison asked. Denise and everyone else in the room looked at him. Hobhouse shrugged and spelled it out, and Harrison nodded his thanks.

"Anything else?"

"Nah. We're good." Herschel tried to find his place in his notes again while Harrison leaned over close to Denise and Gail. "You don't grow up in New Orleans without picking up at least a little French. Malheur is the word for 'calamity' or 'woe.'"

Hobhouse found his place again. "Let me give you a little history about what you're getting into. A French trading vessel discovered the island in the 1600s while sailing toward the East Indies. They left a few of the crew behind to set up a trading post. When the traders came back a couple of months later, they found nothing but destroyed shacks and the bloated remains of the men they'd left behind.

"No one else attempted to colonize the island for another two hundred years or so. The Dutch claim this island as part of their extensive empire in the East Indies. On several occasions, they've attempted to survey Malheur Island, to build outposts there, or otherwise add some sort of administrative center. None of these attempts have succeeded in the slightest. In fact, none of these attempts has lasted more than a month.

"Furthermore, small ships have been known to go missing when they sail near the island. You all saw evidence of what happens to them today. Most vessels avoid the area, in part because there's nothing else out here and in part because the stories have scared most would be explorers off.

"There's a small population of islanders living on Malheur. Occasionally, traders will stop by and swap goods with them for spices, but they've established their village behind a large wall on a peninsula of the island. There have been a couple of attempts to study them by anthropologists, but those expeditions have gone just like all the others. No one has attempted any major venture on Malheur since the Great War.

"Everything on the other side of that wall is untamed jungle and rough terrain. That's where I want you to focus your searches. "

"This sounds like a dangerous place. I'm starting to see why Yersinia is paying us so much," Silas said.

"Indeed. It is dangerous. However, you are the most prepared group to ever set foot on the island. Unlike the occasional hapless Dutch administrator, you all have experience in survival situations. You know how to establish safe base camps, protect yourselves from wild animals, and handle wilderness survival situations. After dropping you off with all your supplies, the *Shield of Mithridates* will retreat to a safe distance away from the island and wait for news from you."

"And what, pray tell, are we actually supposed to be looking for on this island? You still haven't told us what we need to hunt to earn that hundred thousand dollar reward," Creighton said.

"Ahools. And ideally, you won't be hunting them. Not like something you would track for sport at least. Hopefully, you'll be able to capture a few of them alive."

"Ahools? And what exactly is an ahool?"

"An ahool is a legendary species of bat said to inhabit the darker corners of Indonesia. They're large, ferocious predators that live in jungle caves and emerge during the night to carry off just about anything smaller than themselves."

"And just how big are these ahools supposed to be?" Denise asked. The largest bat in the world was the flying fox, with a wingspan of about five feet. However, they weighed less than five pounds. Being generous and outright doubling the size of a flying fox to ten feet across, the animal still wouldn't weigh very much. Most of a bat's size was in its wings. Their bodies were tiny, frail little things. How hard could it be to trap even a large bat and throw it in a cage?

"Imagine a grizzly bear with wings," Hobhouse said.

"Wait. Hold on a minute here. That has to be myth and exaggeration. There's no such thing. A bat that size would be able to carry a person away," Denise said in disbelief.

"Yes. Yes, it would. And the scene on the *Venture* was strikingly similar to how I would imagine the aftermath of a gigantic bat attack."

That shut Denise right up. Most of the reason she couldn't quite accept the *Venture* as an animal attack was simply because there was no animal still there. It was on a yacht. Unless the creature fell into the sea, where would it go? How would it even reach the *Venture* out on the ocean? But those problems went away if whatever had attacked could simply fly away.

Well, shit.

"Okay, so explain this to me. Why exactly do you and Yersinia want giant bats? Yersinia is a biomedical company, is it not?" Gail asked.

"Indeed it is. Yersinia is a global leader in everything from pharmaceuticals to hospital equipment. So I can see how the connection might not be obvious at first. There's essentially four reasons why Yersinia is interested in Malheur Island and the creatures that we hope inhabit it.

"The first reason is more than a little self-serving. We think that anything that exhibits the sort of growth characteristics of an ahool probably has interesting biological properties. That's the reason we're willing to lay so much money on the table. To survive, an ahool would need to reach maturity fairly quickly, which would require almost unprecedented growth for a mammal and put its body under incredible strain. Yersinia wants to study one of these animals up close, to test out its body chemistry. Putting a human through similar growth pressure would almost certainly kill us, so if we can understand how another mammal does it, we might be able to develop drugs that help the human body cope with traumatic physical experiences. That's the goal at least. We might discover something completely different. For all we know, the only economic value of a gigantic bat might be nitrate-rich guano for use in fertilizer.

"The second reason is also more than a little self-serving. Yersinia would love the good press of discovering a new species, especially one as spectacular as the ahools. We would have a wave of interest directed our way, and with it, a secondary wave of investment dollars.

"The third reason is related to the second, but it's a little more high-minded. If your expedition succeeds, and you discover a colony of ahools living on Malheur Island, then we'd like to work with the Dutch government and transform the island into a nature preserve."

Hobhouse looked directly at Denise as he spoke. If he specifically requested her for this expedition, as Roger Pick said, then he must know the reason she had quit the hunting business. He must know that she'd only agreed to go in the first place because this wasn't a true hunting expedition. Curiosity and money had helped get her on this ship, but she still wouldn't have come along if the purpose was just to blow holes in a bunch of animals.

"Think of this as the environmental justice reason. Far too often after mankind has introduced itself to a new species, that species has gone extinct. Dodo birds might have proven economically valuable, if not for medical research then maybe for meat production, if mankind hadn't driven them extinct. But this is about more than that. I think we lose something that can't be measured in purely economic terms when we destroy another species like that. There's something fundamentally unjust about eliminating an entire class of creatures through our own negligence.

"Worse yet are the times we intentionally slaughter a species until it no longer exists. Fourteen years ago, the very last passenger pigeon on earth died at the Cincinnati Zoo. A century before that, up to five billion passenger pigeons existed in North America, sometimes all but blotting out the sun for days at a time as they moved on their annual migrations. What happened? They were considered a cheap source of food, so people would simply aim shotguns up into the sky and kill hundreds at a time. They'd take whatever they wanted and feed the rest to the dogs, if they didn't just leave them to rot. The very last bird in the wild was shot and killed in 1900. Yet, it didn't have to be this way. Even a tiny amount of foresight could have prevented the total elimination of the species, and yet they were senselessly annihilated anyway.

"Bats are already fragile animals. They are the only mammal that flies, an incredible achievement of evolution. They hunt by echolocation, sending out high-pitched noises and using the sounds that bounce back to figure out where they are in the environment and in relation to their food, and they do it all in a split second. Their bodies are amazingly engineered for flight, incredibly light weight, and specially adapted in almost every way.

"Right now, I and my colleagues at Yersinia believe the evidence points to ahools living on Malheur Island. Maybe they were more widespread throughout the island chains of the Dutch East Indies once, but this seems to be the only colony in the world right now.

"If you succeed and confirm that the island is inhabited by ahools, Yersinia wants to work with the Dutch government and ensure that Malheur Island is protected and preserved. It would take very little disruption, maybe even just the dynamiting of a single cave system, to send ahools to the dustbin of history with the dodo and the passenger pigeon.

"We would like to make this a place of preservation and study, the world's greatest chiroptiary."

Hobhouse apparently noticed he was getting a few blank looks from his audience, so he hastened to explain. "A bestiary is a collection of beasts. An aviary is a collection of avians. Birds. A chiroptiary is a collection of chiropterans. Bats. We'd be essentially turning Malheur Island into a giant bat preserve. Any other questions?"

Denise sat at the table thinking. What Hobhouse had said was both frightening and sort of beautiful. Now she understood why all the hunters on board seemed to specialize in different game. There were no experts in hunting and wrangling giant bats. Yersinia had simply assembled a wide field of talent instead.

At the same time, the prospect was actually exhilarating. Since she was a young girl, out on the hunt with her father, the herds of animals across South Africa had thinned. There were fewer elephants, fewer lions, fewer rhinos, fewer of everything that people wanted to hunt. Meanwhile, the ivory trade only seemed to be gathering steam, fueling a seemingly insatiable demand for the stuff and further reducing the numbers of the biggest herbivores. The idea of doing something to actually protect a new animal was enticing.

She did have one question for the Yersinia executive, though. "You said there were four reasons you brought us out here, but that was only three."

Hobhouse smiled. "Oh yes. Of course. I nearly forgot. The fourth reason is actually my favorite. We thought the idea of finding monster bats sounded really, really cool."

FIVE
WE CAN'T HELP YOU

Malheur Island was a paradise. A hot, sweaty paradise. The beach was sparkling white sand littered with shells. The waves washed up and down the beach as the *Shield of Mithridates* launched its motorized dinghies and ferried the hunters to shore. They was no dock to land at, so the small boat simply motored into the surf, and then the crew pulled them onto the sand to start unloading supplies. Everything from tents to crates of food and water to ammunition needed to be brought to shore.

Beyond the sparkling beach lay a jungle so thick that Denise could barely see twenty yards into it. A green riot of creepers, ferns, trees the height of apartment buildings, palms, strangling vines, mushrooms, pitcher plants, ivy, heaps of leaf matter piles feet deep, bushes, fruit trees, tall reeds, bracken, and plants of every variety all fought for sunlight in a huge knot of life that covered the island. Overturned logs provided homes to fungal growths the size of Denise's fist, and battalions of ants marched back to their nests carrying leaf litter and food. Birds sang from the thick forest canopy to the accompaniment of chattering monkeys. The jungle floor stood bathed in perpetual twilight under the overhanging boughs of the mightiest trees, the light above blocked by a sea of leaves.

Denise had seen plenty of jungle before, but this was an astoundingly thick and untrammeled one. In places, it was difficult to tell where one plant ended and the next began. They were all intertwined in an orgy of chlorophyll, practically knitted together until they were one unit.

There were still paths through the arboreal mayhem, though. They wouldn't have to machete their way absolutely everywhere. Game trails snaked in and out of the greenery, trampling through the grass. In some places, the largest trees had killed off nearly all the vegetation around their bases by blocking out the sunlight with their branches.

The center of the island was dominated by a small mountain. From the beaches, the trek to the island's interior quickly became a steep upward slog. Jagged outcroppings and sharp drop offs made the journey even more hazardous.

Only a few trees clung to the summit of the mountain. The terrain was simply too steep and barren to support the lush explosion of biology that existed further down the slope. She wondered if the mountain was actually a volcano, either extinct or slumbering.

So long as it didn't start raining molten rock and burning ash down on them, the idea was rather promising. A volcano ought to have abandoned lava tubes and maybe even an empty magma chamber where bats could live, maybe even extraordinarily large bats.

From where she stood, Denise could see a cliff that had partially tumbled into the sea, leaving a chasm filled with rock and seaweed. She hoped she could find a similar, drier hidey hole elsewhere on the island. The sheer walls and tight fit ought to keep her safe from anything flying overhead that might fancy her as a tasty snack. Given the broken, tumultuous landscape, she figured there were decent odds of finding someplace to set up before nightfall.

For all its splendor, Malheur Island wasn't very large. It was shaped roughly like a trapezoid. At its longest, the island was only ten miles across, and it was about four miles wide. The *Shield of Mithridates* had anchored off the island's eastern edge, which had more beaches and fewer cliffs. Hopefully, the interior was more traversable on this end as well.

A large, off-white boulder lay half-buried in the sand at the edge of the jungle. The rock was about the size of a comfortable armchair, and it was actually a conglomeration of smaller stones that had all been cemented together into a larger mass by some natural process.

What had happened after that was no natural process. Someone had carved the boulder into a stylized face that looked like a snarling demon head. Pitted eyes watched the crew and hunters offload their equipment onto the sand. Fangs the length of Denise's hand grimaced at them. She couldn't tell if the face was supposed to be a stylized human or some sort of animal. Years of erosion had softened the features down until the details were no longer clear.

Hobhouse had said there was a small village on the island and that sailors sometimes traded with the residents. At least they were moderately friendly. Obviously, this sculpture was the handiwork of whatever group lived here.

If Malheur Island really was home to a collection of gigantic murder bats, Denise wondered how the villagers survived. Hobhouse also mentioned they'd built a wall around their village, but that wouldn't do any good against something that could fly.

For that matter, why build a wall at all? If they were the only people on this island, what were they keeping out?

Denise didn't care for that thought. She hefted her Nitro Express elephant gun as she watched the edge of the jungle and waited for Gail and Harrison to make it ashore. They'd already decided they were going to establish their basecamp together. Someone could always be awake during the night that way, and it would be much harder for anything to pick them off while they slept.

She didn't plan to use the elephant gun at all during this trip, but like hell was she going to leave it behind. The Nitro Express fired rounds as thick as a garden hose and as long as her finger. If she held the rifle wrong when she fired it, the recoil could break her shoulder or knock her off her feet. Each one was meant to take down an elephant or an angry rhino. She could probably hunt dinosaurs with it, if there were still any around. She wouldn't be caught dead without it.

Of course, if Hobhouse was right about this island, she very well might be dead if she was caught without it.

Hopefully, she'd never have to fire it, though. In addition to the Nitro Express, she'd also brought a tranquilizer rifle and plenty of netting. The goal was to capture an ahool alive if she wanted the hundred thousand dollars. That meant she needed to trap it and sedate it, not blow it to kingdom come. She was pooling her resources with Gail and Harrison, so if any of them managed to bring down an ahool, they'd split the money by thirds. Thirty-three thousand dollars wasn't anything to sniff at either.

Besides the money, she didn't want to shoot one of the giant bats. Herschel was right. This was an entirely undiscovered species. It would be unfortunate to whittle down their numbers when there was an unknown number to begin with. If this was the only place where they lived, there couldn't be that many. Such a small island couldn't even have enough food to support a particularly large group. No, she'd only kill one of the ahools if she had to.

She waved at Gail and Harrison as they got off a dinghy of their own and started unloading their supplies. Gail came up and hugged her. "We finally made it," she said. Then she noticed the face carved into the boulder nearby and grimaced.

Denise noticed her gaze. "Yeah. The welcoming committee leaves something to be desired."

"We have more company than that," Harrison said, pointing to the edge of the jungle. Denise turned around and scoured the tangle of overgrowth, trying to see what Harrison had spotted.

A man stood at the jungle's edge. He hadn't been there a minute ago. Denise had a lot of experience looking for animals in the bush. She would have seen him if he was there before, and he was making no efforts to hide.

He must be one of the villagers native to this island Denise realized. The man wore a pair of old, faded dungarees and a pair of sandals that looked handmade. The dungarees must have come from traders at some point in the past. His expression looked unmistakably worried as he walked up to Denise.

"You should not be here," he said in lightly accented Dutch. Denise was surprised for a moment, forgetting that the Netherlands had tried to colonize this island before. It made sense that at least some of the locals would understand some Dutch.

Afrikaans was sometimes called Kitchen Dutch, a sort of descendant of the European tongue that had been hybridized and cross-pollinated with some of the African Bantu languages and a few other sources. The Boers that settled South Africa's interior brought Dutch with them, and it slowly evolved away from the mother language. Because there had been some scholarly efforts to clean up irregular grammar in Afrikaans, Dutch speakers could actually understand Afrikaans better than the other way around.

"Hello. We are friends. We will not be here long," Denise said. *"Verstaan jy my?"* she added. *Do you understand me?* She could see the man mentally picking through the Afrikaans.

He said something she didn't fully understand. The gist of it seemed to be about the same, though. *You should not be here.*

The rest might have been about...mouths? Months? Mounds, maybe? Perhaps something about the mountain? The words were all similar in Dutch, and Denise had no idea which one had just been used. They were too close for her to understand.

"Friends," she reiterated instead, making sure that her rifle was pointed well away from the islander. It was hard to look too friendly while holding enough firepower to blow a man's soul clean off.

"You have until tomorrow night to leave," the man said before retreating back into the forest. He slid over a fallen log, and then he disappeared back into the jungle like he had never been there in the first place.

"What was that all about?" Harrison asked.

"I didn't understand all of what he said, but I told him we were friends, and we wouldn't be here long."

"That sounds good," Gail said. "And what did he say?"

"That we had until tomorrow night to leave."

"And that sounds bad," Harrison said.

Herschel Hobhouse came to shore on the last dinghy. There was only a single, large crate on his craft. The crew hopped into the surf and dragged the boat onto the shore before grabbing the crate and prying it open with crowbars. Hobhouse lifted a black, metal box out of the crate and began walking toward Denise and her group.

"Alright, everyone," he said. "In a few minutes, the *Shield of Mithridates* is going to set off and head a safe distance away from the island before night sets in. I want everyone to take one of these radios. If you need to contact us for any reason, you'll be able to do so with these. If you get sick or injured, we can steam in and pick you up. If you manage to capture an ahool alive, we'll pick it up and lock it in the cargo hold to bring back."

He started handing out radios to all the hunters gathered on the beach. They came with a mouthpiece and antenna, and they were encased in hardy-looking black metal.

"Thanks," Denise said.

"Don't thank me too much yet," Hobhouse said. "The *Shield of Mithridates* is going to be eight hours out to maintain a safe distance. If you have an emergency, a real emergency, we can't help you."

SIX
MISS GRITS & THE HOG KING

Denise, Gail, and Harrison picked their way through the jungle and up a gentle incline. Harrison was in the lead at the moment, slicing away at vines and creepers with a machete. Once they reached the apex of the hill, hopefully they could find a good place to camp for the night. None of them liked the idea of camping out in the open when there might be massive airborne predators after nightfall.

"So, Gail," Denise said. "You've never told us exactly what you would do with your money if we actually manage to capture an ahool. With our base ten thousand dollars, you'd have over forty thousand by the time we split everything three ways."

"That's forty thousand before taxes; don't forget. Maybe we can buy some gum with what's left after the taxman is done with us," Harrison said.

"Actually, I'd like to retire from hunting altogether," Gail said. "I'm pretty good at it. My expedition company and fur trading shop makes decent money, but it's never what I wanted to do."

"Really? It was all I ever wanted to do when I grew up," Denise said. "I never knew what else I would do with myself after spending all those years out in the bush with my father."

"Well, my family weren't hunters. They were circus workers, believe it or not. My mother did an equestrian act, basically dancing across the backs of horses as they rode around the center ring. My father was an acrobat with the same circus. When I was born, I just traveled the country with them."

"That must have been an interesting childhood," Harrison said, slashing another swath of tall grass out of the way.

"No. Not really. A lot of it was spent on the train, moving from Podunk town to Podunk town. The circus master thought it would be good for me to learn some sort of unique skill from an early age, something he could market. Otherwise, I was just dead weight to the circus. He was something of a tyrant, but it was because he could never see anything outside of drawing crowds and making money, not real malice.

"My parents didn't want me out trying to ride a unicycle across a high wire when I was six. Go figure. They taught me to shoot instead. By the time I was ten, I could shoot a cigarette out of a person's mouth from thirty paces. Toss a quarter in the air, and I could hit it with a rifle before it touched the ground. I could shoot the center out of a playing card from across the center ring. They advertised me as a sort of miniature Annie Oakley.

"When I was a little older, they improved my shtick further. They gave me a little jalopy, and I did most of the same tricks but from a moving vehicle. The best one probably involved me facing the opposite direction from a floating balloon and using a mirror to sight the rifle backwards over my shoulder while somebody else drove around.

"Technically, I was born in Oklahoma, though I don't think we ever stayed in any one spot more than two weeks. The circus master labeled me Miss Grits: Belle on Wheels. When I reached adulthood, he even had me do the routine in big hoop dresses like some proper Southern lady. The crowds seemed to like it, and I was a big enough hit that the carnival barker would shout about my act to lure more people in."

"I have a hard time picturing you in hoop skirts," Harrison said.

"I don't know how those Southern ladies lived. I was as wide as a hippopotamus, and it seemed like it took all afternoon to put them on."

"So how did you end up here?" Denise asked.

"Well, I was probably the only kid who ever wanted to run away from the circus and join a small town. I didn't like being Miss Grits. Oh, don't get me wrong. I loved the adulation of the crowd. It was always something special to hear five hundred people go quiet when they realized you were about to try an impossible shot and then erupt into cheers when you pulled it off. However, every day was practicing, setting up equipment, doing the exact same thing you've done every day for years, and then picking it all up and carrying it to the next town to do all over again. Every time we packed things in, and I hadn't even gotten the chance to look around, I felt like I could just die. Younger me was probably a bit more willful and a bit more eager to meet some cute city boy somewhere.

"We didn't hit the big cities. No New York or Detroit for us. We were a second string circus, so we mostly did our business in little burgs no one's ever heard of like Blackacre, Vermont. However, we came pretty close to Chicago on our usual summer route.

"When we started that run, I told our circus master that I wanted to quit and head out on my own. He almost choked on the sandwich he was eating. I still remember him hacking a big ball of chewed bread and tuna out onto his card table in surprise. He said he wanted me to stay; he all but begged me to stay. I told him I couldn't, so he asked if I'd be willing to do one last big act, something he'd been thinking about setting up for a while.

"I felt like I owed him, so I agreed. Let me tell you right now. Never feel like you owe something to someone who isn't a close friend or family. If some jerk says you owe him for this or that or some other imaginary obligation, tell him to stick it right in his ear. I worked for the man, but I didn't owe him anything.

"See, the problem was, the circus master had a son who was about my age. He was kind of a mealy thing, and he was being groomed to take over the circus when his father finally retired.

"So for what was supposed to be my last gig, I walk into the big top, and they've got a special podium set up at the center of the ring. The circus master is standing there with his son and a pastor. It took me a second to figure out what was going on, but by then it was too late to just duck out of the back of the tent and run away without looking back.

"Our circus master tells the crowd that they're in for a very special event. They're going to be the witnesses to his son's wedding, right there in the center ring."

"Oh no," Harrison said. "Surely he wasn't going to…"

"Oh yes he was. He told the whole crowd that his son and Miss Grits were going to get married right then and there in a very real and legally binding sense. I don't know how he talked his son into it. Maybe he fancied me to begin with. Either way, it was clearly a really cheap ploy to keep his star attraction from leaving. If I was married to his son, I couldn't very well head out on my own and leave the circus."

"That is a low move," Denise said. "Did he actually expect to get away with that?"

"Apparently, he did. Maybe he thought I'd be too surprised to protest. Or maybe he thought I'd be genuinely thrilled to land that catch."

"So how come you're here enjoying my amazing company and hunting bats instead of starring in circus acts?" Harrison asked.

"I had the rifle I used for my act."

"Please tell me you didn't murder them all and the authorities are still looking for you to this day," Denise said.

Gail laughed at that. "No. Nothing so dramatic as that. I shot out the support ropes that anchored the tent in place and allowed it to keep its shape. About an acre of pin-striped fabric collapsed down on everyone's heads, including the audience. I squirmed out of my hoop skirt while everyone thrashed at the tent. Fortunately, I was wearing something underneath, but I would have done it even if I was buck naked under there so I could run away better. I wriggled out from under the tent and slipped away with the crowd. I never looked back, and I haven't regretted it since.

"I only got into hunting because it was a quick way to make money with my skill set. If you need a dozen quail all shot out of the air at once, I'm your gal. All told, I'd rather do something else, though."

"Like what?" Denise asked. Given that she was looking to get out of the hunting business herself, and she had a dearth of ideas about what to do with herself afterwards, she was happy to poach ideas from Gail.

"I've always wanted to try my hand at painting," Gail said. "After spending so much time either on the move or out in the wilderness, I'd love to just rent an apartment in a big city somewhere and try my hand at it for a couple of years. Maybe Boston or New York, someplace where I can see the ocean. I'd need to sign up for some art lessons, though."

Denise just nodded. She'd never harbored any great yearning to be an artist, and she didn't care for spending much time in cities.

She liked being out under the wide open sky without worrying about bustle and chaos on the streets.

They were almost to the ridge of the hill. They were all sweating already. Behind them, Denise could just barely see the *Shield of Mithridates* as it steamed hard for the horizon. They were officially on their own on Malheur Island.

Another large white rock poked out from a nest of brambles nearby, just like the one on the beach but a little smaller. The pale rocks didn't look like the rest of the boulders and stones on Malheur Island. Aside from these boulders, the rest of the rocks on the island were more or less uniformly dark greys or browns. If that mountain really was a volcano, maybe it spat them out thousands of years ago. Denise had no idea; she wasn't a geologist.

Just like its cousin on the beach, this rock had also been carved into a grotesque face. It looked almost like a crouched gargoyle, all fangs and horns and sneering eyes.

"Alright, your turn." Harrison handed the machete to Denise, and she started chopping her way up the hill. Gnarled tree roots and bushes with grabbing thorns made progress slow.

"So what would you do if you had forty thousand dollars on your hands, Harrison?" Denise asked. Maybe he had some ideas she'd like.

"Me? I'd like to expand my hunting business. Open up some branch offices in other parts of the state. Baton Rouge. Shreveport. Maybe I'd even expand into Arkansas and Mississippi. If I invest it right, I can make and remake that money. I've got Clark to pretend he's the Harrison Quint the business is named after, but I'd need more Clarks for the other offices."

"If you had enough, don't you think you could get away with telling people that you actually own the business?" Denise asked.

"I could. I'm the hog king of New Orleans. However, I'm not going to. Enough people would still hire me, but some of those fellows who like Clark so much would much rather hire some white boy to do the job. In fact, if too many of them hear that some lowly nigger with a smart mouth and a handsome face was too much competition for the good, honest white folks of the neighborhood, they might ask some of their friends to come have a chat with me. The next thing you know, I'm strung up from a tree with a bunch of halfwits wearing their wives' sheets staring up at the soles of my boots.

"It wouldn't be worth it. I wouldn't have to pretend like I was Clark's gopher on every job, but I can drop that act once we get out into the field every time anyway. Nah, I'd just attract the wrong kind of attention. I get by pretty well right now. I'd get along even better with a huge pile of money stashed quietly away in my bank where nobody but me knows about it. The last thing I need is some half-polished turd deciding that I'm uppity because I've got more than him. Nope. No siree, Bub! Clark will still be the Harrison Quint that answers the phone at Harrison Quint Hog Extermination. I'll be the Harrison Quint that cuts Clark's checks, and only him, me, and the bank will know that."

They were just short of the top of the knoll now. Soon, they'd be able to look over a good portion of the island and pick out a good spot to set up their camp.

"So what about you, Denise? What would you do with forty grand?"

"I haven't quite decided yet. I just know I'd like to get out of the hunting business myself."

"Really? Why?" Gail asked.

"It's a long story," she said.

"You better not start it then. I've got an important meeting in five minutes," Harrison said.

Denise laughed. "Well, I haven't gone on any hunting expeditions in a while now. There was an incident. A bad incident. Before this excursion, I wasn't sure I'd ever get back in the field again. Frankly, I wouldn't have come on this one if they hadn't insisted this wasn't a trophy hunt before I signed that non-disclosure agreement."

They reached the top of the hill and looked out over the island in front of them. Denise forgot everything she was about to say as they all stared at the huge thing in the distance.

SEVEN
REAR ADMIRAL HERMANN HOOKSTADT

It took an hour to clamber down to the beach on the far side of the hill and cross a couple of small chasms. Right now, they all ignored the potential base sites, though. They were much more interested in the thing they'd seen from the hill. Now that they were up close, Denise could appreciate the sheer size of the thing.

"Jesus. This thing must be from the Great War," Harrison said.

The SMS *Rear Admiral Hermann Hookstadt* was close to four hundred feet long. The thick steel armor at the front of the ship had torn and ripped open when it ran aground prow-first into shore. Rust covered the parts of the metal where the paint had flaked off over the last fourteen years. The snouts of two heavy duty naval guns poked out over the deck nearly forty feet above Denise's head.

More guns lined the ship's spine further out. The rear of the ship still rested in the water, but the front had plowed a furrow all the way up onto the sand of the beach, almost to the edge of the jungle. Of the ship's three smokestacks, two had fallen off and lay in the water. The third had tilted forward and leaned drunkenly against the back of the bridge.

"Wow. This must be from the German Far East Squadron," Denise said. "I was only a teenager when the war broke out, but I remember reading the news and listening on the radio about the Empire mobilizing for war."

"The war was in Europe. What's this doing here?" Harrison asked.

"The war was everywhere," Denise said. "Some of the areas where my father and I hunted became enemy territory overnight because they were in German East Africa. We didn't have trenches crisscrossing the veldt, but it was scary nonetheless. Sometimes we'd be out in the field, and suddenly, we could hear artillery and machine guns off in the distance."

"So what's the German Far East Squadron?" Gail asked. "I don't remember anything about it."

"America hadn't entered the war yet, so it probably wasn't big news over there. With British casualties, including colonial troops mounting, our news made hay with it. We needed some good news. I always had sort of mixed feelings about it, though.

"When the war broke out, the Germans had one naval base in China. It wasn't a whole lot, but it was their Pacific fleet. Mostly, it was just a few cruisers like this one and a scattering of support ships. Basically, they were just there to support the few itty-bitty German colonies in this hemisphere. They were never meant for a full-out war.

"When they found out that war had broken out, they realized that they were completely cut off. The British Navy had a much stronger presence than their little squadron, and most of the ports on this side of the world were suddenly in territories allied against Germany. The only truly safe ports were on the opposite side of the world.

"A couple of the ships split off and became commerce raiders, basically pirates. Some people in Cape Town were deathly afraid they'd meet up with the German forces in East Africa and start bombarding us, but it never happened. This must be one of the ships that split off from the main group.

"Most of the squadron decided that, rather than surrendering, they would try to make a mad dash all the way around the world to Germany, moving through hostile waters all the way. They'd have to steal coal from enemy ships and fuel up in neutral ports if they wanted to make it, all while playing cat and mouse with bigger, meaner battleships out looking for them.

"They set out from their port before any British ships could block them in and capture them, and then they sailed hard across the Pacific. Their leader, Rear Admiral Maximilian von Spee, and pretty much all the men aboard, knew that they were doomed. The entire ocean was against them.

"At first, they got lucky. They went all the way down to the tip of South America, trying to slip into the Atlantic. That's when the British Navy found them. A couple of big British cruisers zeroed in on them, but the Germans fought back and actually managed to sink the ships, which were comparable to their German counterparts. It was the first defeat of a British squadron since the

Napoleonic Wars. Over a thousand sailors died. Even trying to frame the news in favor of Britain, the local papers sounded grim about it.

"By then, the British knew where the Germans were. When von Spee stopped at the next neutral port, the locals gave him a bouquet to celebrate his victory, but he just told them to save the flowers for his grave.

"Next, the British sent out their best. The ships they dispatched were bigger, faster, and more heavily armored than the German cruisers. The Germans tried to run when the new squadron found them, but the British ships caught up with them and started firing.

"The German cruisers were annihilated during the battle. Their flag ship, with von Spee on it, caught fire and capsized, killing everyone aboard. The British ships didn't attempt to rescue any of the German sailors, and over two thousand of them died. It was just a drop in the bucket compared to some of the battles that were raging on the continent, but the newspapers crowed about it for days because it was such a lopsided victory. Only one of the German ships escaped, and it was hunted down shortly after.

"I guess this is one of the ships that split off early to become a commerce raider," Denise said, looking up at the wreck.

"You almost sound like you admire them," a voice said from the edge of the jungle. Silas Horne sat on a mossy log, watching them. "I see that this old hulk caught your attention too. I was over by the village when I spotted it and thought I'd investigate."

"I do admire them a little," Denise said. She scratched her cheek, eyeing Silas. He'd always been perfectly pleasant to her, to all of them. However, he also preferred to stay with the other main group of hunters, and he often hung around the expedition's only other Englishman, Creighton Montgomery, who had called Harrison a *kaffir*. She didn't dislike Silas, but she wasn't sure she trusted him either. At least he was alone, and not with Creighton.

"Sorry if I may pry, but why? South Africa is a colony of the British Empire. I was drafted into the military but only sat in the trenches for about two days before the Armistice took hold and ended the war. The Germans were our common enemy."

"I always thought there was something..." Denise searched for the right word, "venerable about their decision to steam out against overwhelming odds. They knew they'd be practically reliving Homer's Odyssey, and they decided to go for it anyway. I can respect it. It would have been safe to just stay in their original harbor and surrender. It would have been easy. Instead, they looked out over that watery blue horizon and told safe and easy to get stuffed. Sometimes, that's the only way to live your life. You have to charge into those unsafe waters and accept that the consequences are what they are. We'd never leave our rooms sometimes if we didn't. I'm not sure any of us would be here on this island if we didn't."

"Fair enough. It was worthy of a certain amount of respect, but it got them all killed. I suppose I consider myself a bit more meticulous. Sometimes, I'd rather be alive than bold." Silas eyed her for a moment. "You look uncomfortable."

Denise realized she was standing as stiff as a toy soldier. She forced herself to relax a little. She still wasn't sure if Silas was here just by chance or if he thought it would be fun to pester her the way his colleagues did.

"Don't worry. I'm not here to bother you. Consider this an olive branch of sorts," he said, as if reading her mind. "I was just as curious about this ship as you were. Sorry that maybe the company I keep can be a bit beastly sometimes."

"Well, thank you for reintroducing yourself. The three of us are working together. Are you and Creighton teaming up?"

"Yes. He can be a bit rough around the edges, but we share a passion for fox hunting and a few other hobbies I won't bore you with. He's establishing our camp a bit closer to the native village. It's nice to have company with shared interests, especially in odd conditions. Don't you think?"

"I suppose it is," Denise said. Silas smiled a bit sheepishly. Now that he was by himself instead of with some of the other hunters, he actually seemed rather sweet. Maybe she'd invite him to their base camp for supper later, assuming they could find a good spot.

"You said there's a village that way?" Harrison asked.

"Indeed there is. We can't see much of it, though. It's built on the beach, and the locals have erected a fence of sharpened logs that separates it from the rest of the island. No one has come in or out of the gate."

"We met one of the villagers earlier. He didn't seem very happy we were here," Denise said.

"Oh?"

"He said we had until tomorrow night to leave. Also something about the mountain or the months. I don't know; I didn't understand all of it."

"Well, I suppose I wouldn't be very enthused if I suddenly found a bunch of strangers lollygagging around my property, either. Hopefully, everyone can stay out of everyone else's hair, and we'll be away from this island before they know it."

"Hopefully," Denise said.

"Very well, I should be off to help Creighton set up our equipment. I believe I saw Jubal Hayes setting up somewhere nearby as well, although he seems to be going it alone. Farewell." Silas started off across the sand.

Denise looked back up at the *SMS Rear Admiral Hermann Hookstadt*. It lay on the sand like a beached sea monster, decaying on the beach. "I wonder what happened to the crew."

"Looks like a lot of them are dead," a voice said from inside the ship. Balthazar van Rensburg emerged from inside one of the huge rents in the ship's forward hull. He moved as silently as the big predators he hunted, and he looked just as dangerous. He scowled at Denise. "I found some skeletons inside, some of them still wearing what was left of their uniforms. It looks like maybe the ahools attacked. Some of the skeletons are in pretty bad shape."

Denise processed that. It might make sense why the warship ran aground. The ship came too close to Malheur Island, and then giant bats started to attack the crew. Once they smashed into the sand, they were stuck here.

"I am claiming this ship for my camp," Balthazar said. "It has steel walls, and I can seal off the interior behind heavy doors. It should be safe. You and you are welcome to join me if you wish." He pointed to Gail and Harrison. "But you are not welcome, DeMarco."

Denise felt her temper rising, but she tamped it down. She bit down on her lip and put a Herculean effort into not blowing

Balthazar to dog food with her elephant gun. He was screwing with her, and what was worse, it was actually getting to her.

"We're good. We'll camp with Denise," Gail said.

"Hey, maybe next time you can shake me down for my lunch money too, jackass," Denise said as she walked away.

She stormed away from the German cruiser, not bothering to look back. Gail and Harrison plodded along after her.

"What is with it between the two of you?" Harrison asked.

"I honestly have no idea," Denise said. "C'mon. We need to find a place to shelter before the sun sets and get our supplies there. I just saw proof that there's already one freak of nature on this island. If there really are more monsters, I don't think it will be safe at night."

EIGHT
A SHOT IN THE DARK

Denise checked her dart rifle for the hundredth time in the light of the battery operated lantern. The sights were calibrated. The barrel was clean. The darts were within easy reach. The stock felt comfortable against her shoulder. The bolt action was oiled and ready for easy use. Everything was set for her to take the first watch of the night as the sun sank toward the horizon.

They'd found a small cave wedged into the side of one of the coastal cliffs. Another one of those carved white rocks stood guard near the entrance, snarling out into the sea against all comers. The cave was maybe ten yards deep, and once they'd pulled all the driftwood and rocks out, the floor was fairly even. The entrance led straight out onto the beach.

Normally, Denise wouldn't choose a cave to set up camp. If something went wrong, there was only one way in and one way out. Anything that came at them would also block the only exit as it attacked. However, in this case, it made sense. They were dealing with something that could not only eat them, but could swoop down from any direction at all on silent wings. There was no way for Denise to monitor the entire sky, but she could keep track of a much smaller area just in front of her.

They'd also set up a series of nets outside the cave entrance. The nets had breakaway knots, so anything that tried to fly past or through the entrance would crash straight into one of the nets, which would then collapse around it. Whoever was on watch could then sink a tranquilizer dart into the creature and use one of the radios to contact the *Shield of Mithridates*.

Gail knelt on the floor and unrolled her sleeping bag while Harrison stirred a pot on the burner. Everything else they needed was stashed at the back of the cave, still within easy reach but protected from the elements.

"I can't believe they have the nerve to call this gumbo," Harrison said, staring at the pot. "I could crap better gumbo than this."

"Please don't," Gail said.

"I'm just saying."

Outside, the night was drawing closer as the horizon prepared to swallow the sun. Tomorrow, they'd try to go find the ahool lair, but there was no guarantee they'd be safe wandering the island in the dark. The nocturnal predators would be out soon.

Denise watched the sky turn orange outside, as if the world beyond the horizon had caught fire. It was almost easy to believe here on Malheur Island.

They were four hundred miles from the next closest landmass, and their only connection to the outside world beyond was through the radios that Hobhouse gave them. If the *Shield of Mithridates* sank, no one would even know they were stranded out here. Denise wasn't sure what would be worse, being stranded all by herself or being stranded with the likes of Balthazar van Rensburg.

A bat flitted past the cave entrance as the sky grew darker. Denise jerked and almost snapped the dart rifle up, but the little creature was only a few inches across. It was just a normal-sized bat.

Of course, from a distance, an ahool would like tiny and normal-sized as well. Her hand drifted away from the dart rifle, but she kept the weapon within easy reach nonetheless. In about four hours, she'd wake Harrison up, and it would be his job to watch the cave entrance for a shift.

"Hey, Denise. You never said why you quit hunting," Gail said.

"No, I didn't. I haven't really mentioned it to anyone, I guess."

"I'd rather listen to you than hear about Harrison's ability to make gumbo," Gail said. "If it's something you're willing to talk about, that is," she added.

"I suppose it might not be a bad thing to talk about it to somebody. It feels odd after keeping it to myself for so long, though."

"Hey, I'm happy to listen, too," Harrison said. "I won't even make too many snarky comments."

"Alright, so it goes like this. All I ever wanted to be when I was younger was a hunter, just like my father. He taught me everything I know on the subject, taking me along on most of his trips. He showed me how to track animals across various landscapes, he showed me how to shoot and make a clean kill, he taught me which animals became more aggressive and dangerous during their mating seasons and how to avoid getting flattened or eaten by angry beasts on a rampage.

"I learned all about the habits of animals. Where they congregated. What migration paths they took. What would spook them away and what would attract them. It was all very mechanical.

"When he disappeared on an expedition out in the Namib Desert a few years ago, I already knew everything I needed in order to take over the business. I could track anything across the veldt. Elephants. Rhinos. Lions. You name it, and I could probably find one for you and set up a shooting blind. After that, whoever I was guiding around simply needed to take the shot."

"At the same time, I'd been noticing something, though. The savanna was a different place from when I was a little girl. There simply weren't as many big animals as they used to be. Tracking them was harder because there were fewer trails. At first, I thought maybe it was just in my head, that maybe I was losing my touch, but it was true year after year. Each hunting season, there was simply less and less game. We were all taking too much, and the animal populations couldn't recover at the rate we were hunting them. Pretty soon, I had to guide people further and further north, well away from the main settlements. It was strange, I was doing what I loved, what I always thought I was meant to do, but that meant I was slowly destroying it at the same time."

"I can see that," Gail said. "There's fewer wolves in my neck of Montana than there were even just a few years ago. There's a lot fewer bears, too. People don't like them, so they shoot them on sight, and now they're starting to disappear from some of the more settled areas."

"Yeah, that's what I was seeing, too. I was concerned about it, but I was concerned about it because that's where my livelihood came from. I didn't really think about it beyond that. I mean, Harrison, have you ever been in any danger of running out of hogs to exterminate?"

"I can't say I have been, but they're definitely more common out in the boonies than right near the city these days. Wild pigs can repopulate an area pretty quick."

"Right. But some animals can't do that. A lot of the big game in South Africa doesn't really come back after you clear it from an area. You're just left with hyenas and some gazelles instead of lions and elephants, but that doesn't mean there's any less demand to hunt lions and elephants."

"So, about a year ago, I was leading a hunting party far to the north. It was a group of Belgian dentists that had formed a hunting club and wanted to go on a real African safari for their vacation. Very good money. One of the things they wanted to hunt was an elephant, so I'd been tracking a medium-sized herd for a few days. We were following them through the grassland, using the trampled areas and droppings to tell us where they'd been.

"We finally caught up to them, and I set up an ambush not far away from the nearest watering hole. All we had to do was wait for the elephants to come to us. I'd already picked one out from the herd that was older and slower. My clients would bag that one and then we'd move on. It would be a simple, easy hunt. I'd done the same thing fifty times before.

"I led the group up to the blind, and waited for the elephants to come. It didn't take long, maybe only an hour. The whole herd trundled up to the watering hole to get a drink, and I told the dentists which elephant they should go after. Everything seemed to be going just swimmingly.

"Then they opened fire. I'd rented them each a big bore elephant gun and made sure they knew how to use it. The blasts knocked a couple of them on their asses anyway.

"Apparently, they weren't content to just hunt one elephant. They all wanted an elephant each. I guess they planned it among themselves when I wasn't looking. All at once, almost the entire herd of elephants crumpled. Some of them didn't do down right away due to poor marksmanship. They had holes in their sides you could throw a medium-sized dog through, their intestines spilling out and tripping them up as they tried to scatter and run away, but they were still moving.

"I just remember staring in open-mouthed amazement for a moment. I thought there must have been some miscommunication. But then they started to reload, and I realized that it was just their plan to kill the whole herd of elephants. They wanted the whole enchilada, and they thought I was just in the way of giving it to them.

"I shouted at them, screamed right in their faces to stop, but they just snapped the guns back up and fired again, bringing down the rest of the herd. I wrenched the gun out of the hand of the nearest one. He tried to keep me from getting it, so I just punched him in the face. I think he lost a tooth, and one of his buddies had to fix it back in Belgium."

"That's not exactly playing by the rules of sportsmanship," Gail said.

"No, it wasn't. Some of the elephants were still alive at that point, but they were pretty much all down. You could actually feel the earth quiver slightly as they all fell. The ones that weren't dead yet were all screaming and making awful noises. It's one of the worst things I've ever heard. Frankly, it's pretty much what I imagine hell sounds like. Sometimes, I can still hear them screaming when I go to sleep.

"There was only one elephant still on its feet, a baby. The baby elephant's left ear had been blown off by one of the guns, but I'm not sure that it had even noticed. It was using its trunk to prod at one of the big females, apparently urging her to get up. She was on her side, one of her legs half-collapsed under her, not moving. The baby was standing in a big puddle of her blood."

"That's...an unpleasant image," Gail said.

"I thought so, too. One of the other hunters shot the baby elephant a few seconds after that. Maybe it was best to put it out of its misery then and there. I don't think it was old enough to survive on its own.

"Either way, I couldn't hunt after that. I tried going out a few times after that, but I just couldn't do it. I'd hear those screams and see that injured baby elephant standing in its mother's blood, and I'd break out into a cold sweat and feel like my guts were trying to work themselves into a sailing knot. I was a mess.

"Before, I mean, I understood that the animals I was hunting were living things, but I didn't really think of them as things with lives. Do you see what I'm saying? I could tell that if an animal was wounded, it was distressed and in pain, but I never really thought of myself as someone who inflicted death and agony for a living. That moment just sort of blew me right off my foundations, and I didn't know what to do with myself after that.

"I...I haven't told that story to anyone else. Just thinking about that day is enough to make me cringe up a little bit inside. I could use a drink."

"And I'd buy you one if we were on the mainland," Harrison said.

"Me too," Gail added.

"Did your clients seem to realize what they'd done afterwards?" Harrison asked.

"Oh gracious, no. They thought it was a hoot. They thought they were having the time of their lives as far as they were concerned. Well, except for the guy I punched. He was scrubbing around in the dirt looking for his tooth. I don't think he found it."

"So this is far enough removed from a real hunt that you're okay with it?" Gail asked.

"I think so, yeah. We're not out here to kill things for sport. If that's what Hobhouse and Yersinia wanted, I'd still be in Cape Town. Hopefully, we'll be able to capture an ahool alive without killing it. I'd shoot one if it came down to them or me; that's a different situation. I'll defend myself and you guys too, if it came down to a life and death situation, I just wouldn't like it very much. Maybe the ahools don't even actually exist, and they're just legends. That would take the possibility out of my hands entirely."

The sun was no more than a faint glow below the water now. A small orange light marked the last embers of the day, and all the rest was darkness. Maybe soon enough they'd find out whether or not ahools were real.

"I suppose so," Harrison said. "Maybe we can just have a slow, uneventful night without having too many worries."

A gunshot rang out, followed by a human scream. "Oh Jesus God! I've been shot! Somebody help me! Somebody he—"

The shouts cut off with the sound of another gunshot.

NINE
FIRST DEGREE

Denise, Gail, and Harrison rushed outside. "I think the scream came from over there," Gail said. She pointed into the jungle.

Denise held her elephant gun and watched the skies. Gail and Harrison held weapons, too. It was a bad time to be outside. If there really were ahools on the island, they'd probably be emerging from their dens right now to go on the hunt. With the sky dark overhead, the only way they'd be able to see anything was as it passed across the stars or the nearly full moon. Anything in the air would just be a shadow amongst the shadows.

"Who has a camp that way?" Denise asked.

"I think Creighton and Silas are somewhere over there. Andris, the Russian guy, was setting up a camp that way. Hell, I don't know. I haven't even seen Shinzo since we landed on this island, and I don't know where Jubal or Dr. Marlow ended up," Harrison said.

"Alright, let's see if we can find whoever that was. Maybe we can still help them," Denise said as they moved into the jungle. "Try to stay under the big trees as much as possible. It'll make it harder for something to swoop through the canopy and get us."

Denise held her gun in both hands, swiveling around to make sure there was nothing about to attack from overhead. They followed a game trail through the grass, weaving around bushes and fallen logs. Mushy, decaying leaf matter squished under their feet as they moved quickly and silently toward the source of the scream.

"Can you hear anything else?" Harrison asked, speaking low.

"No," Denise said. Gail shook her head.

"Neither can I," Harrison said. "That's not a good sign."

The jungle around them was dark and claustrophobic. Branches reached out of the shadow to snatch at them like skeletal claws. The earth under their feet was cramped with roots like giant petrified worms, and the soil stank of loamy decay. Logs and rocks loomed out at them from the darkness like the ill-kept tombstones of an abandoned graveyard.

Another big white rock carved like a monstrous head leered out at the three hunters from the darkness. Denise was half-tempted to obliterate the thing with a blast from her Nitro Express, but that probably wouldn't improve relations with the local culture any. She didn't like the weird, angry visages glaring at her from random corners of the island like angry gargoyles.

The silvery light of the moon drifted down from a few of the breaks in the canopy overhead, but Denise stuck to the shadows beneath the massive trees. It was easier to walk through the relatively barren zones under their great boughs, and it kept them safe. At least, that's what she hoped. She still didn't really understand what they were dealing with here. If nothing else, the brightness of the moon helped guide them.

They found what they were looking for on top of a short mound beneath a massive tree whose branches spread like the twisting arms of some stretching colossus. Balthazar van Rensburg was already there, leaning over a body.

The corpse on the ground was Andris Razan. For his camp, he'd dug a sort of foxhole along the top of the hill, giving him a good line of sight all around him and a way to duck down in case something came at him from above.

However, the fortified position was dug with animals in mind, not defending against other human beings. Razan's stomach was a mess of tacky blood where the first bullet must have hit him. Presumably, there was a small entrance wound somewhere in his back, because his belly had been blown apart where the round exited.

Razan's guts and tatters of his shirt were splashed against the side of his tent. He hadn't been hit with a round from an elephant gun, or there would barely be enough of him left to identify, but it must have been a large weapon regardless to do as much damage as it did.

There was a trail of blood, scuffed dirt, and more of Razan's innards where he must have crawled toward the edge of his trench after he was hit. He never made it more than a few feet, though. Another round had taken the top of Razan's head off. The shock of impact from the large bullet had exploded both his eyeballs as the bullet plunged through his skull, scrambled his brain to a pink slurry, and burst out the other side of his head.

Balthazar looked up at them as they moved into the clearing and approached the still-warm corpse of their fellow hunter. Denise's rifle twitched in Balthazar's direction as he got up. He had a rifle of his own, and no one knew what had happened yet.

"Did you do this?" Denise pointed a finger at Balthazar.

His expression was a mixture of disgust and disbelief. "No. I only got here a few minutes ago."

Denise looked at Razan's body. There were no powder burns on the corpse, but that didn't prove anything. It merely meant that the shots were fired from more than a few yards away. The distance could be twenty feet or five hundred, although the longer the distance, the harder it was to put a shot straight through a target as small as a man's head.

"Did you see anybody else running away from the camp?" Gail asked.

"No. I was watching the sky for bats from the bridge of that ship when I heard the first shot and scream. I was only halfway down to the exit when I heard the next blast. I ran over as fast as I could."

Silas and Creighton chose that moment to show up, thrashing their way through a line of underbrush to enter the clearing. "What happened? Is everyone alright? Oh good God!" Silas said as he spotted Razan's dead body.

"I say, this situation looks unfortunate," Creighton said.

"Balthazar got here first. We were just asking him some questions," Denise said.

"How did you get here so fast?" Silas asked.

"It's more or less a straight shot from my camp to Razan's. It's probably a little further than your camp, but I don't have to wind around any of those coastal cliffs to get here the way you do," Balthazar said.

"A 'straight shot' here?" Denise asked.

Balthazar grimaced. "Poor choice of words. Did either of you see anything?" He pointed to Creighton and Silas.

One by one the other hunters arrived. Shinzo showed up last. They'd all heard the shots and screams and zeroed in on Razan's camp. No one saw anything. No one knew what had happened. All nine of the hunters stared at the cooling body on the ground.

"I think there's only one conclusion here," Balthazar said. "Someone on this island is a murderer."

"But why?" Gail asked. "What's the point of killing one of us?"

"It could be a simple matter of dislike," Creighton said. "Andris made himself a difficult man to get along with sometimes. I seem to recall that you and your friends stayed away from him." The Englishman pointed to Denise, Gail, and Harrison. "Perhaps someone thought it would be his just desserts if something bad were to happen to him in a place where the authorities could not easily investigate. Hmm?"

"Oh, shove it, peckerwood," Harrison said. "From my experience, you can trace a lot of trouble back to money. Always follow the money. Me, Gail, and Denise weren't about to start a fan club for Mr. Razan there, but all three of us would have to agree to murder him and then cover for each other. Too complicated. Too easy to go wrong.

"No, I'm guessing this was about the money. Somebody thinks that there's too much competition for that hundred thousand dollar grand prize around here. Maybe if Razan lands an ahool, nobody else will get a good opportunity. Maybe our killer is thinking it's best to thin out the ranks a little, and that will improve his odds of netting some of that sweet, sweet Yersinia money."

"Maybe we should string you up and see how much you really know about this, you loud-mouthed nigger," Jubal Hayes said. "Ain't nobody going to miss your sad black ass if we're wrong."

"I don't know. Your wife would miss it quite a bit. She seems rather fond of it." Harrison glowered at Jubal.

Jubal started forward, but Balthazar knocked him back. "Leave it," the big Boer said. "He's right. It's much more likely to be an individual than a group who is responsible for this. Maybe a couple of people can all make an alibi for each other, but that's a lot harder. You two and DeMarco say you were all together when this happened, and I believe you. Silas and Creighton were in their camp together, and that makes them less likely, too. That leaves four of us who can't confirm their location with anyone else at the time of this murder."

Balthazar looked at Dr. Marlow. Dr. Marlow looked at Jubal. Jubal looked at Shinzo. Shinzo looked at Balthazar.

"You know, it could be one of the island natives." Dr. Marlow said.

"Denise did say one of them told her that we needed to leave the island by tomorrow night. This could be a sort of warning," Silas said.

"And they've sealed themselves off behind that wall of theirs, too," Creighton added.

"I can see the village from the bridge of the ship," Balthazar said. "Nobody came or went through their main gate since I set up my equipment up there. It could be one of the islanders, but it's someone not working with the rest of the village if it is. I'm not sure they'd have access to a big enough gun to do this." He pointed to Razan's broken body. "That's the work of a serious rifle and someone who knew how to use it."

"So what do we do about this?" Shinzo asked.

"I don't think we're going to be able to figure this out on our own just standing here," Denise said. "We're going to need to radio the *Shield of Mithridates*, and they're going to need to come back with the Dutch authorities.

"Until then, we should probably split into groups of three. No one is left alone that way, either to execute more murders or to be preyed on by the killer. Whoever did it will always be outnumbered two to one that way, and he'll always have someone watching him."

Balthazar gave her an odd look. Was that…grudging respect? Or did he just have to sneeze?

"I think that's a good idea for now," Silas said. "Hopefully, that will keep everyone safe, at least until Hobhouse and the *Shield of Mithridates* return. We can consolidate camps in the morning."

The remaining hunters grouped together. Shinzo went with Silas and Creighton, but he wasn't happy about it. His golden eagle would be alone until the morning. Creighton grimaced as they led him away toward their camp.

That left Balthazar, Jubal, and Dr. Marlow together, a regular dream team. After a brief argument, Jubal stood down on insisting they use his camp, and they started toward the beached cruiser van Rensburg was occupying. He won the argument by pointing out that steel walls were much more defensible than a mere tent.

Denise couldn't help but think about the height advantage Balthazar would have up on the bridge as well. She wondered if he could see the entrance to the cave where she, Gail, and Harrison were camped. Would he be able to draw a bead on them from there if he wanted? Did he have a clear shot at Razan's camp from there? Jubal and Dr. Marlow started to walk down the path to the German warship.

"Wait, what do we do about Andris?" Denise asked. She looked down at his corpse, still sprawled awkwardly in the trench. "We should bury him or something, right?"

"Nah, leave him for the maggots," Jubal said. "His troubles are over. I don't want to drag him out of there."

"I would suggest we leave him as well," Dr. Marlow said. "There might be bats in the air, and I'd rather not linger."

"No, she's right," Balthazar said, surprising her. "If nothing else, the authorities should get a chance to examine his body for clues. If we leave him for the scavengers, there might not be much left. We'll take care of this business, and then return." Stepping down into to pit, he grabbed Razan by the legs. Denise and Gail found a tarp, and Balthazar and Harrison lifted the body onto it.

Grabbing Razan's shovel, Denise followed them as they dragged the tarp toward the edge of the beach. They took turns digging while the others watched the sky and kept their rifles handy.

Soon, they had a shallow grave ready, and they rolled Razan off the tarp into the hole. His body *thwumped* into the sand face up, his burst eyes staring at all of them. His mouth hung open in a silent shriek. Denise laid the tarp over top of him, and they shoveled sand on top as fast as they could.

"Hold on. We'll need to be able to find him again," Denise said. She ran back the short distance to Razan's camp and grabbed his pack and rifle. Lugging them back, she plopped the heavy rucksack down over the mound of sand and wedged the rifle vertically through the straps to create a crude marker.

They scurried back to their respective camps like mice under the gaze of an owl. No one said anything. No one needed to. Now they knew that the most dangerous predators on Malheur Island might not be the ahools.

TEN
MOON ROCKS

The next morning was bright with promise. Whether it was a promise of good or bad, it was too early to say.

Denise had barely slept at all last night, even after her watch ended. They hadn't been able to reach the *Shield of Mithridates* on the radios Hobhouse gave them. Whether that was from equipment failure or simply because the ship's radioman was busy communicating with all the other hunting teams about the murder, Denise didn't know. Even though they were using the right channel, and the radio seemed to be working, they never got ahold of Hobhouse to tell him about Razan's murder.

Fortunately, they weren't attacked by anything in the night, human or otherwise. There was no sign of any giant bats on the island, nor had she heard any activity from the other hunters. Apparently, it was a quiet night for everyone after the spectacle of Razan's death.

Hopefully, Malheur Island didn't have any more surprises of that magnitude for them. Denise ate breakfast with Gail and Harrison. They both had dark circles under their eyes as well.

"Alright, so we need to formulate a plan for the day," Gail said.

"Right. First of all, I think we should all stick together. Nobody should wander off on their own," Harrison said.

"Agreed." Denise nodded. She'd gathered some driftwood and started a small fire, which now had a coffee pot bubbling above it. Coffee was good. Coffee was their friend. All hail the savior of the realm, coffee.

"With people grouped up, I don't think the killer will try anything again," she said. "At least, maybe not until nightfall when they could slip away and hide a bit better. Nobody is going to be very eager to let people out of their sights, though."

She had spent the entire night wondering who could be responsible for murdering Razan. Because she knew that neither Gail nor Harrison was responsible, and she could sure as hell rule herself out, that left six suspects among the remaining hunters.

Some of them were pretty rough and tumble, but were any of them willing to murder a man in cold blood, to pop the top of his skull off while he lay on the ground screaming for help?

And of course, they weren't alone on Malheur. There were also the islanders to consider. They were still an enigma. Aside from the man in dungarees at the beach, no one had seen any of the villagers. They'd simply holed up behind their walls like they were expecting a siege.

For that matter, why was the village even walled off? If they were the only population of people on Malheur, they could spread out and live anywhere they wanted. Instead, they'd huddled up behind protection, cut off from the entire rest of the island.

Their radio crackled. "Hello? Anybody there?"

Denise thought about leaving the radio piece where it was and not answering. She recognized the low rumble of Balthazar's voice. Harrison and Gail were watching her. Sighing, she picked the radio up.

"Hello, Balthazar. This is Denise. Why are you calling us?"

There was a pause. "Put someone else on. One of your friends. I don't want to talk to you."

"Yeah? Well, too bad. If you have something important to say, spill it."

There was another long pause. "Put one of the others on long enough, so I can know they're still alive."

"It's cool, Balthazar. We're still fogging mirrors over here," Harrison said close to the mouthpiece. "Now put on somebody else over there, so we can make sure they're still alive, too."

"I'm alright, and so is Marlow," Jubal said over the radio.

"*Damn*," Harrison mouthed to Denise.

"Alright, now that we know nobody killed everyone else off in their sleep last night, what do you need, Balthazar?"

"Were you able to contact the *Shield of Mithridates* last night?"

Denise's grip tightened on the radio. "You mean you weren't able to reach them either?"

"No, we tried to after we buried Razan. The airwaves were clear; there was just no response."

"We had the same problem. There wasn't just nothing. It's like they weren't responding. I'll try radioing Silas and his group. Maybe they were able to get through."

"Don't bother. I asked them first. They couldn't get through, either."

"This is bad," Denise said. Presumably, the *Shield of Mithridates* would come back, but not for another month. It was just supposed to return after a set time or when someone radioed in that they'd captured an ahool.

Until that ship returned, they were all effectively marooned on Malheur Island. Marooned with the killer.

"Stay safe out there," Balthazar said, surprising her.

"You too," she replied. She looked at Harrison and Gail.

There were exactly two other people that Denise trusted on this island, and they were both in this cave with her, pondering the same questions as she was.

"Alright, we have daylight again. I say we use it wisely. Our goals should be threefold. This hiccup in the communications might only be temporary. The *Shield of Mithridates* might have already realized there's something wrong with the radios and is heading back right now, but we have to assume they aren't. Maybe even something happened to them."

Denise thought about the wrecked pleasure yacht, the *Venture*. Even if giant bats were responsible for that, surely they couldn't knock out a ship as large as the *Shield of Mithridates*, could they? Then she remembered the wrecked German cruiser further down the beach. That vessel was a lot bigger and a lot meaner than Hobhouse's floating luxury hospital. She felt a sense of dread creep down her spine.

"First, our number one priority needs to be to stay safe. We go everywhere together. Nobody lets anyone get lost. Nobody splits off. We'll outnumber anyone with bad intentions three to one that way, and I like those odds a lot better than any others.

"Next, we should scout out the island for fresh water and sources of food. We all know how to survive in the wild, but we might be here longer than expected." *Maybe a lot longer if our ride out was attacked,* she thought. "Our canned food and other supplies won't last forever. It will be good to figure out what fruits, nuts, and game we can find here. If there is trouble, it will be to our advantage if we already know where to find enough to live off the land for a while.

"Finally, we should look for any ahool colonies, probably in caves or other dark spaces. I assume that they're like most bats and only come out once it starts to get dark. Maybe they don't even exist at all, but I for one want to make damn sure I know where the big predators are going to pop out of after nightfall. We'll be safer avoiding those places later in the day, and maybe we can set up some traps and capture one of these things by the time the *Shield of Mithridates* comes back to check on us."

"Sounds like a plan," Gail said.

They set off from their cave, carrying just what they needed. Today, that meant a Nitro Express rifle and a heavy revolver strapped to everyone's hip. Denise left her tranquilizer gun behind. If they ran into any trouble during the daylight, it was a lot more likely a person than an ahool.

Denise felt the weight of the rifle in her hands as she stepped off the soft sand, and her feet started across the damp, spongy piles of jungle litter. She hadn't gone hunting since the incident with the Belgian dentists. It wasn't because she didn't want to, which was true. It was because she all but physically couldn't. Tromping through the underbrush carrying a big gun brought it all back.

A coil of unease knotted itself inside her stomach and started squeezing her insides. She tapped her sweaty fingers against the rifle's trigger guard, beating a senseless rhythm. Her breath escaped in hot little bursts, leaving her all but panting.

It's okay. It's not a real hunt. We're just exploring. No one is hunting, she told herself. Her saliva felt hot and ropy in her mouth. She spat a gob on the ground and kept walking as bushes and shrubs scratched at her clothes as if to hold her back from what lay ahead. She reached up and wiped an unbelievable amount of sweat from her brow.

Even though Malheur Island was already warming up with heavy tropical heat, Denise felt a chill. Her muscles felt tense and brittle, as if they might shatter if she fell down.

The scent of omnipresent decay pushed its way up her nose. Rotten fruit. Decomposing plants. Putrid animal carcasses. The jungle was full of them. A jungle was a harsh place to live, but it was also the ultimate recycler.

Everything that fell on the ground would first be picked apart by an army of insects. The heat would make short work of anything left over, all but boiling flesh and meat off the bones and into the soil. The nutrients would then end up sucked into the mighty trees, which would one day die and topple and decay into the earth, starting the process over again. The jungle survived by constantly eating itself, a continuous cycle of auto-cannibalism.

Denise kicked a mound of leaves, and a big, hairy spider scuttled out from under them. She left the angry arachnid alone and continued forward.

Nice deep breaths, she told herself. *There you go.* Taking in deep lungfuls of air and air and letting them out in measured breaths helped her relax a little. The knot loosened a little in her stomach.

She tried focusing on little things, diverting her mind away. She tried to see how many animals she could spot as they walked along. There was a snake slithering across a downed branch. A troupe of monkeys with ridiculous manes watched from the boughs of a tree.

Some of these might be previously undiscovered species. Denise specialized in African game, not the creatures native to the Dutch East Indies. Maybe Dr. Marlow would know. Or maybe not. He seemed like kind of a coot.

Either way, Denise knew she'd be able to identify an ahool if she saw one. She didn't need an advanced degree to recognize a bear-sized bat. That was aberrant anywhere on earth.

To some degree, she still wasn't even sure if she believed that ahools existed. There were a few dusty legends from this corner of the globe about giant bats, but there were also folk stories about vampires and werewolves, and she would have laughed in Hobhouse's face if he told her that's what he wanted her to hunt. He might as well have said Yersinia was interested in capturing a Sasquatch alive for medical study. It was a fun notion, but she wasn't sure that it actually made a single, solitary lick of difference to the reality on the ground.

What evidence had they seen so far that ahools existed? So far, it basically amounted to Hobhouse's say so and a wrecked pleasure yacht. There was no guarantee that the *Venture* and its crew hadn't met some other ill-fated demise, either. If not for the scrapes in its deck that looked like claw marks, Denise would have said that whoever was piloting the yacht simply met one of the dozen or so ways to die at sea. Nothing about the scene really confirmed the existence of a giant bat native to Malheur Island.

The same was true of the *SMS Rear Admiral Hermann Hookstadt*. Obviously, it had run aground, and Balthazar said there were some skeletons wearing German uniforms inside, but that didn't really mean anything. They could have gotten lost in a fog or chased here by a British warship. Some of the crew died in the crash and were never recovered, but it was less of a leap of logic to guess that the remaining hundreds of German sailors aboard that ship were rescued or captured by passing ships, not carried away and devoured by monsters.

Even staying up nearly all last night, Denise didn't see any pterodactyl-sized sky creatures swooping through the darkness. She saw a few normal bats, but there was nothing that looked anything like what Hobhouse described.

As to the Dutch expeditions that came to Malheur Island before? Denise didn't have a good answer for why they all failed. Plenty of colonization attempts didn't work out, though. Disease. Angry natives. Internal disputes. All of them could lead to a Roanoke Island situation in which a colony was wiped off the map before the next supply ship arrived. It wasn't hard to imagine.

That was one of their goals for the day. If they inspected some caves and crevices, and they could find no signs of any giant bats, that was another mark against the existence of the ahool. Maybe she'd sleep a little easier tonight if there was more assurance that she wouldn't be foully eaten alive by some massive, half-blind freak of nature.

And she'd feel less jittery about going out on the island with a rifle. Denise felt a little better distracting her mind from what she was doing by focusing on the task at hand and speculating on the odds of whether monsters really existed or not. It was like unclenching her mind.

"There's something up ahead," Gail said.

Denise looked forward and saw what Denise was pointing at through the trees. It was a cabin, badly overrun with creepers. Looking closer, Denise realized they'd entered an area with smaller, second growth trees. More sunlight dappled the ground around them, and that was because someone had cleared this patch of jungle at some point.

If she looked closely, she could even see the remains of some massive stumps hidden in some bushes nearby. About two acres had been hacked back and tamed, but that was a while ago, Denise guessed maybe two decades or more. The jungle had regained a lot of its crushing green presence since then, so much so that she hadn't even noticed they were walking through a cleared zone at first.

"This must be where the last group of Dutch administrators tried to set up shop," Harrison said. He was probably right.

Now that Denise was looking for signs of human activity, they were subtle but unmistakable. Some decaying wood stuck out in the surf was probably the last remains of a dock that had long since rotted and fallen apart.

She looked over and saw an ax head buried in a tree. The ax's handle had long since decayed and fallen away, but the ax head remained. Since someone started to chop away at the tree all those years ago, the tree had since grown and nearly eaten the blade meant to fell it.

A few upright posts over there were probably part of an old fence rather than the dead saplings she'd originally taken then for. The flattened area over there was probably meant as the foundation for another building, and the pile of stones nearby had probably been dredged up in an attempt to create a field.

The cabin was the only part of the endeavor that had survived, and it was in danger of falling apart. Gaping holes marked its windows, and it sat crookedly on its foundation. Some of the logs used to build it looked like they might crumble into a puff of spores if she stared at them cross-eyed. Vines grew around the building like skinny snakes working together in an attempt to crush the structure.

Further back behind the cabin stood another white boulder, but this one was the largest Denise had seen yet. It was almost ten feet tall and almost as wide. From here, it almost looked like a giant egg from some truly massive bird. Like the other white stones on the island, it had been carved into a nightmarish face, like some macabre version of the Easter Island idols.

Unlike its brethren, this one clearly didn't belong here. Huge straps and chains crisscrossed the stone, wrapping around it like it was in a giant sling. The chains led to the remains of some harnesses and a set of picked-over oxen skeletons. Someone had moved the huge idol here before the nascent settlement fell apart completely, which didn't look like it had taken very long. With only one fully constructed building, it wasn't much of a settlement to begin with.

"Let's check it out," Gail said.

Harrison looked at the crumbling buildings. "I'm mighty curious what this is all about myself."

They all trudged through the once-cleared field toward the cabin. The giant stone head watched them as they walked toward it, but Denise ignored the howling beast face. It was difficult, though. The carved eyes seemed to bore into them as they approached, like some ancient sphinx watching travelers approach and preparing to devour them.

The door to the cabin had fallen off its hinges, allowing them to see inside. Moss and insects had run rampant inside the structure. Most of the space inside was taken up by bunks. This building was probably intended to just be temporary until more structures could be built, but now it was the only remnant of whatever expedition landed here years ago.

A desk and set of drawers lay along the far wall. Denise, Gail, and Harrison stepped inside the mildewed shadows to poke around.

Denise examined the bunks. Animals had torn the mattresses apart, and the jungle had eaten away whatever was left behind. The only thing left were rusty springs inside a frame.

She wondered what happened to these people. Hobhouse said there had been a number of failed expeditions to Malheur Island over the years. Had everyone here died? Or had they packed up, waved down the first ship that sailed past, and made their way back to Amsterdam? Judging from the oxen skeletons outside, they must have left in one hell of a hurry. Or they'd been absolutely and swiftly wiped out.

"Hey, look what I found," Harrison said, pulling something out of one of the desk drawers. It was a small journal, slightly water damaged but in remarkably good shape overall. He opened it up, peeling a couple of pages apart that had become stuck together. "Oh, hmm."

"What is it?" Gail asked.

"I don't really know," Harrison said. "Denise, is this Dutch, or did somebody turn some monkeys with typewriters loose?"

Denise took the notebook from Harrison and looked at the crinkled pages. "This is Dutch." She flipped the book open to its cover and squinted at the words. *Royal Dutch Geological Society – 1902* was printed on the front.

"Can you read it? I was under the impression that Dutch was more of a throat disease than a real language." Harrison looked over her shoulder at the densely written words on the page.

"I can read some of it. Afrikaans is close enough to Dutch that I can puzzle out a good bit of it. Some of this is piled high with scientific terms that I would need a degree in geology to understand, though. Here's what it looks like to me, though. This is apparently the notebook of a Dutch geologist sent by his government to survey the island. It makes reference to a few other people. Looks like there was an anthropologist on the expedition, a couple of builders, a couple of soldiers, and a bureaucrat who was supposed to establish control over the island. I guess they were planning on setting up a waystation and warehouse for the Dutch East India Company, and they wanted to know if there were any interesting minerals here that would be worth mining."

"Anything good?" Gail asked. "If we can't find an ahool, I'd settle for bringing back a small pile of gold."

"A lot of this is just field notes, and I'm having a hard time reading those. Too much jargon. It looks like he found some iron and some...other stuff. I don't know."

"Too bad there's not a treasure map in there, too," Harrison said.

"Wait, I can read most of this part. Looks like our geologist friend took an interest in the weird carved heads all around the island."

"They do have a way of grabbing your attention," Gail said.

"He was less interested in their artistic merits than their composition. Looks like they aren't like any other type of rock in this area. There's some exotic sounding stuff in there. Looks like he got all excited here because there was even a new mineral in them that he was going to name after his wife."

"Doesn't look like he got the chance," Harrison said.

"Whoa. Okay, get this. He was pretty sure that the white rocks are lunar meteorites."

"As in moon rocks?" Gail asked.

"Yeah. He figured that a comet smacked into the moon, blew a chunk of it off the surface, and it ended up falling to earth with a bunch of smaller fragments. He thought it probably exploded in the atmosphere and sent a whole bunch of these white rocks across this part of the world. I guess most of them would have landed in the water, but a good chunk of them landed on Malheur Island."

"Well, huh. I'm not sure Hobhouse will get his giant bats, but he might get something just as interesting from this expedition. Lunar meteorites. Hot damn," Harrison said.

"I'm not sure we should just be walking off with those things," Denise said. "They seem sort of important to the locals. They've carved every single one of them up like something out of a shudder magazine."

"Maybe we can trade them something for one," Harrison said.

Denise frowned. She didn't know if the meteorite statues were idols or warnings or just art, but she didn't like the idea of trying to bargain canned food and guns for one. That felt like a swindle.

"Does the journal say what happened to everyone on this expedition?" Gail asked.

"No. It just ends. There's nothing more after a certain date."

"You think Hobhouse would buy these lunar meteorites? I mean, they must have some pretty hefty scientific value. I don't know of anybody else who just has moon rocks sitting around. Somebody will want to buy them, even if it's not Yersinia."

"You're right. We could get richer off these rocks than the giant bats were supposed to be looking for," Gail said.

"Split the proceeds in thirds, just like our original deal?" Harrison asked.

"I don't think—" Denise started.

"Deal," Gail said.

"I'm not sure we should—" Denise tried to break through her friends' growing excitement.

"But it's important that we keep this absolutely secret between ourselves," Harrison said. "If the others find out that these statues are worth something, things might get complicated."

"Oh, we are going to make a lot of money off this," Gail said. "Boston art school, here I come."

"Did I hear someone say there was money to be made?" a voice asked from behind them. Everyone spun around to see Jubal Hayes standing behind them, blocking their exit.

ELEVEN
HERE BE DRAGONS

"How long have you been lurking there?" Denise demanded.

"Oh, a little while." Jubal grinned. "Long enough to hear that there was some kind of secret plan to make lots and lots of money."

"Back off, Jubal. This doesn't concern you."

"Oh, I think it might. Here we are on an island, with me thinking that maybe one of my friends being murdered and all was a cause for concern, and now I hear you three scheming in this hut here."

"For that matter, where are Balthazar and Dr. Marlow? You're supposed to be with them." Denise didn't like Jubal in the first place, and she didn't like the situation here at all. He was purposely standing in the doorway, their only exit from the decrepit hut.

"They're nearby. I slipped away while they went to look at the village. I don't work well in teams. You three, on the other hand, you seem to work well together, a little too well together. I decided to listen to you to see if you were up to anything. Looks like I was right. Oh how right I was."

"I'm going to tell you again, this doesn't involve you, Jubal."

"Not with that attitude it doesn't. But here's the thing, sweet cheeks. I've got a proposition for you. You can deal me in the easy way, or I can find out on my own. That way would be a lot more fun for me, I think."

Moving with shocking speed, Jubal whipped his hands out and latched them around Denise's neck. He lifted up, applying pressure and lifting her up onto her toes.

Urk. Denise tried to swing her legs out and kick him or spin out of Jubal's grasp, but he had too much reach, and she was already up on her toes. She spat at him, but he merely smiled.

"See, here's the thing that doesn't seem to be going through your pretty little head, here. I only have two goals on this island.

The first is to make lots of goddamn money, the same as everyone else. Hobhouse wants to talk this up as some kind of nature preserve or whatever, but his game is the same. There's money to be made here, and I want as much of it as I can get, and, well, if I have to take it out of your hide, so much the better.

"Next, I want to get off this godforsaken rock alive. I didn't think that would be a problem before somebody put Razan in the ground, but now I have to worry about that, too. And you know what? You're my number one suspect for killing him. You and your friends here never liked the rest of us. I think you're playing the same game as we are, trying to suck more cash out of that money teat Hobhouse offered us by nicking people off one at a time."

Denise could feel Jubal's hard hands clamping down on her throat harder and harder as he spoke. She clawed at his fingers, trying to open up some room between them and her flesh so some air could reach her lungs again, but his hands were like iron manacles.

"Jubal, you may want to put my friend down," Harrison said.

"Eh, why's that? I don't take orders from niggers."

Jubal found out why when Gail leveled her revolver against the back of his head.

The edges of Denise's vision were starting to go black, as if a black fog was seeping out of the corners of the cabin and slowly filling it. She took her hands off Jubal's.

"Here's one reason," Gail said, pulling the hammer back with a cold, hard click.

"I knew it was you three that killed Razan. I knew it. What, are you going to murder me, too? Balthazar and Dr. Marlow aren't a quarter of a mile away. I can snap your little co-conspirator's neck right now. What will they think when they find her dead and me killed by a shot to the back of the head. Eh? Eh? Your game would be up then."

Denise took her hands and pulled them back so they were closer to her shoulders, turning her elbows into spikes. Wriggling around to get a better shot, she suddenly thrust her elbows straight down into Jubal's own elbows.

No matter how strong someone was, the design of the human arm meant that elbows did exactly what they were intended to do quite easily: bend. Jubal's arms had been stretched straight out in holding Denise up, but her explosion of downward forced caused his elbows to creak downward.

That brought her down flat on her feet again, but it didn't release Jubal's grip around her neck. To solve that, she used the forward momentum she'd just gained and magnified it. She sprang forward as soon as her feet touched the ground and bashed her forehead straight into Jubal's nose. The impact hurt a little, but not nearly as much as it hurt Jubal.

The force of her skull mashing straight into his face at full speed broke his nose like a stale breadstick. He howled and released her to bring his hands up to his mashed-in nose. At the same time, Denise lashed out with her foot and kicked him hard in the gut.

Jubal Hayes collapsed like someone had turned off his spine. He fell to the ground with a great whoofing noise and promptly threw up on himself. Blood ran down his upper lip from the remains of his nose and puke ran down his chin as he looked up at her.

"Here's the thing, Jubal," Denise said. "We didn't kill Razan. If we did, you can bet your ass that we would shoot you right now. But see, we're not going to do that. We're going to let you run back to Balthazar and Dr. Marlow, where you're supposed to be in the first place."

"You sure we should do that, Denise?" Harrison asked.

"I mean, he did just put a good effort into strangling the life out of you. What if he's the one that killed Razan last night? We don't know where he was. Nobody does."

Denise looked at her friends. They were both staring down at Jubal, who was still in too much pain to move a whole lot. He looked up at them with wide eyes. Gail and Harrison looked down at him with narrowed ones.

"He did hear us talking about the journal, too," Harrison said.

"No. We aren't killing him. We don't know that he was responsible for what happened last night. If we all start to turn on each other, there won't be anyone left for the *Shield of Mithridates* to pick up."

Her friends looked at her with skepticism. She didn't like Jubal. Maybe she even kind of wanted to stake him out on the beach and use him as ahool bait herself, but she wasn't a cold-blooded killer. She wasn't about to stop her hunting career of shooting animals only to start shooting people instead. If she knew Jubal was the killer, she'd have no problem wrapping him up in chains until Hobhouse returned, but she wouldn't execute him.

"We are *not* killing him," she said again. "You're worried he'll spoil our plans about the moon rocks? Fine. I'll reset the playing field again so we don't have to be paranoid about everyone learning our secrets. If Hobhouse wants to pay for the idols, he'll pay everyone, not just the three of us."

She grabbed the Dutch geologist's journal off the desk and tossed it at Jubal. He winced as it landed next to him.

"I think you're making a mistake," Gail said. "This could be our gold rush."

Denise wasn't even sure what she was doing was a good idea. She didn't like the idea of selling cultural artifacts to Yersinia when they were part of a living society. It felt too much like robbery. Giving the journal to Jubal and spreading word about the moon rocks would almost certainly lead to the widespread pilfering of the statues one way or the other.

On the other hand, they all needed to survive this. If everyone thought she, Gail, and Harrison held some enormously valuable secret, more people than Jubal might turn on them. They could be as hunted as the ahools by the end of the day, and she didn't think any of them would live very long with targets like that on their back. Fear and greed might turn even the relatively even-keeled hunters like Silas into members of a blood hungry mob. Instead of pitchforks and torches, they'd be out with high-powered rifles and flashlights.

It would be good cover for whoever killed Razan to take more victims, too. No, survival trumped any moral victories from preserving the statues on the island.

Off in the distance, Denise could hear voices shouting. "Jubal! Jubal, where have you gone?"

That was Balthazar and Dr. Marlow, looking for their little lost lamb. They'd realized he was missing and had gone looking for him.

Good. That meant he hadn't killed them both and stuffed their bodies somewhere. A day before, Denise wouldn't have even entertained such thoughts, but now that one of their number had been gunned down like a prey animal, it was on the forefront of her mind.

"Take that journal and show it to Balthazar. He speaks Afrikaans. Balthazar might be able to translate the Dutch even better than me. Tell him not to read it until he can find Silas, Creighton, and Shinzo. Then everyone will know what we know. We're leaving, and if I see you try to follow us instead of scampering back to Balthazar with your tail between your legs, I will put a bullet through that mess where your nose is supposed to be. Do you understand?"

Jubal nodded. "Bitch," he said under his breath, although the blood clogging his crushed nose made it come out as *Bish*.

"What was that?" Denise said.

Jubal didn't say anything. He just looked away.

"Answer the lady, honkey," Harrison said.

"I'll take the journal to Balthazar," Jubal wheezed.

"Good," Denise said. She strolled out of the hut and back into the tropical sunlight.

"Denise, you're my friend, but I think you just screwed us," Gail said.

"Maybe."

"I'm not sure there's a maybe about it," Harrison said. "I'm sorely tempted to go back there and club Jubal's brains out anyway."

"We might be screwed now, but I think we'd be twice as screwed if we did anything else," Denise said. "Jubal didn't love us before, but if he's not the killer, he doesn't have any extra reasons to come after us. For that matter, whoever killed Razan won't have any additional reasons to track us down. Harrison, you were the one who thought the killer was probably after more money. Who do you think would be next on his hit list if he thought we had some extra means of pulling out aces here?"

They were walking in the general direction of Malheur Island's central mountain. A game trail wandered through a patch of tall grass in a clearing. Above them, the sun beat down like a molten hammer, and sweat started to stain their clothes. The jungle humidity turned every breath of air into a gasp.

"I don't trust Jubal. He's a bastard and a half," Gail said.

"I don't trust him either."

"We should have at least tied him up or something. If he's the one who killed Razan, he'll probably want to come after us next, even if he knows as much as we do about the lunar meteorites."

"*J'accuse*. Look, I don't know that Jubal is innocent of killing Razan, but I don't know that he's guilty, either. If we let him return to his group unharmed to his group, it shows some good will. If any of us are going to survive on this island, we're going to have to work together until we find out who's responsible for Razan's murder. We'll still play things safe. Travel together. Hold watch shifts at night. If we had killed Jubal without knowing he was the real killer, would we actually feel any safer?"

The painful marks around her neck throbbed as she spoke. Maybe she would feel safer if they had chained Jubal to a tree in some ways. He was undoubtedly a danger, but he might not be *the* danger.

Cripes. She could do with a stiff drink or a dozen right about now. They kept walking, the jungle around them giving way to a clearing of reeds and grass.

The tall grass ahead of them shuddered suddenly. Denise stopped in her tracks. She held the Nitro Express in her hands.

She sniffed the air.

Gail and Harrison seemed to notice at the same time she did. There was a strong odor in the air, something they'd missed during their arguments. It was something strong and pungent. Now that they were paying attention again, their instincts as hunters started waving great big orange neon DANGER signs.

That odor was the scent of decay. More than just the usual odor of the jungle, this was a smell that said a large amount of spoiling meat sat somewhere nearby. Or it was the smell of something that spent a lot of time wallowing in spoiled meat, and there was only one class of animal on earth that strongly smelled of rotting, putrescent corpses.

And that was the type of animal that made a lot of corpses. Large predators.

The grass ahead twitched again.

Suddenly, a gigantic scaly monster burst out of the grass straight toward them, moving freakishly fast on four clawed legs. A tail covered in bumpy osteoderms whiplashed back and forth behind it as it moved. A gaping mouth opened wide, displaying dozens of shiny recurve teeth faceted into the compact, brutish head. Twelve feet of angry reptile surged toward them.

"Run!" Denise turned and sprinted down the path as four more of the massive creatures burst out of the grass. Gail and Harrison followed suit, fleeing as fast as they could.

At first glimpse, Denise had assumed that the reptilian beasts were crocodiles. Big ones at that. She was used to crocodiles at the watering holes around South Africa.

Then she realized that what was chasing them was actually much worse.

They weren't in South Africa anymore. She didn't even know if the Dutch East Indies had crocodiles, but what the Dutch East Indies did have was Komodo dragons.

While they weren't quite as large as a full-sized crocodile, they had some features that made them even worse. Their bite itself wasn't venomous, but their mouths were naturally home to so many aggressive bacteria that broke down animal carcasses that the effect was almost the same as a potent venom. Whenever a Komodo dragon bit anything, it released toxic bacteria into the victim's bloodstream. Even if the prey managed to escape the dragon's clutches, it would likely die from sepsis anyway. The huge monitor lizard could simply trail behind the unfortunate animal and wait for it to die all on its own. Essentially, Komodo dragons had weaponized bad hygiene.

There were too many of the lizards, and they were moving too fast for Denise to hit them all with her Nitro Express. She'd be overwhelmed and torn apart before she could reload.

Gail and Harrison ran beside her. They needed to get up in a tree or somewhere else where the Komodo dragons couldn't reach them. She didn't know how far they could run, but she'd already seen that they could run faster than her. They only had a few moments before the huge reptiles caught up and brought them down in a frenzy of slashing claws, whipping tails, and frothing saliva.

Since they'd entered the clearing, there weren't any trees close by. However, there was an abutment of fractured land. At some point, some geological fault had pushed one section of the island up in a jagged wall of nearly vertical earth and rock. A narrow stream ran between the level clearing and the upthrust wall.

"Over there. Climb! Climb!" Denise pointed and veered away from their current path, vaulting through the tall grass. She dashed around the skeletonized remains of some sort of deer, only a few runny strands of sinew and fly-blackened meat still clinging to its bones. This must be the heart of the Komodo dragons' territory, the killing fields where they outpaced and slaughtered prey. She could hear them scrambling through the grass behind her, gaining ever closer.

Reaching the edge of the creek, she leaped and grabbed onto the craggy surface of the wall. Her body slammed into the hard surface, nearly punching the breath out of her lungs. Her face met dirt, and pebbles scraped open her cheek. One hand still clutching her Nitro Express by the barrel, she launched herself up the uneven surface as best she could. Gail and Harrison were right behind her, launching themselves at the wall and grabbing on.

Denise climbed as fast as she could, nearly ripping the skin off her palms on the rocks. She was afraid that the Komodo dragons might have the claws and the gumption to try moving up the rock wall after her.

After what was only a few seconds but felt like an eternity, she heaved herself over the upper edge of the small cliff. Her friends joined her a second later, pulling themselves up as if the rocks were on fire. She chanced a look down, ready to head for the closest tree in case the huge monitors were following her up the wall.

The dragons circled below in a knot of writhing, scaly bodies. Some of them looked up and hissed at her, but they didn't seem to want to pursue them vertically up the wall. Their beady black eyes stared up at her with reptilian hunger, but she was safe.

Rolling onto her back, she issued a big sigh of relief. The lizards couldn't have been more than a few feet behind her when she leaped for the wall.

"Well," Gail said, panting, "that was a first. Komodo dragons, right?"

"Right," Denise said, bringing her breathing under control as she lay on the ground and enjoyed the feeling of being alive. There was no sweeter nectar in all the world.

She looked down at the reptiles below and frowned. Now that she could get a better look at them, she wasn't sure they were Komodo dragons at all. Komodo dragons didn't have osteoderms, bumpy ridges like crocodiles, down their backs. They were smooth brown scales all over. In addition, these creatures had a small sail running down their backs, like a prehistoric Dimetrodon. The sail was supported by large spines that jutted out of the monitors' backs, and made of a thin flap of skin that ran between them. She'd never heard of anything quite like these guys, though they were probably a cousin to the Komodo dragon.

"You know," Denise said, "those might not be Komodo dragons after all. I think we just discovered a new species."

"I think they discovered us," Harrison said.

Denise pulled herself to her feet, still quivering from adrenaline. Her hands shook a little as she looked down at the mob of angry creatures below.

"Alright, let's find a safe area where we can get back down," she said, moving away from the ledge of the cliff. She walked a few feet, trying to get her bearings, when her foot suddenly slipped right through a thin layer of leaf litter covering a narrow hole.

She screamed as she fell straight down into the darkness below.

TWELVE
CAVERNS MEASURELESS TO MAN

Denise's scream came to an abrupt end as she slammed into the ground about fifteen feet down. She smacked into a thick layer of decaying plant matter that had gathered at the bottom of the hidden hole. Hitting the ground at an awkward angle, she collapsed and went face down on the floor. She groaned. Even with the softer landing from the collection of leaves and old vines, it was a savage fall.

"Denise? Are you okay down there? C'mon. Talk to us," Gail's voice said from above.

"I'm alive," Denise said, checking to make sure her legs weren't broken. "Barely," she added under her breath. The fall had discombobulated her senses. One second she was walking through the sunlight, the next she was plunged into darkness and a sudden full body impact. It felt like she'd been thrown in a paint shaker and then smacked against the wall a few times for good measure.

Her bones didn't feel right under her skin, but none of them seemed to be broken. She knew she'd probably have a bruise over half her body by the next day, though. When that happened, she'd be able to feel individual air molecules colliding with her tender skin.

Pushing herself up, she flopped onto her back and looked up. Gail and Harrison were a couple of shapes silhouetted by the sun further up. The cave she'd fallen into was shaped roughly like a flask, with a wide, flat bottom leading up to tapered sides. A couple of leaves she'd disturbed as she fell into the cave drifted down and landed gently beside her.

A bat, apparently surprised by her sudden entrance into its domain, fluttered away and out through the top of the cave. At least it wasn't an ahool.

Rolling over onto her side, Denise forced herself to move her head around and take in more of her surroundings. Fungal growths hung from the walls. Water dripped from the ceiling and formed a number of small puddles nearby. There was a pile of…

Denise snapped alert as if she'd been given an electric shock. About ten feet away from her sat a pile of massive bones.

If she curled her knees up to her legs, she could probably fit inside the ribcage. The skull was almost as long as her entire forearm, and the jaws were rimmed with pointed needle teeth like a giant eel. Most amazing of all were the elongated bones forming the wings.

The long, thin bones looked like a horribly mutated hand, which was really what they were. Bats were mammals, just like humans, dogs, and dolphins. Hands, paws, and flippers were all skeletally similar in a lot of ways. A lot of the bones were basically the same in all of them, just compacted or stretched and rearranged slightly.

Bats simply took the evolutionary system one step further. The bones that formed the paws of their ancestors stretched themselves into a complex lattice to form wings. Each of the supports that ran through the wings was really a bizarre sort of finger.

This was a unique specimen, though. The creature would have had a thirty-foot wingspan when it was alive. It was easy to tell why it wasn't, though.

A large rock had given way from the ceiling and crushed most of the giant bat's pelvis and left wing. Even for all its size, the creature was probably quite delicate in a lot of ways, and the minor cave-in had killed it.

"Can you see this?" Denise called upward, pointing to the massive skeleton. Jesus, the ahools did exist, and they were absolutely horrifying. A creature like that could easily carry off a full grown man.

She thought again about the *Venture*, adrift and empty near Malheur Island. She'd been skeptical before, but now it was all too easy to picture a couple of ahools swooping down on the yacht as it sailed too near to the island at night.

"We see it alright," Gail said.

"Stay where you are," Harrison said. "We have some rope back at camp. Gail and I will go back and get some and get you out of there."

She looked around. A variety of tunnels and open spaces led away from the chamber she found herself in. This whole area must be a karst system, full of caves and sinkholes where soluble rock had washed away and left behind empty underground chambers.

There were a dozen chambers leading off from where she currently found herself. Some of them were so narrow she would only be able to crawl through them on her belly. Others were big enough to drive a truck through. Or for anything that lived in these tunnels to scurry through.

Denise didn't like that idea. She didn't like it one bit. Obviously, at least one ahool used to live down here, and everything she knew about bats said they lived in colonies. There might still be some living specimens down here, and they probably wouldn't be happy to see her.

"Alright, get that rope fast, though. I have a bad feeling about this," she said.

Gail and Harrison disappeared from the little halo of sunlight above her, and she was suddenly very glad for her Nitro Express rifle. She looked down at the teeth on the skeleton beside her again. They were as long and thin as her fingers, and they absolutely filled the creature's maw in a jagged row.

She sat in the little pool of light and listened to the sounds of the cave. There was the steady drip, drip, drip of water coming from all around. From overhead, she could hear the calls and cackles of birds and monkeys. The crevasse smelled of wet earth and damp decay, like a Seattle graveyard. The air inside the cave was just as damp as above, but it was much cooler.

A clicking noise sounded from somewhere deeper inside the cave. Denise recognized that sound. It was the sound of bats sending out echoes. She pulled a miniature flashlight out of her vest and clicked it on.

From here, it was impossible to tell where the noise was coming from. It could be close or it could be distant. For that matter, the creature making that noise could be small or it could be very large. Very large indeed. She looked down at the nearby skeleton again.

Biting her lip, Denise pulled herself to her feet. Her body protested after already receiving some rough treatment today, but it obeyed with only minimum creaks and pops. She patted the breast pocket of her vest to make sure that the massive bullets for her Nitro Express were still in there, readily accessible.

The clicking noise came again. Perhaps it was her imagination, but it sounded closer this time. Her finger crept inside the rifle's trigger guard.

Gail and Harrison told her to stay put. Normally, that would be the smart thing to do. They'd come back to this same spot with rope and get her out.

However, it would take them a while to get back to their camp from here, and it would take just as long to get back. Meanwhile, Denise might be trapped in here with something else, something that might be seeking her out with echolocation right now. If she stayed here and waited for Gail and Denise, there was no guarantee they'd get back in time to find any more of her than whatever parts the ahool didn't feel like eating. Or maybe it was just a little bat curious about the commotion of her falling in.

She reached over to another pocket and pulled out a number of speed loaders for her revolver. The bullets were still large, but they were BB pellets compared to the huge rounds for the Nitro Express. Her revolver was a weapon of last resort, meant for personal defense in case she ever found something sinking its teeth into her arm. If that ever happened, she'd pull the revolver out, stick the barrel in her attacker's eye, and pull the trigger.

Pulling bullets out of the speed loaders, she held the cool brass in her palms. She looked back again as another flurry of clicks sounded from somewhere else in the cave system.

That settled it.

She stepped up to the largest tunnel leading away from her antechamber. Leaning down, she put one of the revolver rounds on the ground, the tip pointing back the direction she'd come. Now she'd have a trail of high-caliber bread crumbs to lead her back to her starting point if she needed to turn around.

Marching deeper into the darkness, she felt along the slimy walls to guide her way. Here and there, little patches of sunlight shone down from above where the ceiling of the chamber broke through to the surface. Most of the openings were no bigger than a postage stamp, though, not nearly large enough for Denise to crawl out of.

Every time she crossed an intersection or the entrance to some new chamber, she laid down another bullet, always pointing the way she'd originally come.

However, she was rapidly running out of bullets. The inside of the cavern system was like a giant sponge. Chambers and antechambers and passageways all led away from each other in an endless maze. Whenever she could, Denise chose a path that looked like it led more or less upward.

Hopefully, there was a large exit leading up to the surface she could crawl out of. Then she could meet with Gail and Harrison back at their basecamp again. Right now, she only had twelve bullets left before she'd have to start using her Nitro Express rounds as place markers, and she didn't want to do that. She wanted to save those in case she really needed them. If she reached the end of her bullet supply, she'd turn around and start collecting them again and then start off in another direction.

Another round of squeaks and clicks from somewhere in the cave reminded her why she didn't really want to do that either.

Something flitted past her cheek on leathery wings, and she nearly squeezed the trigger of her Nitro Express in surprise. The tiny, normal-sized bat zipped past her, chittering as it zigzagged through the air. The animal jerked and jinked through the air like it was engaged in an invisible dogfight before taking a sharp turn to the right.

Denise looked down that tunnel. It was low and narrow. She'd been taking the larger, more open pathways, assuming they led out into a bigger chamber and possibly an exit.

Maybe the little insectivore knew something she didn't, though. The tunnel the bat took was low and narrow. Denise would have to move through sideways, and even then, it would be a tight fit. If she became stuck, she'd die down here, her bones lost forever until they dissolved into cave slime. Then again, nothing large would be able to follow her through the small opening either, and not being eaten alive was even further up on her list of things to avoid than dying wedged in a fissure. If things got too tight, she could hopefully scooch her way back out.

Laying another bullet down, she slid into the gap between the rocks. The walls were cold and damp, as if she were crawling through the guts of some dead sea monster. Cold stone pressed at her as she shuffled along, grimacing at the tightness around her chest and stomach.

The path tightened further, but she could see the far side now. There was a way out. If she could just slither a little further along... Denise sucked in her stomach and scrambled sideways down the alley of rock.

Was it just her imagination, or was it brighter in this section of the cavern? The occasional crack and crevice in the ceiling allowed in a little light, but she thought she could see more details as she moved closer to the end of the path. She'd been moving steadily closer to the surface. If there was a large enough hole, maybe she could crawl her way out.

Her own breathing was loud in her ears. It was all too easy to imagine some minute shift in the earth squeezing her chamber a little closer together, pinning her in place. Maybe all it would take was a single, badly timed rumble down in the earth's guts, a mere burp from the fire-filled earth's core. Then she'd be stuck.

Or in the alternative, the walls would just keep closing. If they slipped another foot closer, her head would be squished like a melon in a vise. The earth could swallow her whole, reducing her body to pulp and red gruel through the merest shudder. She wondered if that sort of thing happened suddenly, if she'd be instantly reduced to a thin film of meat without a moment to wonder what had just happened, or if it would move slowly, crushing her like a giant wine press until she burst.

Clamping down on such thoughts, Denise pushed herself forward. She couldn't think about getting stuck down here or what might be following her. Those thoughts would paralyze her. Getting out was what was important. She had to focus on that.

Almost there, she told herself as her left arm and shoulder squeezed out into the next chamber. Another foot, and she'd squirm free of this stone vise.

She suddenly jerked to a halt. Her belt buckle was caught on a little nub of rock. Denise couldn't look down. She could barely move her head at all. A swarm of horrified thoughts tried to fill her brain like flies buzzing around hot turds.

She tried moving back into the tunnel slightly. No dice. That little stub of rock was hooked into the metal, and it was holding her fast.

Denise closed her eyes, but visions of her rotting corpse stuck in that fissure tried to swim up to taunt her. Gritting her teeth, she wriggled as close to the opening as she could. Taking slow, measured breaths, she slowly let more and more air out of her lungs. When there was almost nothing left, she lunged as hard as she could.

Metal scraped in protest, but she managed to break free. Tumbling out into the next chamber, she fell down on her side, free.

Taking another revolver bullet, she pointed it toward the opening. Not that it mattered. She didn't think she'd be able to fit back through from this side. Now that she was through, there was no going back.

Hopefully, it didn't matter, though. Now that she was through, she was positive it was brighter on this side of the fissure.

She could hear something too, the trickle of water. This wasn't just a drip, this was more like a small stream, and that meant it had to be coming from somewhere.

Marching forward, she followed the sound of the water as best she could. As she did so, the caverns grew brighter and brighter. Shifting from near pitch blackness, the walls became merely shadowy. She flicked her flashlight off and stuck it back in a pocket of her vest.

Just ahead of her lay a shallow stream, leading off to somewhere deeper in the darkness. The water was flowing downward, so in theory, she only had to follow it back to its source to find the surface.

She rounded a bend, and was suddenly struck in the face by a ray of golden sunlight. Denise squinted and smiled. Up ahead lay a wide opening and beyond that, a field of beautiful blue sky. It was like peeking out of the throat of some massive beast and staring out through its mouth at the outside world.

A slight slope led up to the entrance. The cavern smelled rank and filthy, but she didn't care. The thin wisp of fresh air from above was refreshing enough to ignore all the other underground odors.

Denise started up the short hill toward the cave exit. Suddenly, she became aware of another sound, something she hadn't originally heard over the burble of water rushing toward dark oblivion below.

There was a restless rustling noise from overhead, like the constant adjusting of sheets in an insomniac's bedroom. Denise froze in place. Her hand crept back to her vest and grabbed her flashlight again. Pointing it upward, she clicked it on.

The ceiling was covered with bats, thousands of bats. They gazed down at her with little black eyes, pondering her intrusion into their realm. She shone the little light around, revealing more and more bats.

She sighed in relief as she realized that there were no ahools, though. Even though the chamber was big enough to support a colony of bear-sized monstrosities, these little guys were tiny. They shifted and climbed over each other in a constant wave of motion as Denise played her light over them. It was like the ceiling itself was a single mass of rippling, living flesh.

The floor of the cavern was covered in a thick layer of guano, bat poop. Entire battalions of insects were busy crawling through the filth, chewing the nutrients out and turning the guano field into a rich layer of dirt. Wetas scurried through the filth, and large millipedes scurried after the wetas. There was an entire ecosystem down there simply based on the constant stream of bat crap from overhead. As Denise tread over the hillocks of shit and insects, she thought there might be a metaphor there somewhere, but she was too tired to suss it out.

Her feet sank a half inch into the debris with each step. Dozens of tiny creatures, from nearly microscopic mites to horrific-looking cave scorpions moved to get out of her way as she made her way toward the light.

There were bones in the bed of filth, too. Most of them were young bats that had fallen from their mothers and plunged to the ground before they were ready to fly. The insects had overwhelmed the bat pups and stripped their flesh off, leaving only the bones behind to be slowly covered in shit. There were a few adult-sized bat bones too from individuals who died of disease, old age, or injuries while they roosted and fell to the ground. The bugs below were happy to feast on them as well.

She didn't see any more ahool bones like in the first chamber she'd fallen into, but there were still larger bones here too. A human skeleton lay half-submerged in guano a little further ahead. One arm was out, flung in a hopeless effort to protect the victim's face. A huge crater in the skull and scratch marks on the bones looked like they corresponded with the fang size of the ahool bones she'd seen.

Was this one of the villagers? It looked like an ahool was probably responsible for this death, even if there weren't any here right at the present.

A little voice in Denise's head screamed at her to get out of the cave while that was still the case. She had a clean shot at the exit, and it was possible that something bigger than her current chiropteran company could arrive at any moment.

She shone her light on the human skeleton again, though. There was something attached to its wrist. Most of the person's clothes had either rotted away or been chewed apart by insects, but it looked like there was a leather strap still attached to the arm.

Stepping a little closer, she finally managed a good look at the object. It was a watch, an expensive-looking one.

She wouldn't expect any of the natives to have watches, not unless some passing ship traded a few, and nobody from the 1902 Dutch expedition was likely to have watches, either. No one really wore a watch before fighter pilots in the Great War started strapping their pocket watches to their wrists so they could check the time without taking their hands off their controls.

Bending down, she paused before touching the bones. Instead of grabbing the skeleton with her bare hands, she pulled her revolver out and used the barrel to prod the arm bones around. Where the bones weren't shattered outright, they were crisscrossed with deep grooves where huge teeth had chewed the flesh off.

The bones flopped over, and Denise got a better look at the watch. Its face was shattered, and unsurprisingly, the hands had stopped. There was an engraving on the underside, though. Denise could just barely make out the letters.

Moving carefully so as not to touch the skeleton, Denise undid the watch strap and pulled it off. She felt vaguely guilty, like a grave robber sneaking through the night with a shovel and a pocket full of rings still attached to fingers. However, she was more than simply curious. Maybe the engraving would help her identify whatever poor soul met his end down here in Satan's butt crack.

She flipped the watch over and shone her light onto the back. *To Robert for thirty years of service with Yersinia. 1894-1924*

What in the hell?

No, seriously. What in the actual hell was going on here?

It was dated from last year, and it was from Yersinia, Hobhouse's business organization. The same group that would be paying them for their expedition.

And there had been Yersinia personnel on Malheur Island recently that Hobhouse never mentioned, people who evidently died. And died badly at that.

Denise pocketed the watch. She needed to show Gail and Harrison this. No, she needed to show everyone this. If there was a previous expedition to Malheur Island that ended in disaster, that was something they should all know about.

She scurried up the rest of the way to the mouth of the cave, bugs crunching under her feet as she moved. The sunlight was warm and welcoming as she emerged from the cave. Even the listless tropical humidity felt good on her skin after being trapped underground for far too long. She was about halfway up the side of a hill, overlooking the sea.

Looking up, she glanced at the sun. It was well after noon. She'd been down there longer than she thought. Marking the passage of time was all but impossible in the stygian darkness below. In a few hours, it would be dark again. Picking her bearings, she saw the *SMS Hookstadt* off in the distance as well as the walled-off islander village.

That reminded her. The man in denim they'd met on the beach had said they had until tonight to leave the island. Well, they were going to miss that deadline.

Maybe she could speak to some of the villagers, though. They had to know something about any previous Yersinia operations on Malheur Island. Maybe they could tell her what happened to the dead man in the cave. She would have to find a way to get in contact with them, no matter how adamant they seemed about staying behind their wooden palisade.

Denise felt something whizz past her nose. It ruffled her hair in its wake. Then she heard the gunshot echoing through the jungle.

She ducked, her reflexes already too late. If that bullet had found its way home, she'd already be dead. Whoever killed Razan was now taking potshots at her. They'd seen her standing prominently on the ridge of the hill, and now they were trying to draw a bead on her.

She did the only thing she could do. Denise leaped down the side of the hill, throwing herself into the underbrush. Tree trunks, grass, and vines would obscure the shooter's vision.

In the distance, she could hear shouts. Everyone else had heard the shots, too. The shooter would be forced to relocate soon.

She paused in her scramble through the underbrush. If she could just look around for a moment, maybe she could see who was doing the shooting.

Slowly, carefully, she brought her head up above the grass line. She slid up the side of a tree to protect most of her body, giving her some cover.

The jungle was thick. She scanned the environment for movement, searching for anything out of place. Creepers swayed from the tree boughs as small primates moved through the branches. Birds bobbed through the air and hopped along the ground, looking for fallen fruit.

Nothing looked like it was out of place. She couldn't see anything wrong. Maybe the shooter had already beat a hasty retreat.

The wood in front of her chest exploded into a hundred splinters. Some of them sprang out and embedded themselves in her arm. She cursed and ducked back down as the sound of a second gunshot reached her ears.

Blood trickled down her arm as she slithered back in the direction of her basecamp. More shouting marked the approach of the other hunters, converging on the killer's direction.

If he was smart, he'd already have moved. It would be all but impossible to tell who actually fired the shots once all the hunters arrived in the same area and tried to sort out who had been there first and who could have fired and then doubled back.

Whoever it was, though, Denise was sure they would rue the day they tried to kill her.

THIRTEEN
UNDER THE PHANTOM MOON

Denise was already sitting in the base camp when Gail and Harrison walked through the cave opening. Even after almost an hour to calm down, Denise nearly shot them. Her nerves were frayed, and she'd spent the last hour half-expecting the killer to track her here and make another attempt at shooting her.

Harrison put his hands up in front of him when he saw the Nitro Express rifle pointed at him. Everyone took the business end of a Nitro Express seriously. Denise put the rifle down when she saw it was them, and she breathed a big sigh.

"Hey, there, Balthazar told us what happened. We were out looking for you after we found that cave you fell into empty."

"Yeah, sorry about that. I could hear things, and I thought it might be best to try to find a way out on my own." After reaching her base camp, she'd tried to radio the *Shield of Mithridates* again. No dice, the same as last night. When she couldn't get any response from the ship, she tried radioing the other groups.

She reached Silas, Creighton, and Shinzo first. Silas and Creighton were together when the killer tried to shoot her, but Shinzo had been following his golden eagle. He said he needed to let his bird hunt to feed her, but nobody could confirm exactly where he was when somebody started taking potshots at her.

It took her longer to reach Balthazar's group. They were separated when Balthazar picked up his radio unit, and she couldn't be sure where any of them were when the shooting started.

She told him what she told Silas and Creighton. They were all going to have a meeting tonight. Neutral ground. Everyone would come to the abandoned shack where she discovered the Dutch geologist's journal at sunset. If anyone didn't show, there would be hell to pay.

That left her with four immediate suspects among the hunters. Balthazar. Jubal. Dr. Marlow. Shinzo.

However, that was just among the hunters, though. If the islanders really and truly did not want them here, it could be them, too. For that matter, she had evidence of a previous Yersinia expedition as well. It was possible there was some survivor from that group that had snapped and decided to target the new arrivals on Malheur Island.

She didn't feel like she was any closer to figuring out what was happening here or who had killed Razan and nearly killed her. If anything, she felt like she was further away from the truth than ever.

Right now, she barely trusted anyone, Gail and Harrison included. A fevered, paranoid part of her mind was all too eager to point out that she had no idea where she was when those bullets started zipping past her, and right after they'd disagreed about giving the journal about the lunar meteorites to Jubal, too.

But that was madness. Gail and Harrison were with her when Razan was killed. They obviously hadn't shot him.

Although, they could have tried to kill her and shove blame off onto the original killer. It would be the perfect plan. She shut off the little voice in her brain that wanted to whisper seductive conspiracy theories to her. That voice wanted her to crawl off into the brush and shoot anyone who came too close. Survival at all costs and at any price. Anyone could be the enemy.

"It's about time to head off to the meeting site," Gail said.

"We should spread out as we move. Everyone will be there, but everyone will know just where to set up an ambush," Harrison added.

"Hopefully, no one will try anything. We'll all be converging on the same area in groups. If anyone is missing, the folks who are supposed to be with them should figure it out pretty fast."

"Yeah, that worked out real well with Jubal earlier," Gail said. She had a point, but if everyone ended up in the same area at the same time, it would become real obvious real fast who was missing, and that was as good as an admission of guilt.

"We need to get tough against whoever's doing this," Denise said.

"My father always said that once people start talking about getting tough on X, you should start betting on X," Harrison said.

Denise bit back a snippy response. This day had been far too long and confusing. More than anything, she just needed some quiet time by herself somewhere she felt safe. The only problem was, she didn't think a place like that existed on Malheur Island.

"Let's go," she said instead. They walked along the edge of the jungle just before it gave way to beach. That made the going pretty easy but also allowed them some space to dive for cover if they needed it.

Denise felt like a soldier caught out in no man's land, knowing that someone could be watching and waiting for her to walk into range. It was an eerie sensation, and she could feel tension bunching up between her shoulder blades as if that was the very spot some sniper was aiming at.

The decaying cabin came into view. Balthazar, Dr. Marlow, and Jubal were already there, half-crouched near the huge stone head. Dr. Marlow waved at them when he saw them. Neither Balthazar nor Jubal bothered.

"Leave your rifles in the hut," Balthazar said. "Ours are already in there."

"I think everyone will feel a lot safer if no one is pointing long guns around," Dr. Marlow said.

Denise didn't object. They all still had their side arms, and the rifles were close enough in case something went awry. Leaving them a little out of reach was probably wise in case passions flared.

Jubal looked worse for wear. Someone, probably Dr. Marlow, had reset his nose, but it was swollen and misshapen. Wads of tissue paper were stuffed up his nostrils, and they were tinged with red. He glared at Denise, but she ignored him.

"So, you three were separated when the shooting happened today?" She already knew the answer. Balthazar had told her as much over the radio when she contacted them. The big Boer frowned and turned his head away, refusing to answer her.

"I was taking a short nap after setting Jubal's nose," Dr. Marlow said. "I hadn't slept well after last night's events, and we weren't going anywhere, so I didn't think it would do any harm. Balthazar went back to the *Hookstadt*, and Jubal was supposed to be there with me, but obviously I can't really confirm that if I was napping."

"Oh, come off it," Jubal said. "I was there. You know I was there. I listened to you snore the whole time. My face still hurt too much for me to go anywhere."

"You weren't there when I woke up."

"A man's gotta take a piss sometimes. Lay off. I was back a minute after those gunshots. It was Balthazar who was gone the whole time."

"And where were you?" Gail asked, pointing at Balthazar.

"Jubal had given me the journal. I could translate a lot of it, but some of the technical vocabulary is too different from Afrikaans. I needed the Dutch translation dictionary from my trunk in the *Hookstadt*. I was translating the rest of the journal when I heard the shots."

Denise sighed. No one had an ironclad alibi here, but no one was obviously the killer, either. Dammit, she needed some hardnosed police inspector here. She didn't know what to ask to ferret out the truth. She thought clues and evidence were supposed to go off like mental flashbulbs and all come together until they formed a complete picture. Instead, all she had was a jumble of information, none of which added up to anything more than a mishmash of speculation and paranoia.

The sun was low in the sky. Soon, it would be dark again, but at least the full moon would be able to guide them. She wanted to be back in her basecamp before it got too dark, though. Now that she'd seen proof that ahools were real, she didn't want to spend any more time out at night than necessary.

Silas, Creighton, and Shinzo came through the brush a few minutes later. She questioned them about where they'd been when someone started shooting at her. Shinzo said he needed to take his bird hunting in order to feed it, so he'd been briefly away from camp. Silas and Creighton had been back at their own camp, waiting for him to return when they heard the shots.

She eyed Shinzo. Of all of them, his story was probably the flimsiest of all.

They all stood around the huge, carved moon rock for a moment pondering each other. A small green lizard scuttled across the surface of the lunar meteorite, stopping every few inches to evaluate the human intruders in its realm. Its tongue flicked in and out in furtive reptilian movements, tasting the darkening atmosphere.

The moon was starting to rise as the sun went down. It crept up over the horizon like a gigantic eye spying on them. Denise reached into her pocket and pulled out the watch she'd found. She could see the moon reflecting in the scratched face of the watch.

"There's something else I want to bring up," she said, holding the watch aloft. "I don't think we're the first group Yersinia has sent here." There was a babble of confusion before she hushed them. "I found this in a cave on a dead body. It's from last year, and it's clearly from Yersinia."

She showed everyone the inscription on the back of the watch.

"I wonder if this is why Hobhouse isn't answering our hails on the radio," Silas said.

"That's what I'm starting to think, too," Denise said. "I think there was a lot about this expedition that he didn't tell us. Truth be told, I think pretty much everything we were told was probably one long line of crap. Hobhouse should know by now that we're in trouble, but it could well be by design."

"What, you think Yersinia planted an assassin in with us?" Silas asked.

"Poppycock," Creighton said.

"I don't know. Maybe. This doesn't make a whole lot of sense to me, frankly."

The little green lizard continued its trek across the surface of the statue, enjoying the warmth of the last rays of the sun. The reptile slipped in and out of the crevices that formed the intricate design.

"Not to crap all over everyone's parade or anything, but I want to bring something up myself," Jubal said. "Even if Hobhouse screwed us over, I think we're ahead of him anyway. We've got these babies." He patted the gigantic carved head, causing the little lizard to flee into the statue's carved out pupil for cover.

"Yes, Balthazar was kind enough to translate for us," Silas said. "Lunar meteorites. Most remarkable."

"And valuable," Creighton added.

"Right, so how do we want to divvy these bad boys up?" Jubal asked. "There's no way Hobhouse has a copy of that Dutchman's journal. Even if Yersinia wants to play games with us, we can still come out of this ahead so long as we play it straight. Some scientists or universities will pay through the nose for these." Jubal grinned and dabbed at his own broken nose.

"I never thought I'd say this, but I agree with Jubal," Harrison said.

"We are *not* going to just steal these things from the island," Denise said. "We need to at least find out what the significance to the villagers first before we simply cart them off. It would be like taking all the idols off Easter Island."

"Listen, Denise," Gail said, "you're my friend, and I agreed with you on your first point. Yersinia is trying to screw us one way or the other. There's something up. If they're going to play dirty, we don't owe them a single thing. No obligations to people who don't deserve it. We can still beat them at their own game and make more money than we would have otherwise."

"And we won't have to go up against an ahool. Those things looked nasty," Harrison said.

"You saw one?" Shinzo asked, the first thing he'd said in a long time.

"Well, a skeleton of one. They're big. Like, really big. I say we go for the easy money. Even if Hobhouse just sails away and abandons us, we can still hail other passing ships with our radios and hitch a ride off this island. We take these rocks with us, and we make a fortune regardless. When there's no real guarantee that I'm going to be paid for it, I'd rather not get up close to one of these bats."

"These stones aren't ours to take," Denise said. "Maybe if we alerted a museum or laboratory, and then they negotiated with the villagers and paid us a finder's fee, it would be fine. You all just want to snatch the meteorites up like they're our natural bounty."

"You know what? I do. I do want to do that," Jubal said. He whisked a long knife off his belt and used the handle to bash a chunk of rock off the statue. The end of a carved fang came away with a sharp snap. Jubal stuck the rock in his satchel.

"Hey," Denise said, knowing just who ineffectual it sounded.

"Want to put it to a vote?" Jubal grinned. "I'm getting some of what's coming to me no matter what. You dicks are welcome to leave the statues alone and allow me to take the full supply off the island by myself."

Balthazar surprised Denise. "The DeMarco woman is right, Jubal. These aren't ours. Taking them without permission would be theft."

She wished Balthazar would just use her actual name instead of referring to her as *the Demarco woman,* but Denise was happy to have support from at least one corner. Maybe working in South Africa, where cooperation with the local African tribes was helpful in the bush, meant she and her fellow countryman shared some views on this issue at least. She'd take her allies where she could get them.

"Oh yeah? And who's going to stop me? You?" Jubal chipped another piece of the statue away.

"If I have to. The problem here is that the islanders probably like their statues. Somebody put a lot of time into carving them. I'm guessing they don't want people chipping pieces off. If they see that imbecile started defacing the statues, they might get very mad, and then they might try to kill us. They haven't exactly been cordial so far, and you're not improving our chances of getting off this island alive. Now, you can either put those two pieces you took on the ground, or I can snap you in half."

Jubal blinked. "You son of a bitch. You can't tell me what to do." His hand crept toward the pistol on his belt.

Balthazar moved his hand toward his revolver.

The group watched in aghast fascination. Denise didn't know what to do. Surely, they weren't about to fight to the death over this, were they? Even if she agreed with Balthazar, she didn't want to settle the point through bloodshed. But Jubal and Balthazar continued to size each other up, each with their hand on the butt of their weapon.

It didn't come to that, though. Something much worse happened instead.

FOURTEEN
BREATH OF THE MOON

At that moment, the full moon came fully over the horizon, shining its light down on Malheur Island. Denise felt it before she noticed anything else. It was almost as if some immense power switch had been flipped on underneath the island. The hair on the back of her arms stood on end, and goosebumps sprang up on the back of her neck.

She had a curious sensation, as if the very atmosphere was alight with some strange energy. The only thing she could compare it to was as if something very old and very powerful had just drawn its first breath in a long time.

Everyone else noticed it too, even if they couldn't immediately tell what was happening. Everyone looked around except for Jubal and Balthazar, who kept their eyes locked on each other instead. Even they looked suddenly unsure, though.

Then the noises began. To Denise's ears, the cries sounded like the panicked shrieks of animals running from a brush fire. She looked around, but there was no orange glow that signified flames anywhere on the island. There was only the bleached light of the moon.

The howls and screams reached a new intensity, as if every single animal on the island was being skinned alive. As she listened, the noises came from all over the island, both near and far. The whole of Malheur Island was alive with wretched noises like the full choir of hell singing a hymn of damnation.

Near Jubal, the little green lizard that had scurried out of sight reemerged into the moonlight. As soon as it appeared, the reptile began writhing as if someone had broken its back. Thrashing and squirming, its eyes bulged and dark red blood wept from around the rim of each socket. Normally so graceful and tenacious, the lizard's claws lost their grip on the stone, and it fell to the ground.

The group of hunters cried out, too. "What in the hell?" Harrison asked, his head cocked to one side listening to the ungodly ruckus that had broken out over the whole island.

On the ground at the base of the statue, the lizard jerked and thrashed. It hissed like a match dropped in a puddle. Ropes of saliva sprayed from its jaws as its body jackknifed back and forth. The convulsions looked like they would tear the animal's body apart.

In fact, something strange was happening to the lizard. The flesh on its body almost look as if it was boiling, barely able to contain some horrible eruption going on inside.

Additionally, the lizard was getting bigger. The growth happened slowly at first, so slowly that Denise thought it might be a mere figment of her imagination. But then, as if overcoming some initial barrier, the lizard's size exploded. Where before the lizard was no larger than a few inches in length, it was now several feet long, the size of a full-grown iguana.

Bones burst through its flesh only to be reabsorbed, the skin knitting back together in the span of a second as the animal grew at an uneven rate. One leg grew far faster than the others, only to be overtaken by the other three as they suddenly swelled in size. Bones snapped and crackled as they rearranged themselves, seemingly with a mind all their own. Now the lizard was the size of a small crocodile, and it had just as many teeth.

Inhuman eyes glared out at the surprised hunters as the lizard's body morphed and contorted into something that was no longer recognizable. Scales as thick and hard as dinner plates covered the creature's back. Fangs like ten-penny nails filled its gaping mouth. The huge muscular back legs looked like they belonged to a bodybuilder with some unnatural skin condition. Arms tipped with massive talons scrabbled at the dirt as the rate of transformation began to slow down.

Shinzo shot at the thing first. He whipped a revolver off his hip and fired point blank into the beast's armored hide. The bullet sank in with a squirt of blood, not even thick scales could stop a large revolver round, but the lizard-thing barely seemed to care. It was almost like its body ate the bullet. A second later, the skin healed over like water sloughing up the beach.

The lizard snarled as more of the hunters pulled their sidearms out and fired off a dozen rounds at the beast in the span of a few seconds. Normally, a hail storm of bullets like that would put down almost any animal.

But this wasn't a normal animal anymore. This was a monster now. Denise wasn't used to thinking about animals in those terms. She was used to thinking about the natural habits and patterns of animals. They were just another part of nature, something she'd spent her whole life studying, in her own way.

This thing was distinctly unnatural. She couldn't even think of it as an animal anymore. It was a hissing, spitting ball of living malevolence. The lizard monster shrugged off the wave of bullets like they were bee stings. Its flesh rippled with every new slap of brass, but the scaly skin always grew back right before their eyes.

Rearing up on its hind legs, the lizard was almost seven feet tall. Bellowing and roaring, it grabbed at the hunters. Balthazar ducked away from the grasping claws. Creighton dodged backwards.

Shinzo wasn't so lucky. He tried to back up as the lizard rounded on him, but he smacked into the meteorite statue instead. A huge claw, easily big enough to grasp a large watermelon, raked out and latched onto Shinzo just below the ribcage. Two inch long claws sank into the flesh of Shinzo's stomach.

The man shrieked as the claws punctured through his skin like tissue paper and latched onto his guts. Roaring in triumph, the lizard lifted Shinzo up to its mouth. Shinzo screamed, his face contorted in pain and horror. The lizard stared at Shinzo for a second before opening its bear-trap jaws wide and clamping them down on the hunter's head.

There was a crunch like the world's largest potato chip, and then the lizard tore its jaws back with a savage jerk. The front part of Shinzo's head came away in the monster's fangs. Blood, teeth, and shredded flesh sprayed in every direction.

Shinzo wasn't quite dead yet. The lizard had taken his lower jaw with it, and Denise could see what was left of the man's tongue flopping in the red hole where his mouth used to be. His arms flailed to where his eyes had been and touched the gummy mess of blood and crushed bone. A small streamer of pulped brain matter leaked out of Shinzo's shattered skull. Some wet gurgling sounds emanated from Shinzo's dripping mouth hole.

Then the lizard leaned forward and closed its jaws around Shinzo's throat. With a single twist of its jaws, the creature nearly tore what was left of Shinzo's head off his shoulders. A few strands of sinew and gristle prevented the head from falling off completely as blood jetted up into the night. However, Shinzo's partially decapitated head flopped off to the side, faceless and unrecognizable.

Most of the hunters had already unloaded their side arms into the horrible thing, leaving the air thick with the scent of spent cordite. A .357 magnum round caught it in the side of the chest and temporarily knocked it off balance.

Instead of dropping dead in a heap as any sensible creature would do, the lizard whipped around and hissed. Its long, sinuous tail slammed into Gail and knocked her down. Heaving Shinzo's body away like he didn't weigh more than a dead kitten, the lizard rounded on Gail.

Still moving awkwardly on its hind legs like some sort of drunk Australopithecus, the lizard walked closer to Gail. Even hunched and gnarled into its unnatural stance, the lizard loomed over her.

"Bollocks. Let's get out of here," Creighton said as his pistol ran dry.

"Creighton, wait," Silas said, but the other Englishman was already gone, moving toward the beach. Silas took one glance back at Gail and then fled, too.

Dr. Marlow looked around with blind panic in his eyes. Nothing had even slowed the lizard down. When he broke and ran, Jubal went with him.

That left just Denise, Harrison, Gail, and Balthazar to deal with the lizard. However, Denise had one last hope. While the lizard was tearing Shinzo apart, she ducked back to the cabin.

Grabbing up her Nitro Express, she aimed it at the lizard and fired. The recoil from the .600 caliber rounds nearly threw her to the ground. If the rifle's roar was like the end of the world, then the kick felt like the end of the solar system.

A couple of rounds the size and shape of chili peppers blew across the clearing at over two thousand feet per second. When they struck the lizard a split second later, they struck with enough force to pierce the armor of a small tank. The rounds were intended for much larger targets.

The lizard all but flew apart. Its midsection exploded in every conceivable direction, spraying gobbets of viscera and shredded organs against the nearby stone statue and Gail. Spinning through the air, the head landed almost thirty feet away, still snapping its jaws. Fragments of bone went every which way like sprinklings of stardust.

Gail scrambled backward on her knees as the remainder of the lizard collapsed in front of her. Clotted blood stuck in her hair, and the front of her shirt was dripping with crimson back splatter. She was alive, though.

There was no guarantee any of them would be for long, though. The jungle was alive with the cries of thousands of mutated beasts. It was as if everything on the island was simply waiting for the full moon in order to shed their skin and reveal the monsters beneath.

Denise didn't have nearly enough ammunition to deal with everything on the island. The eight remaining hunters combined didn't have nearly enough ammunition to deal with this situation. Malheur Island had flipped the tables on them. Suddenly, they were the smallest, weakest prey animals around.

Pieces of the lizard continued to twitch and writhe on the ground, but it showed no signs of healing again. It was well and truly dead after shrugging off dozens of direct hits from pistols and revolvers.

Denise felt her stomach twist into a knot. She knew fear. She'd seen rhinos charge at her jeep and lions pounce out of the grass at her. Fear was nothing new. Every expedition was an exercise in fear versus knowledge and experience. She could counter fear. Finding herself suddenly on the bottom of Malheur Island's new food chain was terrifying, but it was a familiar sort of fear, and she could already feel her inner resources chewing over their best survival strategies. She was born to overcome this sort of fear.

No, the feeling that punched her in the gut when she looked at the dead lizard was something else. She'd killed again; she'd killed something unique and never before seen. This was a mixture of black regret and blood red triumph.

The emotions fought inside her. She'd killed the lizard because it was about to slaughter her friend. That was good, but that wasn't the whole feeling. It felt *good* to pit herself against something and come out on top. She used to relish that feeling after a successful hunt, only to come to hate it. Her mind conjured up that baby elephant again, one ear blown off as it tried to nudge its mother back to life.

That was a horrible moment, but it was also a moment of clarity, a realization that this wasn't what she wanted to do with her life. She wanted to add things to the world, not just help to wipe out some of its most magnificent wonders.

She would do what she needed to do to protect herself and her friends on this island, but Denise hoped she wouldn't surrender to that savage triumph again. There would be a lot more spilled blood tonight, and a tiny sliver of her was looking forward to it. She hated that part. Trying to kill it with drink hadn't worked these last few months, and now it was back and stronger than ever.

Hopefully, it wouldn't overtake the rest of her by the time this night was over. Hopefully.

First, she had to actually survive the night, though. As she offered Gail a hand and pulled her to her feet, Denise could hear movement in the night. Noise and the smell of blood had attracted more creatures.

FIFTEEN
BATS OUT OF HELL

"We need to get back to our camp," Denise said. "Maybe we can use the radio to contact some passing ship. I'm not sure we'll make it if we're stuck on Malheur Island." As if to underscore her point, the noises in the jungle were coming closer and closer. Growls, grunts, and snarls sounded throughout the darkness.

"Right, hopefully we can make a stand there," Harrison said, already moving.

Gail didn't say anything, but she grabbed her rifle from the cabin. Her hands left bloody prints on the stock.

They moved through the jungle as quickly as they dared. Their view was already limited by the tangles of creepers and warring plant life. Factoring in the darkness made the trek of identifying what lay ahead of them that much harder. There was only the cold light of the moon to guide them.

"What the hell happened back there?" Harrison asked. "I mean, what was that thing? It started out as a lizard, and then it was just...a monster. Son of a bitch. I've never seen anything like that before."

"It didn't happen until the moon came out," Denise said. "Everything was fine until then."

"It was fine last night, too."

"Yeah, but tonight's a full moon," Gail said.

"What, you mean everything on this island is like a loup garou?"

"A what?"

"It's sort of a French legend imported to Louisiana. Like a bayou werewolf."

"Maybe. There's apparently a large concentration of moon rock on this island. Maybe it worked its way into the ecosystem. Time weathered some of the rocks down into the soil, plants took in the nutrients, animals ate the plants, and now the animals are affected by moonlight."

"I have no idea. After seeing what happened back there, I'm ready to go ahead and just label the place cursed. That wasn't any kind of natural back there." Harrison shook his head.

"What do we do if we can't reach anyone on the radio?" Gail asked. "Even if we can, it might take them all night to reach us."

Denise hadn't thought of that. They might be able to hold off the freakish fauna that had overrun Malheur Island for a little while, but they'd be in deep trouble if too many monsters attacked at once. From what Denise could hear behind them, there were a lot of monsters out there, too.

"The village," Harrison said, snapping his fingers. "Maybe they'll let us in. It seemed weird to me that they had that wall when they were the only people on the island. I think we know why now."

He had a point, but Denise wasn't sure it would work. "What if they don't let us in? There's no guarantee they'd be eager to open their doors at night, especially if we have something hot on our heels."

"Better ideas?"

"Maybe. What about the cave system I was in earlier? Some of the passages are too small for anything as large as that lizard to fit through, and it's blocked from the moonlight. Maybe things are still normal down there."

"Our normal was pretty screwed up before, but I'll take it," Harrison said a second before something huge and hairy lunged out of the darkness and knocked him down.

Everyone screamed in surprise. The man-sized spider clacked its mandibles together in response.

Harrison tried to beat at the huge arachnid, but it had one of his arms pinned beneath its six-inch-long tarsal claws. Its many, many black, emotionless eyes reflected the light of the moon like little white pupils. Thick, sharp bristles sprang off its exoskeleton in every direction.

Denise lifted her Nitro Express, but she didn't have a clear shot. The chattering monstrosity was directly on top of Harrison. Any shot that hit it would likely also hit him.

Pincer-like chelicerae snapped at Harrison's face. He cursed and drew his machete with his free arm and started hacking at the spider's face. Ichor sprayed out with each strike, but the opening in the spider's exoskeleton sealed back up with barely a groove almost as soon as the blade withdrew.

"Try to roll out of the way," Denise shouted. But Harrison was pinned underneath its hideous bulk. There was no escaping.

Suddenly, a screeching noise erupted, and a shadow crossed over the moon. Denise felt a rush of wind as something swept past her. She instinctually ducked, but the shape was already past her, talons gleaming.

The ahool zoomed past on great, leathery wings. Denise only caught a glimpse of huge sickle claws, massive ears the size of trash can lids, and slavering teeth before the enormous bat was off again, the beating of its wings raising a short windstorm.

Each flap of its wings took it higher and farther into the night until Denise lost sight of it beyond the jungle canopy, the flailing spider still caught in its claws. She'd seen the skeleton of an ahool, but the full-sized living specimen was even larger and more alarming.

Apparently, the island's bats were just as affected by the full moon as anything else on the island. Ahools never existed, not really. There was never a distinct species of giant bats. They were just the regular bats of Malheur Island grown to titanic proportions under the light of the moon. The legends spread because bats from the island sometimes wandered off and were seen elsewhere in the Dutch East Indies. They were the only animals on the island capable of easily reaching any other stretch of land. If lizards or spiders had wings, there would be legends of giant lizards or spiders instead.

Harrison got up and brushed himself off as best he could. There was a long cut on his arm from the spider's tarsal claws, but it wasn't too serious. He shuddered in revulsion.

"Are you alright?" Gail asked.

"That thing isn't slurping out my innards like a smoothie right now, so yeah, I'm pretty alright. It's hard not to feel alright when that's the alternative, I guess. On the other hand, it's going to be a long time before I feel okay about anything again." He put his hands on his face as if to make sure it was all still there.

Denise nodded. Harrison looked shaken, but he was still mostly in one piece. "Let's get out of here before another bat comes by and decides we look tasty, too," she said.

Harrison picked his rifle up off the ground and stuck his machete back in its sheath. If they could just make it down the rest of the way to the beach, they'd be able to get to their base and the radio. Then maybe, hopefully, there was someone out there who could rescue them.

Denise could hear shooting in the distance, the heavy roar of more big game rifles. At least some of the other hunters were still alive, allow she didn't know which ones or where they were. Most of them were probably retreating toward their own base camps and their stockpiles of firepower.

She wondered if any of them would make it through the night.

SIXTEEN
REACHING OUT

They reached the cavern inside the coastal cliff a few minutes later. One at a time they ran from the edge of the jungle to the cave entrance while the others covered them. The open stretch across the sand was short, and Denise couldn't see anything roaming the beach, but they would be totally exposed as they ran. If there was something waiting for a shot at them, the beach would be its best chance.

Gail went first. She sprinted out of the underbrush, sand kicking up behind her. Denise watched the skies.

High up, seemingly close enough to touch the stars, dark shapes cavorted across the sky. They flitted and swooped, occasionally diving into the trees to scoop up some smaller creature.

As she watched, an ahool emerged from the ground cover maybe a mile down the beach, carrying something in its claws. The shape struggled and squirmed until the ahool brought its claws up to its fangs and took a massive bite. Then the shape went still.

Two other ahools saw their companion with its prize and took off after it. The first bat flapped away, but the others caught up to it. They fought with fangs and claws, zipping through the air in a twisting dogfight.

Finally, one of the other two ahools managed to wrest the food away and started to fly away with it. The process started all over again as the robbed ahool immediately joined with the other to pursue the food thief.

Gail slipped around the ahool netting they'd strung up around the cave entrance and disappeared inside. She poked her head out a moment later and beckoned to Harrison and Denise.

Harrison went next. He moved fast and low, trying to make himself as tiny a target as possible. Presumably, the ahools didn't have great eyesight if they were relying on echolocation to navigate, but the ahools weren't the only things out there tonight.

There was something tromping through the underbrush behind Denise. It wasn't too close yet, but it was getting closer all the time. Sometimes, the steady rustle of grass and foliage would stop, and she could hear a loud snorting noise, like the creature was following a scent trail.

Denise didn't care for that idea one bit. Gail was covered in lizard blood. Harrison had a cut on his arm. And they no doubt all reeked of fear and adrenaline. Anything with a sensitive nose would be able to track them.

Another loud snort came from somewhere behind Denise. She risked a glance backward, but she couldn't see anything amidst the black jungle. The footsteps resumed again, zeroing in on her.

She forced herself to look forward again to cover the last few steps of Harrison's dash across the sand. The ahools continued to swoop and circle overhead, chittering and screeching.

A few seconds later, Harrison too ducked around the netting in front of their cave. He and Gail both gave the all clear sign for Denise to go. They had their long rifles ready to cover her as she made her way across the sand.

The footsteps behind her stopped. Gail and Harrison's expressions both changed from encouragement to something radically different at the same time. They were no longer looking at her. They were looking behind her.

Denise didn't need to guess what that meant. She took off running at full speed without a glance back.

In response, something bellowed like a freight train in mating season. The noise was all fury and power.

Thunderous footfalls started up behind her, each one causing the ground beneath her feet to tremble. Huffing-chuffing breaths grew louder and louder until she couldn't even hear the sound of her own hard breathing.

A smell hit Denise that made her want to double over and gag right there. Her brain reached for a comparison, and the best she could come up with was if someone filled the zoo monkey house with sewage and cigarette butts and then set the whole thing on fire.

Her legs pumping, her feet struggled to gain traction in the soft sand. Swinging her elephant gun in front of her as she moved, Denise felt like she was trapped in one of those nightmares where no matter how fast she ran, it was never fast enough.

Ahead of her, Gail leveled her own elephant rifle. A blast of sound smote Denise's ears, and a wind like a passing truck blew past her.

Behind her, a blood-curdling wail filled the night. It was even louder than the blast of Gail's elephant gun. Whatever the creature was, it must have lungs the size of small cars to make a noise like that.

She didn't look back, though. Looking back would slow her down. Even if the huge bullet killed the thing behind her, she didn't want to slow down.

The rifle blast might stop the thing behind her, but it would only attract more attention from elsewhere. Up above her head, dozens of creatures with amazingly sophisticated ears and senses of direction were circling Malheur Island.

If even one of them swept down and grabbed her by the shoulders to carry her off, she was toast. No, scratch that. She wasn't even toast. She'd be burnt crumbs at the bottom of the toaster.

Another roar sounded behind her, but the footsteps tapered off. Somehow, the elephant gun hadn't killed whatever was back there. Good grief. An elephant gun could fire through a brick wall, pass through a military vehicle's engine block, and then kill an elephant. What the hell was back there?

The footsteps started booming again, and Denise tried to pour even more speed out of her legs. She was almost to the cave and safety. Almost there. Then she realized that the footfalls were getting softer and quieter, moving further away.

She almost breathed a sigh of relief as she dodged around the netting and stepped insides the rocky confines of their basecamp. "What the hell was chasing me?" Denise asked.

"It might have been one of those cute little tree monkeys at one point," Harrison said.

"Back when it was about twenty feet shorter," Gail added.

"Did you hit it?"

"Yeah, but it wasn't a kill shot. I took a big chunk out of its flank, but it started sewing itself back together almost as soon as the bullet was through."

"Maybe those things are like werewolves, and we're supposed to have silver bullets and garlic or something to kill them."

"Wolfsbane," Harrison said.

"What?"

"Wolfsbane is for werewolves. Garlic is for vampires. And Clark said all those pulp magazines would never do me any good."

"Unless you happen to have some wolfsbane or silver bullets stored away somewhere, they still aren't doing you any good."

Harrison opened his mouth to come up with some sort of witty comeback when the ahool attacked. The monster swept down from the sky and aimed right for the mouth of the cave.

Before it could get there though, the humongous bat slammed directly into the netting the hunters had strung up. Just as they'd hoped, the knots tethering the rope to its anchors gave way under the impact. The ahool collapsed onto the ground, half-tangled in the net. The rest of the rope fell down on top of it, fully encasing it. Roaring and spitting, the ahool chewed at the fibers, trying to break free.

Gail raised her rifle again as the ahool sprayed saliva and flailed at the rope. It tried to flap its wings, but they were tangled up in the nets.

"No," Denise stepped in front of the rifle. "I have another idea."

"What the hell are you talking about, Denise? It's going to get out and kill us."

Instead of answering, Denise grabbed up her tranquilizer rifle. She'd left it behind for the meeting at the abandoned cabin. She picked up a dart, inserted it into the chamber, and slammed the bolt back in place.

She looked up and saw the ahool had already managed to rip through part of the net, sticking its snout through and trying to shred the rest of the fibers as it thrashed and screeched. Sand flew everywhere as it wrestled with the ropes.

Denise raised the tranquilizer rifle to her shoulder and fired. The dart shot out with a *poofth* and hit the ahool near its shoulder. Instead of sinking into its flesh, the metal injector snapped off against the monster's hide.

The ahool looked directly at her and shrieked. Its eyes locked onto her, and it redoubled its efforts to escape the nets.

"Uh, Denise?" Harrison backed away from the cave entrance. The bat was scooching forward, its head filling the entrance. Teeth and eyes and flaring nostrils filled the space in front of them.

"Damn, damn, damn, damn," Denise chanted under her breath as she grabbed another dart and inserted it into the rifle. In another few seconds, the bat would be able to get its entire head out of the net and stick it through the cave entrance, effectively trapping them all inside.

Slamming the bolt back into place, Denise raised the rifle again. However, she didn't pull the trigger. Not yet.

The bat stared at her, working another knot in the rope with its teeth. Gail and Harrison were both backed up against the far wall, their rifles raised.

"Denise, what are you waiting for?" Gail hissed.

The bat snarled at them again, displaying a row of teeth that looked like they could chew through a car.

She fired. The dart sprang out and embedded itself in the space underneath the bat's long, curling tongue. The ahool's eyes went wide and fiery, and it tried to turn around and flap away. Instead, it only managed to roll onto its side, still trapped by the heavy duty net.

Struggling to spit the dart out, the gargantuan bat hacked and coughed and gagged. Denise wondered if she'd gotten the dose correct. She hadn't used very much sedative. The ahool was enormous, but it didn't have very much body mass for its overall size. Most of it was just thin membranous wings. Maybe she'd used too little. Or maybe the bat was all but immune to the effects of the sedative with the moon fueling its bloody transformation.

A moment later, a change took hold in the ahool's eyes. They lost their focus, their unwavering urge to kill. They started to gloss over. Great strands of drool started to dribble from its maw. It made a coughing noise and tried to squirm out from under the net again, but all the will had gone out of it. More saliva spooled out of its mouth as it wobbled.

The ahool's head hit the sand with a heavy thud. It continued to jerk and fidget for a minute, fighting the tranquilizer with all its might, but the drugs were taking their toll. With a final half-hearted attempt to bite at the ropes, the bat fell onto its side and lay still. Aside from the steady up and down motion of its chest, it might have been dead.

"Now we have an ahool, captured alive. Let's see what that gets us. Use the radio and call the *Shield of Mithridates*. If Hobhouse is listening, this ought to grab his attention. Maybe this is our ticket out of here."

Harrison picked up the radio and tuned it to the appropriate channel. "Hello? This is the hunting team on Malheur Island. Things have gotten a little complicated here, but we've managed to capture an ahool. Do you read us?"

There was a pause.

"Hello. This is the *Shield of Mithridates*. We read you. We'll be able to pick you up in about four hours."

SEVENTEEN
TOO MANY LEGS

Denise paced back and forth near the cavern entrance, watching the ahool breathe. It had been a few hours since they managed to reach the *Shield of Mithridates*. Hobhouse himself had promised to help them. He said that an electrical fault aboard the ship had prevented them from communicating earlier, but it had since been fixed.

Really, it was all rather convenient that the fault was only repaired once Denise had an ahool sedated. She didn't trust Hobhouse anymore. He'd dazzled her with his speech about preserving the island, but too many things didn't add up.

She didn't bother to mention that she knew there had been a previous expedition to the island. In fact, she still had the Yersinia watch in her pocket. Nor did she bring up the lunar meteorites scattered across Malheur Island and what they were doing to the wildlife.

If Hobhouse could get her off this rock, she'd bring those issues up once she was safely back in Cape Town. Until then, all she really wanted was rescue, and asking a bunch of impertinent questions right now might jeopardize that goal. It was easy. All she had to do was play dumb, use the ahool as their ticket out of here, and then make it back to the mainland. She'd hold their feet to the fire after they saved her. Saved her from the mess they'd gotten her into.

They were still a few hours out, though, and Denise had seen a number of creatures wandering the beach through the cave entrance. None of them looked in the least bit friendly. So far, they'd managed to stay safe with their prize, but they'd have to make some sort of break for it when Hobhouse got here. For that matter, she had no idea how they intended to load the sedated ahool into the *Shield of Mithridates*.

She stared at the bat slumbering in front of their cave entrance. Hobhouse was right about one thing. This was probably the greatest zoological discovery of the past hundred years, and not just because it was an unusually large bat. Bigger wasn't necessarily what made it better, though that was impressive in and of itself.

The amazing part was the transformation. Earlier today, this thing had been a normal-sized bat. It had been feasting on insects no larger than Denise's thumbnail. Now the bugs were the size of marines, and the bats had grown to match. Something about the full moon had turned Malheur Island into a menagerie of nightmares. Yersinia would make a fortune if it could figure out how that worked and secure patents on it. There would be scientific prizes for everyone involved.

She supposed that was why Yersinia was willing to pay the hunters so much. They knew from their previous expedition that there was something extraordinary about the island, even if they hadn't passed the bulk of that information along. No doubt, she was never supposed to learn there was a previous expedition.

And she was less sure than ever what to make of the fact that Razan had been murdered and someone took a shot at her. Was there really a survivor of the previous expedition who had simply snapped? Did the islanders want them to leave? Was one of the other hunters just angling for more money by eliminating the competition? All she had was pure speculation.

"Do you see that?" Harrison asked, pointing outside.

"What?" Denise looked out over the horizon, hoping to see the lights of the *Shield of Mithridates* approaching. The horizon was dark, though.

"By the surf." Focusing her attention closer, Denise squinted into the darkness. The infernal full moon reflected off the churning waves, turning the foam an eerie alabaster. The rest of the sea was black satin, constantly writhing and moving.

Then she spotted it. There was a, for lack of a better term, a lump by the water's edge. Shaped roughly like a sloped pyramid, the lump was about three feet tall and as wide around as a manhole cover. Was it a large rock? No, it hadn't been there a few minutes ago, she was sure of that.

The rock moved, and Denise got a better look at it. Scuttling armored legs carried the lump further up the beach. Black, alien eyes took in the beach from inside hardened turrets. Scrap shearer claws clicked and clacked.

It was a crab, albeit an unnaturally large one. This was yet another creature transformed by the light of the full moon. Even the sea life right around Malheur Island was affected. Denise supposed that made sense. There were probably a few lunar meteorites below the waves, too.

At least this creature didn't look too terrible compared to some of its comrades. Given that it was only the height of a small child, it was practically tiny. Denise still wouldn't want to go up against those claws at close range, but hopefully it would stay well away from the cave entrance. If it did decide to attack them, the elephant guns would turn it into crab pate easily enough.

"I think we can deal with a lone crab," Denise said, patting Harrison on the shoulder.

Another lump emerged from the water and heaved itself up onto dry land. Denise watched. Okay, no big deal. A couple of crabs wouldn't provide any more trouble than a single one. This was still completely manageable.

Another glistening carapace emerged from the water, and then another. Seaweed and sand clung to their shells as the crabs moved inland. Denise stared as even more crabs emerged from the sea.

Six.

A dozen.

A gross.

Thousands.

It was like watching one of those experiments with bacteria where they spread across a petri dish in the span of a few hours. Only this wasn't the span of a few hours. This was the span of a few minutes. The number of crabs grew exponentially, soon filling the surf line.

"That isn't good," Denise said. She'd heard of this sort of thing before. Some islands experienced crab migrations, meaning millions of crabs would sometimes take over the shore in a vast-moving carpet of chitinous armor. Roads near the beaches could become inundated with marching crabs so that anyone driving a vehicle would inadvertently crush thousands of them beneath their wheels.

When the crabs were only a couple of inches in size, it was little more than an inconvenience. When they were as tall as fire hydrants, it was another matter.

The wave of crabs started to move inland, pushed ashore by the untold legions who were still beneath the waves.

"Oh hell," Gail said as she came up to the cave entrance. The scene outside looked like some sort of alien invasion story. Only instead of arriving in gigantic Martian tripods, the invaders chose squat little tanks.

One of the crabs wandered to within twenty yards.

"I think we might have to get out of here," Denise said.

"And go where?" Harrison whispered. His eyes were wide as he stared at the tsunami of segmented bodies working their way forward. The amphibious invasion showed no signs of relenting any time soon.

Denise didn't even know if crabs had ears to hear with, but she answered in a whisper, too. "I can take us to the cave entrance I escaped from. It's only about a quarter of a mile from here through the jungle."

"I don't like the idea of going through the jungle again."

"I don't either, but I don't think we can stay here much longer," Gail said.

Denise looked around. "Grab as much ammo for the elephant guns as you can without weighing yourself down. Leave everything else. It'll only encumber us, and we only need to hold out until the *Shield of Mithridates* gets here."

"Do you think Hobhouse and Yersinia are prepared to deal with the things on this island?"

"Probably not. But if they can just land a dinghy, we can fight our way to it and then motor away."

The crab at the head of the army, some bold Leonidas or George Washington of crustaceans, discovered the sedated bat in front of their cave entrance. Denise opened a box of Nitro Express rounds and dumped them into her pockets. Gail and Harrison did the same as they watched the crabs move closer and closer. They were heading back to the caves, so she threw a coil of rope onto her belt, too.

Clacking its claws together, the lead crab poked and prodded at the ahool. The gigantic bat didn't stir, but apparently the crab decided that the ahool was too big to attack. Instead, it marched on, leading its battalions behind it.

Its eyes, black little orbs that revealed no emotion or thoughts or even a familiarity with either concept, locked onto their cave entrance. Snapping its claws together, the crab started straight toward them. Soon, the whole army of crabs would be at their doorstep, and Denise wasn't sure there was enough ammunition in the world to stop them.

She raised her gun and blew the crab apart. Pieces of shell and legs flew across the beach. Other crabs immediately fell on the pulped remains and stuffed them into their nictitating mouth-holes. They swarmed over their dead leader, snatching up every chunk and quivering blob and devouring them.

Denise slid out of the cave, hoping the crabs would be too distracted to notice her. Gail and Harrison followed a step behind.

The crabs surged forward as soon as they saw human prey, though. They were finished eating their friend almost before all his parts landed. There were simply too many crabs, and apparently, they were all hungry.

Bullets jangled and flopped in Denise's pockets as she ran. She didn't stop to fire at any of the crabs following them, though. Any space she cleared in the horde of clacking monstrosities was as likely as not to be filled with twice the number of crabs a few seconds later. She'd be overrun before she could even make it to the edge of the jungle.

Instead, she did the only thing she could. She ran for her life. Behind her, she could hear tens of thousands of legs pumping after her. The crabs moved like a magma flow, rolling over each other and fighting as they went. They jousted with their claws even as they tore after their prey.

As she reached the edge of the jungle, she heard a shriek as an ahool swept down and tried to snatch up one of the crabs. She turned around and saw the ahool lift up, one of the crabs crushed in its talons. Dark ooze leaked from the crab's pierced shell, but it still reached up and tried to snip at the huge bat.

A few more crabs latched onto the bat's legs with their pincers as it lifted off. The ahool flapped its wings and took to the air again, several crustaceans clinging to its legs and the base of its wings. The bat shrieked in distress and pain at the pinching claws, gaining altitude as quickly as it could.

One by one, the unwanted passengers fell off their host as the bat flapped away into the sky. The crabs tumbled off from hundreds of feet up, smashing into the beach at incredible speeds. One of them landed directly on top of another crab, obliterating both creatures in an explosion of ichor. More crabs swarmed around the fallen bodies and tore them to shreds, eating them as quickly as they could in a festival of mass cannibalism.

The crabs didn't stop at the edge of the jungle. They surged after Denise and her friends, trampling the foliage in front of them in a great rolling wave.

"We have to keep moving," Denise shouted, watching the crabs flow into the jungle behind them.

Before, they'd been able to easily outpace the scuttling sea creatures. Now, they had to deal with the oppressive density of the jungle all around them. Branches scratched at Denise's face. Vines threatened to strangle her. Massive trees turned the very ground into an uneven patchwork of ankle-snapping holes with their labyrinthine roots. Moving uphill toward the cave entrance was harder than running across the flat surface near the beach, too. The crabs were steadily gaining ground on them with their compact bodies that shrugged off impacts with obstacles.

She glanced behind her again, and when she looked forward again, she smacked straight into something sticky. Denise would have pitched forward onto her face, but the sticky substance halted her forward momentum. Swinging in place for a second, she tried to figure out what had just happened. Her arms and legs didn't want to work.

Then she realized what had happened. She was caught in a web, a truly gigantic spider web. She thrashed at the sticky silk holding her, but it clung to her like tape. All she succeeded in doing was creating panicked waves in the web.

The motions must have alerted the web's occupant. A set of legs unfolded themselves from further up in the tree.

Whereas the spider they'd seen earlier was stout and hairy, this one was all legs and glistening exoskeleton. The smooth, flawless finish on the arachnid's surface looked like something that had rolled off a Detroit luxury assembly line.

Long, multi-jointed legs worked their way down the tree trunk, claws sinking into the wood with each step. Denise caught her first glimpse at the spider's dribbling mouth, and felt the bolts come a little loose on her sanity.

"Denise, we'll get you down. Just hang on," Harrison said as he grabbed his machete.

That was an apt choice of words. What else was she going to do but hang on, a voice in Denise's head tittered. She mentally grabbed onto her mind with both hands and forced it to focus on solutions rather than simply going blood simple with fear.

Harrison hacked away at the web, but the spider silk was strong. Behind her, Denise could hear the swarm of crabs marching closer with each passing second.

Another swing of the machete, and Denise could suddenly move her left arm. Above her, the tree spider put one leg onto its web and then the other, finding its grip on the thin strands of silk. Tiny black eyes stared down at her, as dark and impenetrable as a miser's heart.

Harrison worked on some of the other strands, but they stuck to the machete and gummed up the blade. Gail was also working with a large knife of her own. Denise's left leg came free.

Denise looked up again and immediately flinched back. The spider was only a few feet away, its mouthparts rubbing together in excitement.

She was familiar with how spiders ate. They injected their victims with a venom that liquefied their insides, then they slurped out the resulting slurry of juices. Denise could see a set of mandibles attached to the spider's mouth, ready to sink into Denise's body and pump her full of sizzling hot acid.

A remote part of her brain wondered what the sensation of having one's flesh and muscle slide right off the bone as meaty goop would feel like. Would it course through her body in her bloodstream and send her brain dribbling out of her ears after the first bite? Or was it more localized, and she'd get to watch as her organs melted to chunky-style spider soup right before her eyes? She'd get to find out in a minute. The spider's fangs were no more than a foot away.

Riiiiiiiiiiiiiiiiiiip.

Gail cut through another strand, and the structural integrity of the web around Denise gave way. She fell on her face as the remaining strands tore under her weight. Rolling across the ground, she moved out of the space directly beneath the spider.

She looked behind her. The leading edge of the crab army was no more than ten yards away. Denise snatched up her rifle.

"Thanks," she managed, but Gail and Harrison were already running again. Denise took off after them.

Behind her, one of the crabs in the front of the group slammed directly into the remains of the web. The silken weave swung and vibrated like a demonic harp.

Alerted to new prey, the huge tree spider moved down the last few feet of its web and snatched up the crab. Its fangs punctured straight through the crab's shell. The crustacean flailed its legs, but its distant arachnid cousin kept a firm grip with its own graspers. Thick goo started to ooze out from between the cracks in the crab's carapace, its own melting innards seeping out through its shell. The spider slurped out crab goo with its mouth parts from the hole in the crab's shell.

However, the spider's victory didn't last long. The other crabs that encountered the web snipped at it with their claws. After a few seconds, the already-damaged web collapsed completely, taking the spider and its dinner with it.

The spider landed on the ground in a heap and tried to scramble up the tree. It was already too late, though. More crabs converged on the larger beast. Their claws clamped onto the spider's legs. Some of them slipped off the thick, smooth surface. Others managed a better grip.

Chitin shattered as the crabs punched through the spider's armor. They snipped through one leg along the equivalent to the spider's ankles, tearing a clawed foot off. The spider wobbled but adjusted to its other seven legs as the crabs fought to stuff the foot into their gobbling mouths.

Then the crabs managed to wrench away another foot. And another. The spider collapsed, and crabs immediately swarmed across its flailing body. They tore its legs away from its abdomen. They ripped its chelicerae out of its face and fought over them. The spider was an unrecognizable hulk of pale, blobby flesh a minute later, and it had vanished completely another minute after that.

Most of the crabs didn't even stop to consider the spider, though. They kept moving up the hill after their human prey.

Denise was almost to the cave entrance now. If they could just make it inside, hopefully they could hold off the onslaught of crabs. Hopefully.

She could see the cavern entrance up ahead, looming wide. It was just one long sprint to get inside and to comparative safety.

Suddenly, she felt the ground rumble beneath her feet. Denise's first thought was that they were experiencing an earthquake on top of everything else. A tree as tall as a four-story building uprooted from the earth with a mighty tearing noise and fell nearby.

Then Denise saw that the tree hadn't just uprooted due to the tremor. The tremor wasn't even an earthquake. It was just another footstep from the thing that uprooted the tree. Denise looked up at over fifty feet of scales and fangs. She hadn't seen it before only because her brain had processed its legs as just more tree trunks.

She'd forgotten all about the new species of Komodo dragons they met on the island earlier that day.

"We cannot get a break tonight," Denise said.

EIGHTEEN
HUMANS ARE ALWAYS THE GREATEST PREDATOR

The Komodo dragon stood on its hind legs like a tyrannosaurus, except much larger. Its long body was counterbalanced horizontally by the tail, and a sail stood tall and proud across its back.

It stood hunched, its arms dangling close to the ground underneath the bulk of its body. Each of the claws looked big enough to pick up a car.

High above them, the dragon's head was the size of a delivery truck. Teeth like traffic cones studded its mouth. The eyes stared down at them from a height normally reserved for large apartment buildings.

A carrion stink wafted off its body in great waves, like the scent of a warzone mass grave. The dragon took another step, and the earth shuddered as if in fear.

"Balls," Gail said.

"Yup."

Even the crabs seemed to notice the huge monstrosity in front of them. They slowed their relentless march up the hill and stood, clicking their claws. Their shells caught the light of the moon. Where nothing before had even given them pause, even their primitive little crustacean brains seemed to recognize that the Komodo dragon was bad news.

Denise didn't even know how it would be possible to kill the dragon if she had to. Maybe a barrage zeppelin. Not even the elephant guns would be able to take that thing on.

"Over here. Hurry!" a voice called. Denise's head whipped around.

Dr. Marlow stood in the cave entrance. He waved to them urging them toward the cave. Obviously, he'd found his way here after the group scattered after the moon came out.

The Komodo dragon roared at them, its breath like a blast furnace of heat. It took a step toward them, shoving a tree out of the way as it did so. The top of the tree snapped off halfway up and plunged to the ground. Greenery fell to the earth with a roar of crunching branches vines tearing away like high tension wires.

Denise didn't wait. She was already breathing hard after bashing her way straight through the jungle. Denise threw every reserve she had into dashing toward the cave entrance, though. Giant bats weren't going to stop her. Giant crabs weren't going to stop here. Giant goddamn spiders weren't going to stop her. Humongous, gigantic, oversized Komodo freakin' dragons weren't going to stop her tonight, either.

The sound of the wind in her ears was swiftly overtaken by the booming sound of footsteps. She could smell the Komodo dragon coming closer. The scent of decaying meat filled her nostrils. It clung to her tongue as she tried to breathe.

Each step the dragon took carried it a dozen yards forward. The creature was so massive that each stride carried it across the landscape like the Statue of Liberty out for a stroll.

The cave entrance and Dr. Marlow were close now, so very close.

Twenty yards. The ground shook underneath her feet. Denise could actually hear the earth itself compressing beneath the creature's feet as it moved.

Ten yards. Now she could see the dragon's head hovering over her. Rather than trying to bend down and scoop them directly into its mouth, it was going to snatch them up in its oversized claws instead and then lift them up to its fangs, popping them into it mouth like hard candy.

Five yards. Denise could feel a wind at her back, the breeze from something massive approaching. It was from the creature's scaly hand. It was the wind of the reaper's scythe.

With a final burst of energy, Denise dove through the cave opening, Gail and Harrison right behind her. She landed in the dense field of guano just as a set of claws scratched at the entrance. The talons scrapped at the rock, digging deep grooves into the stone, but they couldn't rip the stone away.

Bugs swarmed toward Denise as she lay in the filth. Some of them were as big as her fist. A foot long millipede trundled over to investigate as she drew herself to her feet. She cursed and stomped her feet to frighten the insects away. She finally stepped on a particularly plump weta that refused to be dissuaded, and it popped under her boots. Behind her, Gail and Harrison brushed themselves off while the Komodo dragon raged outside.

Dr. Marlow cringed as the huge creature outside continued to roar and scratch at the cave entrance. "I haven't seen anyone else since…since that lizard killed Shinzo. I thought I might be the only one still alive. The whole island is filled with things like that."

"Do you have a rifle?" Denise asked. She noticed Marlow didn't seem to have one on him.

"No. I left mine behind when I ran, I'm afraid. It's still in the abandoned shack near where we met earlier tonight. I found a much smaller opening in the rock near the village, and I crawled inside because I didn't want to stay out in the open."

Denise took it as a good sign that Marlow had survived in here without major firepower. That meant there couldn't be too many awful things down here. The bugs were larger than they should have been, and more aggressive at that, but they weren't as colossal as anything outside. They couldn't get a full dose of the moonlight down here.

"Do you have any idea what's making these things transform? You're a zoologist," Gail asked.

"I can speculate, but I've honestly never seen anything like it. I've never even heard of anything like it. I would call it remarkable if it wasn't so very horrifying."

"We figure it's probably the moonlight that does the trick," Harrison said.

"That's what I'm assuming as well. I haven't had anything to do with myself except think and hope nothing found me. Everything only went to pot after the full moon came up. Most likely, the lunar meteorites on Malheur Island have affected the wildlife here in some way."

"Do you think you know how? I mean, is there any way we can stop it or something? Maybe ward them off? Like wolfsbane or something?" Harrison asked.

"My guess is that the lunar meteorites left some sort of chemical on Malheur Island that worked its way into the ecosystem. Think of it like plants and chlorophyll. When the sun shines on plants, they convert the energy into a form they can use. On this island, if enough moonlight shines on the creatures, it activates the chemical, and they experience exponential growth. It's built into their very cells, so they're both very powerful, and they experience unnatural rates of healing. It could be a chemical or maybe even a virus that commandeers the cells when it received the right kind of energy, namely a strong exposure to moonlight."

"Yeah, but is there anything we can do to stop them? The old proverbial silver bullet?"

"Maybe. I'm sure these things have weaknesses, even if they can take an enormous amount of physical trauma. Conventional poisons would probably work in high enough doses."

"We definitely don't have a stockpile of arsenic and chlorine gas sitting around."

"And while it would be interesting to test and see if the old folktales are true, I didn't bring along any silver bullets, either."

"My Nitro Express has done the job on pretty much all the smaller creatures," Denise said. "I don't think we can do anything about the behemoth out there, though."

"Yes, I suspect you would need an armored division to do much about that situation."

"We should go deeper into the cave." Denise pointed with her rifle toward the darkness that lay beyond.

"I already came from that direction. It's not entirely safe," Dr. Marlow said.

"I was in these caves earlier, and the ceiling here was crammed full of bats. They're all ahools now, flapping around out there. They might still come back before the moon disappears, though, heading back before dawn. I don't want to be there when that happens."

Dr. Marlow turned a shade of pale. "No, I'd rather avoid that myself."

"And I wouldn't mind putting some distance between myself and those crabs," Gail said, kicking away a rat-sized mite that tried to chew through her boot. Even if the full power of the moon couldn't shine down into the depths, it was still having an effect on the creatures down here. Thankfully, most of them seemed content to go about their business of harvesting guano. Only a few seemed truly interested in attacking the much larger humans.

"I can take us back the way I came," Dr. Marlow said. "You, Mr. Quint, you should be our rear guard just in case something follow us. We can protect the ladies that way."

"The ladies can take care of themselves just fine. You're the one without a rifle."

Dr. Marlow *harrumphed* over that, but he didn't seem in the mind to argue.

Denise suddenly remembered something. The *Shield of Mithridates* was coming to pick them up. They needed to get back to the coast if they were going to have any chance of reaching that ship.

"Were you able to grab a radio? We need to contact Hobhouse. He's coming back to the island."

"No. I didn't take anything with me when I retreated but here. Hobhouse is coming?"

"Yeah. We managed to get through to him after we sedated an ahool. He's coming to pick us up. We never got a chance to contact him again before those crabs chased us out of our camp, though."

"He won't be able to reach us up here in this cave. We need a way to get back to the coast." Harrison looked back outside the cavern entrance. They could all still hear the massive Komodo dragon snorting and moving around out there. Nobody was going back that way.

"You said you got into this cavern system from near the village? I wonder if we can meet up with Balthazar and anyone else still alive. We can all get picked up together and surround ourselves with a bit more firepower to boot."

"I heard some shooting earlier from that direction," Dr. Marlow said. "I don't know who else is still alive, if anyone."

"Balthazar probably tried to get back to his camp on the wrecked German cruiser. Maybe Jubal, Creighton, and Silas made it there with him."

"Maybe," Gail said. Even though they were all experienced in the field, this island was still a collection of nightmares. There was no guarantee anyone was still alive. Experience only went so far when it was tossed against the unknown. Still, Dr. Marlow had survived, even without a weapon. He was practically defenseless, and he was still alive. Perhaps there was hope after all.

"Maybe some of them managed to regroup at the village," Harrison said.

"The locals didn't exactly seem friendly before," Dr. Marlow said.

Denise finally understood the warning the man in dungarees had given them when they landed. He'd told them they had until the next night to leave the island. It wasn't a threat; it was an attempt to ward them away from Malheur Island before this happened. The full moon was a regular event here. They knew what was going to happen. That's why they had a wall in place.

She also understood the part her translation skills had garbled now. At first, she thought the man was saying something about the mountain or a mound. Maybe even mouths. Now she knew the word that hadn't quite registered. He was trying to warn them about the moon. The words were similar enough that she couldn't tell the difference when they were spoken aloud.

"It's possible the village took in some of our friends tonight. We'll check it out if we can. It ought to be another safe place if they'll let us in, too. We can wait for the *Shield of Mithridates* there if we have to."

"Think you can lead us that way, Doc?" Gail asked.

Marlow looked back. "We just follow this stream most of the way. I think I can get us through the last bits of the caves. It's not far from where we split off. Then we just follow some old lava tubes. Simple enough. There's a couple of places where light comes down from the ceiling, though. I never saw anything, but I heard things a couple of times." He fiddled with the pistol on his hip apparently without realizing he was doing it.

"I think we'll manage," Denise said, hefting her Nitro Express. She felt more confident about moving through the caves this time than her last visit. They had guns. They had ammo. They had lights. She even had a coil of rope this time that she'd taken from their base. So long as the tunnels weren't infested with creatures, and they shouldn't be with the moon blocked out, they were fully prepared.

Moving out, Dr. Marlow pointed the way ahead. Their flashlights played over the damp stone walls. Moss, insects, and slime covered almost every surface.

They walked beside the little underground creek as the water gurgled and worked its way down into the earth. More water dripped from the ceiling and stalactites and spattered against the earthen floor. Some of the cold cave water dripped on the back of Denise's neck, and she nearly jumped.

Something small and pale splashed in the water as they walked past. Everyone swung their flashlights around to see what had made the noise, but it was already gone.

The inside of the cave was even more eerie knowing what was happing just above at the surface. Denise could sometimes hear muffled thumps and roars that came to them more as subtle vibrations than real sounds.

Suddenly, Denise heard something moving behind them. A rock dislodged and struck the floor somewhere further back in the cave. Denise swiveled around and pointed her Nitro Express in the direction of the sound.

There was nothing there. Her light played across the rough stone, but nothing leered back at her. Nothing leaped out of the shadows. She bit her lip and kept moving. Maybe it was just the cavern settling or perhaps a bug had knocked a rock loose. Hopefully, that was all it was.

They came to a pool of deeper water where the stream they were following backed up. Something was blocking it. There must be a tight space up ahead where it couldn't all escape down some crevice, like a clogged sink.

The stone around them also changed. Up ahead, the rock was dark and lumpy, like the black basalt left behind after a volcanic eruption. They'd just found some sort of volcanic intrusion.

However, parts of the ceiling were open to the naked sky. Several holes and rifts let the moonlight in to glitter on the water. Denise looked around again, but she still didn't see anything. She hadn't heard any more activity behind them since that stone striking the floor either. Maybe they were in the clear after all. None of the gaps in the roof of their cavern were more than a few feet wide, either. Certainly nothing as big as an ahool could get down here with them. She was thankful for that at least.

This was a completely different part of the cave system than from where Denise fell in earlier. She wondered just how far the tunnels extended. Did they creep beneath the whole island, extending past the land's edges and under the sea at some point? How far deep did they go? From here, it was easy to imagine the endless warrens as the desiccated arteries of some great and awful being, winding and twisting deeper and deeper into the earth until they reached a rotted heart that needed only the light of the moon to beat again.

"I came in through that lava tube over there." Dr. Marlow pointed at one of the tunnels branching off from the chamber they were currently standing in. "We're going to have to wade across this little lake here. Don't worry. The deepest part only comes up to about your knees. After that, it's more or less a straight shot to an exit. It's a tight fit to get in or out, but we can do it if we take our time."

Denise started into the lake, moving slowly. The water was shockingly cold, and it soaked right through her boots. She grimaced as the freezing water turned her socks into clinging wads of fabric. It felt like she was wearing dead squirrels around her feet.

"It's colder than a witch's belt buckle," Harrison said, making a face.

Gail started to take her boots off before wading in. "I wouldn't do that if I were you," Denise said.

"Why not? I'd rather keep these dry so they don't chafe later."

"I don't see anything, but there could be something in the water. Maybe not anything big, but the moon can get in here. There could be worms or biting fish or God knows what else. I'd rather they took a bite out of my leather boots than making off with one of my toes or something."

Denise heard another sound behind them. She stopped moving in the water. It was a stealthy, almost sub-audible noise. She wasn't even entirely sure she had heard it in the first place, but it sounded like a leathery scraping noise.

The sound was followed by a hiss that echoed and reechoed off the walls.

"Did you guys hear that?"

"Yeah," Gail said in a low voice as she relaced her boots. She hefted herself to her feet and pointed her rifle behind them.

A head emerged from the tunnel they'd just emerged from. It was sleek and scaly, and it filled up nearly the entire tunnel. A forked tongue darted in and out of the lipless mouth, and a pair of amber eyes just as cold and hard as the surrounding rock stared out at them.

It was a snake, hunting them through the tunnels based on their scent. The huge reptile was hunting them like they were baby rabbits left alone in a burrow. With a hiss like air escaping from a leaking zeppelin, it slithered closer to them.

Most snakes "tasted" the air with their tongues, following scent trails as easily as blood hounds. Some could even sense heat signatures, allowing them to track potential prey even through barriers. Denise didn't know what this snake was using, but it had managed to follow them through the entire labyrinth of tunnels and found them here.

This one looked like a big, pebbled boa constrictor. It wasn't one of the venomous snakes that used elaborate cocktails of poison to kill or incapacitate their prey. Instead, it would wrap around them, use its entire body as one big muscle and slowly, slowly crush the life out of them. Constrictors didn't squeeze all at once. They waited for their prey to exhale, and then they wrapped themselves a little tighter, making each and every breath harder to draw. Eventually, the prey's lungs simply couldn't muster the power to keep moving against that kind of resistance. They couldn't inhale any more, and then the snake just waited a few minutes until the feeble squirming finally stopped.

Then it was just a simple matter for the snake to uncurl and fit its jaws around the unfortunate victim. Snakes were infamous for their double hinged jaws, which allowed them to consume absolutely enormous meals. They could fit impossibly large items down their gullets, the outlines of a dead meal sitting in their belly as a big lump.

Some of the big constrictor snakes had other features in addition to just their elaborate jaws, though. They had teeth. They weren't fangs for squirting venom, and they weren't the sort of teeth that chewed. They were long curved things that looked like filleting knives. The snake sank them into their prey as it maneuvered its mouth around its prize, trying to find the best way to consume it, just in case the animal somehow wasn't dead and tried to thrash away. Even then, the snake would be able to keep a firm grip.

If it unhinged its jaws, Denise could probably walk right into this snake's stomach without so much as a need to duck. Had the reptile sat at a cave entrance with its mouth open, they might have all marched right in before they realized that the curved spikes overhead weren't simply more stalactites.

The snake slithered forward. The damned thing had to be over a hundred feet long. Denise doubted the water would stop it. Most snakes did quite well in water, actually. It was probably a bigger hindrance for her than the snake.

"Get moving," Denise said. She leveled her rifle, but she didn't fire. If she could help it, she wouldn't kill anything else on Malheur Island unless she had to. She hadn't wanted to kill anything at all when she came on this expedition.

Still, if it was between her and the snake, she knew which she'd choose. The Nitro Express could blow the reptile's head off and tear through most of the length of its body.

She waded through the water with everyone else, sloshing toward the opposite end of the chamber. There was still plenty of room between them and the snake, so if they could just get out through the opening Dr. Marlow knew about, it shouldn't be a problem.

Suddenly, Denise felt a tug at her legs. At first, she didn't understand what was happening, but then the water started to flow away from her, as it was going down a giant bathtub drain somewhere further down the tunnel. Whatever blockage was damming the water up must have cleared.

But what could possible cause…?

A leech the size of a cow reared up from the water and landed on Dr. Marlow. Its sucker mouth flared open and landed over the zoologist's head, cutting off his gasp before it could turn into a scream. The leech engulfed the entire upper half of his body.

Denise realized what had happened. The boneless invertebrate had been lying flat below the water, covering up most of whatever cistern the water naturally flowed to. When it sensed prey moving through the water further along, it moved and unblocked the water, causing it to suddenly drain away.

Marlow's legs kicked and thrashed, but the leech started sucking almost the instant it latched onto the man. Suddenly, Marlow's legs kicked straight out as if someone had stuck an electrical current through him. Denise could actually see the skin tighten against his bones in the matter of a couple of seconds as he was completely and utterly exsanguinated.

His skin lost all its color, turning a feeble grey in which only the veins stood out. Then, one by one, the veins and arteries collapsed in on themselves. Marlow's body went as limp as a wet rag, slumping inside the grip of the leech's mouth.

Harrison leveled his rifle and fired. The huge round basically cut the leech in half. Chunks of pulpy black flesh flew across the cavern like blackberry jam. A torrent of blood, a lot of it probably Marlow's, gushed out as if someone had just torn a blood transfusion bag in half.

Both halves of the leech wriggled and writhed on the ground. Dr. Marlow slid out of the leech's mouth. His body looked like something that had been buried in the desert for a very long time. Dozens of pinhole marks ringed his upper body as if he'd been kidnapped by a mad acupuncturist. The red perforations were the only color on his otherwise grey skin.

The sheer force of the leech's sucking had ripped Marlow's eyeballs out of his skull. One dangled by a stalk, but the other was simply gone. His skin looked as fragile as damp origami paper as it hung on his body in loose flaps.

Gail shot the leech's front half again as it tried to flop its way closer. The leech's head exploded into a million little chunks. Ribbons of damp flesh the consistency of unfinished rubber landed everywhere like some sort of grotesque confetti bomb. The rear half of the leech continued to flop mindlessly all on its own, completely unaware that the rest of the leech was spread across the entirety of the chamber.

Without the water to wade through, there was nothing to slow them down. Denise, Gail, and Harrison ran across the now empty chamber to the opposite side. Their boots squelched and squished as they ran.

Behind them, the snake moved at its own leisurely pace, apparently quite confident that it could chase them into a corner and consume them all at will. Maybe it was even right. The huge reptile stopped for a second to investigate the dead leech. Its tongue flickered in and out of its mouth, in and out. The scent of blood was all but overpowering where it flowed out of the exploded leech and flowed in little channels toward the same dark crevice the water had escaped into. Marlow's blood would slip beneath the world's surface and disappear down into the depths, flowing in some black river never to be seen by man.

A moment later, the snake resumed its slow pursuit of the hunters, moving no faster than necessary to follow them. Its body flexed as it slithered, moving effortlessly over the stone in a long trail of flesh.

Ducking into the lava tube Marlow had indicated, Denise, Gail, and Harrison moved as quickly as they could in the tight little tunnel. The walls were black and sharp with jagged volcanic glass in some places. Brushing up against some parts of the tunnel was likely to flay some of the skin right off. The snake didn't hesitate to follow them inside, though.

"I think I see the exit right up there," Harrison said, pointing. Sure enough, Denise could see a little pinhole of light up ahead. The hateful moonlight shone into the tunnels ahead, though the moon was now lower in the sky than before.

Denise shone her light on her watch for an instant and realized that Hobhouse and the *Shield of Mithridates* would be at the island in less than ninety minutes. All they needed to do was find reliable shelter until then. They were so close to being rescued. So close.

And yet so far. The snake hissed again behind them, as if realizing their plan. A lot could happen inside of an hour, and on Malheur Island, a lot of it was likely to be bad.

They had to walk single file, with Harrison in the lead. He reached the end of the path first and stood next to the little borehole were the lava tube met the outside world. The hole was not very large. Denise would have to struggle to fit through it. She could see Harrison thinking the same thing. Would he be able to fit through at all?

"Gail, you're the smallest. You go first."

"Maybe you should try first just to make sure you'll fit."

"No. If I get stuck, you'll never be able to push me through from this side. If you and Denise fit, you can help pull me through from the other side. Now go."

The snake was fast approaching, its tongue still flicking in and out at them. Denise wondered if it could smell their desperation.

Gail leaned down and stuck her arms through the narrow hole. It was maybe three feet to the outside world, with the smallest section at the very outside lip. She crawled inside and used her feet and hips to wriggle her way through. Denise could hear her scraping and sliding along. Maybe thirty seconds later, she heard Gail's voice. "Alright, I'm through."

Harrison motioned to Denise. She took her Nitro Express and threw it through the hole. She was a little bigger than Gail, and she didn't want the big, bulky gun slowing her down or snagging on anything. Then she tossed herself into the cramped little hole, probably formed when some big air bubble in the molten rock burst and left a void in the cooling stone.

She grunted and moved as quickly as she could. Her hands weren't very useful in pulling her forward because there was a bare minimum of room to use her elbows. She had to generate most of her forward movement with her legs and knees.

The stone poked and stabbed at her the whole way as she moved. Behind her, she could hear the sound of the snake moving against the walls of the tunnel, sliding forward as surely as a dollop of sap down the side of a tree.

"Are you through yet?" Harrison asked, his voice betraying his nervousness.

"Almost." Denise reached her hands through the opening, and Gail grabbed her wrists. A few seconds later, with a lot of pulling and wriggling, she popped free.

"Okay," Gail called. "Get out here, Harrison."

His equipment flew through the opening first. First his rifle, then his vest full of gear and ammunition. Denise looked into the tunnel and saw Harrison's face squirming toward her out of the darkness. His eyes were wide, and he was breathing fast.

"My legs aren't quite through yet, but that scaly son of a bitch is almost here," Harrison said. "Grab my arms and pull. Pull, dammit."

Denise grabbed one arm and Gail grabbed the other, and they hauled with all their strength. Harrison moved forward a few feet. His head emerged from the tunnel, then his shoulders.

Then he got stuck. His chest was slightly too wide for the opening. He gritted his teeth and cursed. "My feet are still out in the open. Get me outta here. Quick. I can feel that thing sniffing around my boots. Pull me out quick."

Denise hauled on Harrison's arms until she could feel his tendons creak. He was wedged in the hole far too tight.

"Guys. It's right there. It's right there. Pull me out." Harrison's voice rose an octave.

"Denise, take both his arms," Gail said. "Get ready to pull. Harrison, this is going to hurt." She moved over and put her hands on Harrison's chest. "Okay, pull now."

Gail shoved her hands down, compressing Harrison's ribs. He made a gagging noise, but he came slightly loose from his confinement. She kept dragging him, pulling him all the way free from the lava tube. He flopped out onto the ground and lay there for a few seconds.

"That wasn't fun," he finally said, lifting himself up onto his knees. "Not fun at all."

Inside the caves, discontented hissing echoed out of the rock. Denise looked through the opening she'd just pulled Harrison through. All she could see was a huge amber eye rimmed by scales.

She looked out toward the sea. The village was perhaps only a half mile away. Torches guttered behind the walls, casting little pools of shimmering light.

There were other lights, though. She could see a tiny set of lights out at sea. That had to be the *Shield of Mithridates*, moving in to pick them up. It would be here within the hour. They were so close to being safe, so close.

The route down to the village was comparatively short, an easy walk. All they had to do was stay low and find a way past the village palisades and then wait for the *Shield of Mithridates*.

"We made it," Denise said. "We made it." She almost didn't believe it herself. They'd survived the onrush of crabs, the giant tree spider, overlarge insects, the leech, and a snake as long as several city buses. This part would be easy.

Then someone shot Gail.

NINETEEN
WELCOME TO HELL; ENJOY THE BUFFET

The bullet caught Gail in the jaw and blew out the back of her head. A fragment of bone shot out and buried itself in Denise's cheek like a tiny shred of shrapnel. Gail dropped to the ground and twitched once...twice...and then went still.

Denise dropped to the ground. Harrison hugged the earth beside her. Gail was clearly gone. The high-powered rifle shot had taken most of her head off. She checked for a pulse, but it was clearly futile. Hot, angry tears burned in Denise's eyes, but she willed them away as shock gave way to boiling rage.

"This must be the same bastard that tried to shoot me earlier today," she finally managed to say. Her voice came out thick and husky before she cleared her throat.

"Why in the hell would they do this? Gail never hurt anybody. Why?" Harrison's voice was off, too. "Too bad nothing on this island managed to eat them."

"If I find out who it is, they're going to wish the monsters got to them first." Denise looked around. Finding where a shot came from was almost impossible in the jungle. She could roughly tell the direction of the shooter from the way the bullet impacted her friend, but she hadn't seen a muzzle flash. For that matter, the dense, thick coating of greenery that ran across the island absorbed sound differently than a gunshot on the open savanna.

"Did you see where the shot came from?" Harrison asked.

"No. I think it was from somewhere closer to the coast, but I couldn't give you an exact location."

"Whoever it is, they know where we are a lot better than we know where they are."

"If we try to flush them out, they're a lot more likely to gun us both down before we even get a chance to get close."

"That's what I was thinking."

"So what do we do?"

"I say we try to make our way to the village. It's close, and we can move low through the jungle most of the way, which gives us a lot of cover. If we stay here, it's only a matter of time until something finds us, either animal or human. I'm guessing that neither one will be friendly."

Denise noticed the shard of bone stuck in her cheek and plucked it out. "Sounds like a plan," she said. "Then we can wait for the *Shield of Mithridates* to pick us up."

"What about the others?"

She was thinking the same thing. One the one hand, she very much wanted to tell Hobhouse to hoist the anchor as soon as they made it aboard. Hauling away from Malheur Island sounded like a good idea. As far as she knew, the only other person aside from Harrison she could definitively say had survived the night was the shooter. Leaving him behind wouldn't be any great loss. Let him fend for himself on the island of freaks.

On the other hand, Denise didn't know for sure that the shooter was the only survivor. If both Jubal and Balthazar were alive somewhere on the island and they were also trying to get to the *Shield of Mithridates*, how would she positively identify which one was the assassin? She didn't have any real evidence against anyone. It would take a ballistics expert and a medical examiner to even begin to determine who was responsible, and neither of those was readily available anywhere near Malheur Island.

If they both demanded to be let aboard, how would she stop either one of them? How would she stop the right one? She certainly didn't want to be trapped on a small ship with the killer. That might be even more dangerous than remaining on the island until dawn, when things would presumably revert back to normal. How was she supposed to figure out what to do?

She cast those thoughts aside for now. Thinking too much about problems that hadn't arisen yet would only slow her down now. And she still needed all her attention and skills just to survive the next ten minutes. Instead, she broke the most immediate problem down into steps.

Gazing out at the village wall, she plotted a course through the trees that would minimize their exposure. She put together a point A to point Z map in her mind, figuring out how to cover the distance while still staying low. There would be only one major point of difficulty.

The village was located on a spit of land branching off from the beach, a narrow peninsula that isolated it from the rest of the island. To get to that little panhandle of land, they'd need to cross the open sands of the beach. Denise didn't see any crabs loitering in the surf, but that wasn't her only concern.

If the shooter had his peepers ready to follow them, something that wouldn't be impossible with the swaying of grasses and bushes that would be involved with traveling through the underbrush, he could pop them both when they started across the sands. There were still ahools in the sky as well, and they might think that two humans scurrying across the sand looked like tasty meals.

And there still wasn't any guarantee that the villagers would want to let them inside the gates.

"The way I see it, we don't have a ton of options," Denise said. "We can either hunker down here and probably end up dead one way or the other."

"And the other option?"

"Quite possibly end up dead somewhere between here and the village, trying to get to some semblance of safety."

"Well, I for one would rather see an outcome where we make it to safety, and then I shove my foot so far up that sniper's ass that he can trim my toenails with his teeth. Let's see if we can get to the village."

"I was hoping you'd say that." A few seconds later, they crawled through the grass and briars. Thorns and thistles clawed at Denise's face and hair, but she brushed them aside the best she could.

She couldn't hear any human noises in the rest of the jungle. There were animal shrieks and howls as beasts never intended to live in the natural world clawed and eviscerated one another. However, Denise was more worried about the rogue hunter trying to shoot them. Her ears strained for the sound of stealthy footfalls, the snap of a twig as someone walked closer, or the jangle of a bandolier. Even though she knew it didn't make any sense, she was also listening for another gun shot. If the killer was as good as he seemed to be, she would never hear the shot before it struck home. But she couldn't help but try to listen for it anyway.

A large tree loomed ahead. Denise looked around just to double check that its branches weren't loaded with fat-bodied spiders or gigantic, bald-faced monkeys looking to eat her alive. She didn't see any immediate horrors, so she slithered up to the tree and moved into a crouch.

Peeking up above the large, gnarled roots, she looked to get her bearings to the next spot they needed to find to stay out of the killer's sights. Hopefully.

They skittered between low-lying patches of ground, turning natural divots in the earth into temporary foxholes. The tall grass became camouflage, and the sturdy boughs of trees became shields. Denise had used the same strategy to sneak back to their base camp earlier that day. With luck, it would work again.

Finally, they reached the ragged, bare edge of the jungle. From there on out, it was just a low clumping of hardy shrubs, and then the earth gave way to hard, packed sand. Moving across that would be the riskiest part of the whole venture.

If they were lucky, the rogue hunter wouldn't even know they had made it to the beach. They could just slip through the village wall without being shot at. That would be nice. Very nice indeed. Denise wasn't counting on it, though. This wasn't shaping up to be a nice night.

She could see the wall that cut the village off from the rest of the island maybe one hundred yards away. It looked well-made. The wall was primarily made of large logs, about thirty feet tall, that had been sunk vertically into the ground. They were placed side by side so that there was barely an inch of space between any of them. Each of the logs had a coating of pitch, preventing rot and probably making the surface more difficult to climb.

At the top, each of the large logs had been sharpened to a brutal-looking point. Anyone who slipped while attempting to scale the wall could find themselves impaled like a butterfly on a pin at a museum.

Even reaching the top of the wall would be difficult, though. Boreholes had been hammered through the logs at a steep angle near the top, and sharpened wooden spikes had been inserted through. In profile, the wall would look something like an upside-down "7," with the foot of the letter slanted to an acute angle.

Maybe it wasn't as effective as a coil of barbed wire along the top of a chain link fence, but it served a similar purpose. Even animals that could climb up the vertical siding of the wall wouldn't be able to surmount the angled spikes very easily.

Finally, the base of the wall was surrounded almost six feet high with a mound of compressed and dried clay and mud. Gravel and boulders had been added into the matrix to provide further stability. The simple cement would provide increased stability for the wall, making it harder to tip over.

Denise had to admire the engineering that went into the wall, even if it was the very same barrier between her and safety. A lot of work and maintenance had gone into the making and upkeep of the structure.

She could only see two entrances, places where there was no mud retainer buttressing the wall up. The first was clearly the main entrance. A wide double gate sat closed. No doubt the people who lived here normally carried firewood, captured game, and waste in and out of that gate. It was wide enough for a horse and carriage team to completely turn around in the space.

The other entrance looked like a more promising way to get inside. It was closer and much narrower. Only one person could walk through the gate at a time. Essentially, it was the back door. Opening that would be a much less time-consuming endeavor than rolling open the gigantic front gates, which looked like they were made of several tons of wood in their own right. Getting in fast would be a top priority if they had someone shooting at them.

"Alright, here's how we do this," Denise said. "On the count of three, I say we run for the smaller gate over there. Ready?"

"What if they don't let us in?"

"We'll find a way in one way or the other. I'm not going to take no for an answer on this one."

"Okay. One." Denise felt her muscles bunch up, preparing for the all-out sprint to the gate.

"Two." She slung her elephant gun over her shoulder by its strap so it wouldn't bounce against her side as she ran. She wanted both hands free to move as fast as she could.

"Three." Both Denise and Harrison were up and moving before she even finished the word. In the space of a few feet, the dense jungle foliage turned to open sand, like an oasis turning to desert. Her feet kicked up little geysers of white, postcard-perfect sand as she moved. So far, there wasn't any rifle fire spitting at their heels, which was a good sign.

Her heart thudded in her chest like an abused bongo drum. Breathing in sharp pants, she hurled herself across the beach. The sand almost seemed to glow the same silvery color as the moon under the accursed light from overhead.

What couldn't have been more than a few seconds later but felt like all of eternity plus another week, they reached the small gate. Denise barely slowed down. She slammed directly into the side of the wood and started pounding on it with the flat of her hand.

"Hey! Hey, we need someone to let us in. Please help. We're stuck out here. Open the gate." She tried again in Afrikaans, smacking the wood. Throwing a glance behind her, she didn't see anything. Neither the glint of a rifle lens or the approach of a huge, slavering beast, but that didn't mean that either threat was off the table. "Help us," she called.

No one came to the gate. No one opened the way in for them. Denise stuck her eye to a gap in the wood.

She didn't see anyone on the other side, no one at all. Not even a guard. Everyone must have retreated to some inner sanctum for further protection against the beasts that roamed during the full moon. She could see a number of large structures that looked like they were designed to shelter the island's population.

What she was really interested in, though, was how the door was locked. As she expected, there was a big black streak across her vision along one section of the slats. There was a thick wooden log serving as a bar on the door. Even if the wall itself was quite sophisticated, the main lock on this door was pretty simple. There were just a couple of supports on both sides of the door which the log rested on, preventing the door from opening.

Maybe she could use the rope she had, slip it through a crack, wrap it around the log, and jimmy the support a little loose.

A loud *whump* sounded behind her. She turned around and saw an ahool sitting on the ground not twenty yards away. Its fangs glistened in the moonlight as it stared at them with hungering eyes. The creature must have seen them scamper across the beach but couldn't just swoop down and snatch them up when they were pressed tight against the side of the wall.

Whump. Whump. Whump.

Several more ahools landed in the sand behind the first. They gazed at the humans cornered against the wooden palisade for a moment, and then they started forward. While they could soar with the majesty of eagles in the air, they moved in an ungainly crawl while on the ground. They walked like commandos trying to infiltrate under a string of barbed wire after ingesting a slew of powerful drugs. The massive bats clearly weren't comfortable moving on the ground, but they didn't need to be when their prey was so conveniently cornered.

"Uh, Denise? Please tell me you have a plan."

"Working on it," she said. She unslung her Nitro Express, but she didn't aim it at the ahools. She didn't want to kill them if she could help it, and she suspected the scent of fresh blood would only draw something worse in a matter of seconds.

Instead, she aimed it at the door and the bar keeping it closed from the other side. A pull of the trigger, and the elephant gun roared loud enough to deafen Denise. Behind her, the bats all flinched as the noise assaulted their sensitive, oversized ears, but they didn't stop coming. They hissed and squeaked at each other, but all Denise and Harrison could hear was a high-pitched ringing noise.

Denise looked at her handiwork. She'd blown a fist-sized hole through the door and taken an equally large chunk out of the bar holding it closed, but that wasn't enough to push the door open. She needed to saw all the way through the bar, or to at least blow a big enough hole in the gate that she could stick her arm through and shove the bar aside.

She reached into her pocket and pulled out two more shells. The Nitro Express released a little puff of smoke as she snapped it open and removed the spent casings. Slapping the new rounds into place, she closed the rifle back up and raised it again.

The bats were less than ten yards away now, within lunging distance. Denise fired the elephant gun a second time, and the closest bat backed up a step. It shook its head as if shrugging off a painful injury. The monster's ears flattened against the back of its head, and it shrieked at the hunters.

Denise shoved at the gate, and the last few centimeters of the bar that were still holding together disintegrated with a snap. The bar fell away where she'd cleaved it in two. She grabbed Harrison and practically heaved him through the now open door, following immediately behind him.

Realizing that their prey was about to escape, the ahools surged forward. Denise's vision filled with the sight of hundreds of flashing teeth all coming for her at once as she turned around and slammed the door shut.

With the bar destroyed, there was nothing to lock the gate with, though. Denise braced the door with her body a second before the impact.

The first ahool slammed into the door with its full weight. Denise suddenly found herself airborne as the door banged open even against her attempt to stop it. She landed on her chest, barely getting her hands out in time to cushion her fall and prevent her from smashing her face directly into the ground.

With a cry of victory, the ahool stuck its head through the now open doorway. Glaring at Denise, it tried to fit the rest of its body through, too.

"We're the only party crashers coming through here tonight," Harrison said. He leveled his own heavy rifle next to the ahool's head, a few inches away from its ears, and fired a round into the night.

The bullet whizzed harmlessly off into the jungle, but it did its job anyway. Startled by the deafening noise, the ahool leaped backwards and clawed at its ears. The roar of such a large rifle so close must be like an explosion directly inside its skull.

With the space suddenly clear, Harrison threw the gate closed and slapped his rifle in place where the bar had been. A second later, the gate slammed on its hinges, but the metal barrel of the rifle was just as strong as the thick log it had replaced to keep the gate closed against such intruders. Enraged shrieking issued from the other side of the gate as the ahools all spat and bit at the gate and at each other.

Harrison rubbed his palms together in apparent satisfaction. "Eh? Eh? What do you think of them beans?"

Denise picked herself up off the ground. She found her own rifle a second later and grabbed it, too. Her whole body felt like it had been laid out on a road and run over by truckers all day, but they'd finally made it.

"Thanks for not killing them, Harrison. It really means a lot to me."

"Yeah, well, you're welcome, I guess. But if I had to choose between being eaten and protecting myself, I'll shoot anything on this island."

"I know. I would too, if I had too. I'd just regret it later if there was some other way."

"Look, I know you don't like the idea of hunting anymore after what happened with those elephants, but nature isn't always all fun time and cuddles. Nature red in tooth and claw and all that jazz. Things eat other things to survive."

"Right. I know. That's the natural order of things. I just don't want to kill anything unless I absolutely have to. I might consider an exception for whoever shot Gail, though."

"I'll hold that son of a bitch down while you shove that rifle barrel up his nose. Here's the thing, though. Between the two of us, you're the only one with the heavy weaponry now. I just want to make sure where we both stand. If it comes down to me or some freak of nature, I want you to shoot whatever it is that's coming after me. I can respect your principles even if I don't share them, I just don't want to end up dead for reasons I don't agree with."

"You won't. You're my friend. You just saved my life, and I'll do whatever I can to return the favor. We're in this together. I'll do what I have to in order to keep it that way."

"Alright. I can definitely get behind that. I don't want to make you choose between your ideals and me, but it's that sort of night."

"No. I agree. I think in a weird sort of way, this night has shown me some things. I like being out in the field, even when things are rough. I almost need it, and I have a bad time of things when I just hole up somewhere. But at the same time, I'm not worried that I'll revert to being the same person I was before. I won't be going on any more sport hunting expeditions. I can assure you that, but I can do what I need to do to survive. And make sure my friends survive. I just prefer to do things my way from now on."

"Good. Good. I'm not sure I see things your way. I'd probably set this whole damn island on fire and be done with it myself, but you have your own path. That's fine. So long as we both end up alive long enough to see dawn, I'm fine with that. Do you know what you want to do with yourself if you won't be going on hunting trips?"

"Yeah, I think so. I'll tell you later once we get inside somewhere safe."

"Fair enough." Harrison looked back at the locked gate. His rifle shuddered in place as the ahools banged against the door from the other side, but it held.

Denise looked around the village. Most of the buildings appeared to be houses. The buildings were made out of a combination of compressed mud, like adobe, and a combination of woven reeds and bamboo. There were other structures too, but one thing struck her about the village.

It was completely abandoned.

TWENTY
GRAPPLING HOOK

"Where is everybody?" Harrison asked, looking around. He had noticed the same thing as Denise.

Even though there were torches guttering from a few holders around the village, there was no sign of actual human habitation. No one came out of any of the houses to see what all the shooting had been about. There were no guards manning the wall to warn of possible breaches. A sea breeze wafted through the village, causing the torches to dance.

Denise had been expecting some sort of reception, and probably not a friendly one. They'd made a lot of noise in the process of getting in here, and they'd damaged the gate. She thought for sure she'd have to try to beg forgiveness and shelter through a combination of Afrikaans and pidgin Dutch.

"Hello?" She called.

There was no response except for another gust of breeze and the waving of the torches. She walked up to the closest house and knocked on the side of the wall to get the attention of anyone staying inside. There was no movement from inside. Some buildings were immediately obvious when they were empty. The subtle vibrations and thrum of life could be sensed, and it was clear when it was missing.

Denise stuck her head through the door just to be sure, but there were no signs of any inhabitants. Grass mats and a fire pit sat in the middle of the house.

Stepping inside, Denise walked over and poked a finger in the dead fire pit. There was still a small amount of residual warmth. Someone had doused the fire a few hours ago, probably shortly before the full moon rose above the horizon.

Moving back outside, Denise saw some larger structures closer to the beach. They looked like they were probably used for food storage or perhaps some sort of communal gathering place. The islanders must have taken shelter inside.

The only other option was that they had abandoned their safe walls, and every last soul had moved into the jungle interior for some reason. Denise didn't think that was particularly likely. They must have all gone to the safety of the largest building, a small area they could actively defend.

Now that she looked at the thick mud walls of the large building again, the more it looked like a fortress to her. The tall, windowless walls, heavy-looking doors, and imposing size of the structure would make it difficult to breach.

"I'm guessing everybody is in there," Denise said, pointing.

"Should we go introduce ourselves?"

"Probably. I'd rather stay in there with them until the *Shield of Mithridates* gets here than out here in the open. It's not too late for more ahools to come by and realize they can swoop down here and grab us. I think they could knock down one of these huts if they really wanted to. That structure looks a lot more secure."

"Let's head out, then," Harrison said. They moved between the houses, always trying to stay in the doorways. Denise watched the skies, hoping that there wouldn't be any more black, winged shapes drifting through the dark ether to hunt them down.

She held her rifle in the firmest grip she could manage, but her hands were trembling. Now that she wasn't running everywhere and crawling away from gunfire, she had more time to process what had happened earlier.

A whole range of emotions tossed and heaved inside her. The sorrow of Gail's death ate at her like acid, and pure, razor-edged anger was just behind that. At the same time, she felt relief that they'd found safety and a different kind of relief that she starting to put her life back into some kind of order. She had a purpose and goals again. First she needed to survive the night. Then, she needed to track down whichever son of a bitch shot Gail.

Gail was dead, and they'd left her body for the island's creatures to find. Not that they'd had a choice, but it still felt wrong to leave her there. She was Denise's friend, and she would have at least liked to hide her body somewhere the animals wouldn't get it. At least they'd had the chance to bury Razan's body when he was shot. It wasn't much, but at least it afforded a tiny scrap of dignity.

God. It had barely been twenty-four hours since someone shot Andris Razan. Since then, the killer had murdered Gail and nearly killed Denise. All that, and the whole island had gone straight to hell.

"So who's left?" Harrison asked.

"Huh?"

"Somebody killed Razan. That lizard thing tore Shinzo apart. Dr. Marlow is dead. That same bastard who shot Razan probably killed Gail. There were only ten of us on this island to begin with. Now we're down to six, if that. I want to figure out who killed Gail, and I want to leave them behind. Let them sit things out until the next full moon. See how they like that. I feel pretty comfortable saying that neither one of us is the murderer, so that leaves us with four suspects."

"I've been trying to figure that out myself, and I don't have anything."

"There's our friend Jubal Hayes. Nobody knows where he was when Razan was killed."

"And he slipped away from Balthazar and Dr. Marlow the next day to bother us."

"And Dr. Marlow was asleep when somebody started firing at you later that day. Jubal could have been anywhere."

"He could have been."

"I may not be a betting man, but Jubal is what the boys in blue tend to label a suspicious character. He's kind of a shit, too. I think maybe he's our man."

"Could be," Denise said.

"You don't exactly sound convinced. I mean, he nearly strangled the life out of you this morning. If we run into him, I'll seriously think about putting a hole in him just as a precautionary measure."

"There's three other hunters on this island, too."

"I'd just shoot him a little bit. Wing him. He could probably do with a lesson anyway."

"He probably could. That doesn't mean we know it was him, though."

"So you don't think it was him?"

"I said I don't know it was him. There's a difference. I think it's a fifty-fifty shot."

"Fifty-fifty? Shouldn't it be a twenty-five percent chance? There's four other people on the island. Maybe. Hard to say who else is still alive, honestly."

"Silas Horne and Creighton Montgomery are probably still together. They were sharing a camp. I figure there's a pretty good chance they're still alive if they're working as a team. I'd have been dead a couple of times over already if not for you and Gail."

"Yeah, our English pals were together when Razan was killed. If one of them was a psychopath, I think the other would be the first to know. Ol' Creighton Peckerwood Montgomery wouldn't be my first choice for a friend, but Silas seems like an okay guy from when I talked to him. Maybe even a little embarrassed by Creighton's antics. So, yeah, we probably don't have to worry about them. So that means you think it's down between Balthazar van Rensburg and Jubal?"

"Pretty much."

"I have to admit, I'd still place my money on Jubal. I never had any beef with Balthazar. I know the two of you didn't see eye to eye, but I never found out why."

"To be honest, neither did I. He's disliked me since the very first moment we met. He made his feelings pretty clear that he didn't want me on this expedition when we set out from Cape Town that first morning. I don't trust him."

"You think it's a fifty-fifty shot between Jubal and Balthazar mostly because you don't like Balthazar?"

"No, it's not just that. We don't know where he was when Razan was killed, either. He said that he was aboard the *Hookstadt* looking for a Dutch translation dictionary when somebody started shooting at me. Nobody was watching him. And who brings a Dutch dictionary with them on a hunting trip anyway?"

"He is a Boer. Maybe he likes to keep fluent."

"Maybe," Denise said. She'd known Balthazar for years, and he'd been uniformly unpleasant that entire time. Did that mean he was capable of cold-blooded murder, though?

"I know the two of you don't like each other, but you've known him a lot longer than I have. Do you think he's capable of something like this? Jubal may be a sorry excuse for a human being, but I wouldn't want to drop him if I should actually be looking at Balthazar more."

"Dammit, I don't know if Balthazar could be the killer. I never picked up anything murderous from him over the years, but I don't trust him, either. I can't tell if that's my gut trying to tell me something, or if I'm just biased from too many bad turns with him. But what was it you said originally?"

"When?"

"Back when we discovered Razan had been killed. You said it always made sense to follow the money. Jubal seemed like he was mostly interested in the money he could get out of this expedition. That's why he wanted to know about the meteorites. Once everything went to pot tonight though, everyone's best strategy for getting off the island alive was probably to stick together. We only get paid if we survive. Jubal is, if anything, else likely to gain anything by killing off the other hunters on the island."

"Jubal doesn't exactly strike me as the sharpest light bulb in the shed."

"Maybe not, but I don't see what he gains out of this, and that was his main motivation all along. I've known Balthazar a lot longer, and his reasons for disliking me are still pretty opaque. I don't know what makes him tick. I don't think Gail's killer is doing this for money. At least, I don't think it's directly about the money we're receiving for hunting ahools. I think there's something else going on here, something we don't understand. Balthazar's the one I don't feel like I understand between the two of them."

"Alright, fair enough. I trust you. If we see Jubal, I won't shoot him on the spot. Not even a good winging, no matter how much he deserves one. You can bet I'll be watching him like a hawk, though."

"If we run into him, and he starts acting like he's here to stab us in the back, I'll plug him myself. If he killed Gail, I'll put his head over my mantle."

"If he killed Gail, I'm not sure that much of him will be left after we're done with him."

They walked up to the largest building in the village. The thick mud walls reminded Denise of the architecture in Timbuktu, with its massive mosques and libraries and their hardened earth exteriors.

There was only one set of doors, large wooden ones that had been painstakingly carved with intricate designs. Denise could see stylized depictions of men with spears fighting beasts of every size and shape. Hairy monsters, winged monsters, scaly monsters, and every other manner of horror was depicted on that door. Rather than carving a heroic picture of the men slaughtering the monsters, a lot of the human figures in the foreground were being torn apart in messy ways. Only the figures in the background, who were less distinct and given fewer details, seemed to be having any luck at all surviving the onslaught of ghoulish nightmares.

The door lock was an intricate-looking thing. It was another bar, but this one was more complex than just a simple log laid across the doorframe. Instead, it was a thick beam of smelted metal with an elaborate series of grooves. The positions of the brackets holding the bar in place meant it couldn't simply be slid to the side, either. It had to be precisely rotated around so the pegs didn't become unaligned from the grooves.

Really, the system looked quite clever. A mere animal wouldn't be able to knock the metal bar off. Deliberate rotation was the key. The bar was attached to a sort of lever mechanism that disappeared through the side of the wall and into the structure, allowing the people inside to unlock it from within or jam the rotation entirely. A great deal of ingenuity and craftsmanship both had been expended on making this door.

"Here, I think we can get inside if you just take that end, and we work together," Denise said. Harrison grabbed one end of the metal bar. She grabbed the other end. The metal was incredibly heavy, meant to thwart attacks from even large creatures. It would be impossible for her to work it from the outside by herself.

"Okay, start twisting it this way," Harrison said. They both grunted and strained, working the metal through the various pegs and joints.

More grunting and more heaving freed the metal bar from the door. Denise and Harrison lifted it away and set it on the ground.

"I hope they're not too unhappy with us intruding," Harrison said.

"I hope so, too." Denise wasn't sure how the villagers would react to playing host to the two of them. Hopefully, they wouldn't be too perturbed to have a couple of strangers stay with them until the *Shield of Mithridates* could pick them up. They were just a couple of beggars looking for shelter at this point. Even if they weren't thrilled about it, Denise was sure she could use her Afrikaans skills to navigate some sort of agreement.

She pushed open the heavy doors. They creaked and groaned as they moved, sounding like the wind through the graveyard.

Denise realized something odd. The doors swung inward, into the building. A lot of engineering and thought had clearly gone into this structure. The doors should have swung outward. If they were meant to defend against something battering against the doors, the doors should be designed so that the creatures would have to beat the doors all the way down in order to open them. If the bar somehow came loose, all it would take would be a simple push, and the animals would be inside.

That's when she realized that the door and its security mechanism weren't meant to keep animals out of the structure. They were meant to keep the inhabitants inside until daybreak.

Oh hell.

The snarls reached her ears before she saw anything. Inside the structure, it was pure blackness. Not a single torch or fire burned, so only the sounds reached Denise. The sounds and the smell. The smell hit her like a slap to the face. It was sharp and musky, like some sort of rare cheese made only by cultists in French caves. As the light filtered in, Denise saw dozens of glowing eyes looking at her.

"Shut the door. Shut the door," Harrison said, trying to lift the metal bar back into place. Denise made a grab for the door, but a huge, hairy hand shot out of the darkness and grabbed onto the wood. Long, black claws jutted out of each finger, sinking deep into the wood. The hand wrenched the door out of Denise's grip.

"Run," she shouted. Harrison dropped the bar and started moving. They'd been wrong. They'd both been so wrong. The village wasn't a place of safety. The same effect that caused the other animals on the island to break out into horrible monstrosities also affected the humans living on the island.

The moonlight had an effect like poison ivy on everything on Malheur Island, the people included. One brush with it, and things went bad fast.

The only thing that saved them was how narrow the door was. Several *things* that used to be people all tried to shove through at the same time, causing a jam. They bit and slashed and thrashed at each other, all trying to get free. Dozens more of the twisted beings pushed from behind, all baying like the grim reaper's hounds out hunting souls.

Denise raised her rifle and almost fired out of pure reflex, but she pulled her finger back at the last second. Right now, that howling mob of awful things didn't look like anything human, but in the morning, they'd be people again. Her Nitro Express could shoot straight through any of them. She might kill twenty with one shot if she fired straight down the middle. Maybe she could live with herself if she needed to do something like that to save her life. Maybe she couldn't. She didn't intend to find out unless she had to.

"How do we get out of here?" Harrison asked as they ran. He looked at the gate they'd come in through. It was still banging on its hinges as the ahools smashed against it. She and Harrison could both hear the giant bats still shrieking their awful wails after them. Opening that door would offer a quick yet unpleasant death.

She looked to the main gate. It was huge and heavy. Opening it looked like it would take several minutes and a lot of sweat and effort. That's why they didn't use that gate in the first place. They didn't have several minutes.

In fact, they had no time at all. The log jam of huge, hairy bodies finally freed itself behind them.

Denise could see now that the wall was meant as much to keep the villagers in during the full moon as it was to keep everything else out. The wall certainly couldn't keep flying threats like the ahools from sailing over it, but in case the villagers broke out of their enclosure during the full moon, they still couldn't scatter to hither and yon on the island and risk being eaten by spiders or Komodo dragons.

Both the regular entrances were out of the equation. Even if they opened the main gate, they wouldn't be able to close it in time before they were overwhelmed by the transformed villagers.

What options did that leave? None of the buildings were strong enough to withstand any sort of siege from the villagers. Most of the houses didn't even have doors. They were simply open to the elements, separated by a thin curtain of woven fabric or nothing at all. Even the buildings with a way to block off the entrance wouldn't last long. Their walls were made from woven fronds and bamboo. They wouldn't last more than a minute. If the creatures following them didn't simply crash straight through the walls, they could claw them apart in less time than it took to scream.

Denise mashed her brains together. Behind them, the creatures bounded forward. Some of them walked on two legs, others used all four limbs to go leaping forward. Flashing eyes and grotesque snouts and sharp, hungry teeth all aimed for Denise and Harrison. Even though they were both running at full speed, the things that had once been human were faster. They would catch up soon.

Suddenly, Denise had an idea. "Make for the wall," she said.

"Which part?"

"Any part." Denise reached back and grabbed the length of rope she'd taken from their base when the crabs attacked. She thought they might need it when they moved through the caves, but she'd completely forgotten about the coil of tough fibers since then.

They found themselves facing a length of the wall a few seconds later. Denise screeched to a stop. Her hands moving with terrible, frantic speed, she tied a knot with one end of her rope around the middle of her Nitro Express rifle. She pulled it tight and snug, and then she took the rope and started twirling it like a lasso.

"What are you doing? They're almost here." Harrison watched the oncoming horde of things with wide, horrified eyes. His hands twitched at his sides, yearning to have his rifle back in their grip. With Denise's rifle at the end of a rope, they were all but defenseless.

"The spikes," Denise said. She hurled the gun upward, trying to send it sailing over the top of the wall. It struck the crenelated peak and tumbled back downward, thudding into the dirt. She grabbed the rifle up and started twirling it again.

"What spikes?"

"The ones drilled through the wall every few feet to the other side so nothing can climb up." She threw the rifle again, letting the momentum from the rope do most of the work for her. The rifle sailed up, up, and then it cleared the top of the wall.

Denise pulled on the rope before the rifle could fall all the way to the ground on the other side. She reeled the rope in as quickly as she could. A few seconds later, the rifle caught on something, and she couldn't pull it any higher.

The outside of the wall was covered in downward facing spikes. By throwing the rifle over, she'd caused it to snag between two of them. She'd essentially created a sort of grappling hook. Now they had a rope leading up over the top of the wall. All they had to do was climb it.

"You go first," Denise said, pushing the rope toward Harrison.

"No, you're smaller." There was no time to argue about it. The creatures were almost upon them. A slobbering, howling mob shot straight toward them, blood in their inhuman eyes. The moon sent their shadows loping across the sand in front of them, and their shadows had already reached the wall.

Grabbing the rope, Denise hauled herself straight up. She planted her feet against the side of the wall and used it to help boost herself up. Going hand over hand, Denise pulled herself up as far as she could at a time. Slipping and falling to the ground would mean death. The hard, frazzled rope bit into her hands as she moved, but she kept going.

Directly below her, Harrison took the rope in his hands. The snarls and grunts and howls were close now. Denise didn't look down, but she could hear the pounding footfalls following them. It sounded like a constant, low rumble. There were hundreds of feet behind them, all pushing their owners as fast as they could to tear Denise and Harrison apart.

Denise was perhaps twenty feet up the side of the wall when Harrison screamed. The sound punched into her ears and shot straight down to her soul. For a second, her grip faltered on the rope.

Harrison kept screaming. Denise looked down and instantly regretted what she saw, knowing that it was something she would take a very long time to forget.

They had Harrison. He was too low on the rope when they reached the wall, and they were able to jump up and grab him. Furious claws ripped and pulled at him. Teeth like something out of a medieval fairytale chomped down.

Denise kept moving, reaching the top of the wall a few seconds later. Harrison had stopped screaming in just those few seconds. The screams had been replaced with wet ripping noises and chewing. The screams had been replaced with the sounds of limbs being torn free from their sockets. The screams had been replaced with the snap of bones as the marrow was sucked out.

Even above those noises, more of the creatures shrieked for Denise's blood. They gazed up at her like hounds eying a stray caught up on a fence, and they brayed for her death. A couple of the creatures pulled on the rope.

For a second, Denise thought they were about to climb up after her, but apparently they didn't possess their full human intellect, just animal cunning. They tugged on the rope, straining it. The rope went as taut as fishing line that had just snagged a killer whale. Denise could hear it creak a little under the strain. A couple of them bit the rope, but none of them shimmied up it. Several tried to climb the wall directly, but they always slid down, leaving furrows in the wood with their claws.

She sat at the top of the wall for a moment, her presence taunting the creatures below. Oh God. Harrison.

Had she been too slow climbing up? Could she have done something different to save him? Was there something she'd overlooked that might have led to a different outcome?

She didn't know. Everything happened so fast. Denise closed her eyes and tried to concentrate for a moment, but the growls and sounds of meat being peeled from bones below wouldn't allow her to put her thoughts in order.

If nothing else, she knew she needed to climb down the other side of the wall without falling and breaking her neck. She reeled in her rope and let the rifle fall to the ground on the other side with a thud. She swung her legs around.

The wall was thirty feet high and sheer. She took the rope and tied it around one of the spikes where she'd anchored the rifle. Working her way down, she moved as best she could rappelling off the side of the wall.

She dropped the last few feet. Denise could see through the narrow gaps between the logs. A swarm of hungry movement seethed behind the wall, scratching at the wood, still trying to get at her.

Denise looked down at her Nitro Express rifle on the ground. The barrel was bent from supporting her and Harrison's weight and then the tugging of the things on the other side of the wall. The metal now had a very slight curve to it, nothing dramatic, but enough to ruin the weapon. If anyone tried to fire it at this point, the elephant gun would probably explode and blow the face off anyone holding it.

That was the end of it. Denise didn't have any shelter. She didn't have any defenses. She didn't have any friends.

The end would come swiftly now.

TWENTY-ONE
FROM THE GRAVE

Denise picked herself up. She was in a bad spot. Everything hurt. Her body and emotions had both taken a pummeling in the last twenty-four hours. She had barely slept in that time, and her body could only run so far on adrenaline alone.

She had to keep going, though. Her only other option was to sit out here in the open and die, and that she refused to do.

What was nearby? Where could she find some sort of shelter?

Razan's abandoned camp was the closest, but it was through the jungle. Denise didn't think she'd be able to make it through there again. The jungle offered some shelter, but it also provided dozens of ambush opportunities for other predators. Walking into that black thicket with only her revolver would be tantamount to suicide.

Then she remembered. Razan's gun. His supplies. They'd carried them out to the beach to mark where they'd buried him. A rifle would at least give her a chance to defend herself again, and she wouldn't have to set foot in the jungle to get it.

It wasn't much, but it was a start. Denise started moving. She slunk across the sand to the ridge where the jungle itself began. She stayed far enough away that she wouldn't be easy prey for something that wanted to lunge out at her, but she didn't want to walk exposed along the beach either.

Even though she knew it wouldn't do her much good, Denise held her revolver in her hands. The standard bullets wouldn't stop anything that wanted to eat her, but they would give the shooter something to think about if she ran into him. She wasn't going to survive all this only to be gunned down while totally defenseless. If this night was her time to go, she'd do it fighting.

Fierce howls and shrieks emanated from the jungle, but most of the action seemed to be deeper in the interior. There weren't as many animals who lived right near where the environment transitioned. Off in the distance, she could hear the steady booming of something truly gigantic walking through the jungle, probably another Komodo dragon.

Razan's grave lay just ahead. Denise wouldn't have been able to recognize one spot of trampled sand from another if not for the pack of supplies they'd laid down as a temporary marker. And there on top of the pack lay Razan's modified Savage Model 99 rifle.

Normally, the Savage was more of a military-style rifle, not designed to shoot oversized elephant gun bullets. It used a rotary magazine, almost like a giant revolver, but it could hold several bullets at the ready, which was an innovative design.

At some point, Razan had swapped out a lot of the parts, though. Where before the rifle shot .303 rounds, Razan had taken a new barrel and magazine and repurposed them to shoot .450 rounds. The custom work made the rifle look like something stitched together by Dr. Frankenstein if he had become a gunsmith rather than a doctor, but Denise was plenty happy to find it regardless. Even if it wasn't quite as fearsome as her Nitro Express, it could still lay waste to just about anything she pointed it at. She grabbed up the box of ammunition sticking out of Razan's pack.

"Denise?" voice asked from behind her. She spun around and raised the rifle.

"Hold on. It's just us," Silas said, raising his hands. Creighton stood next to him, holding a rifle of his own and giving her a grim stare. A few feet behind them, Jubal Hayes stood with his hands tied behind his back.

"What are you up to?" Creighton asked.

Silas waved his colleague away. "Are you alright? Is there anyone else with you?"

"No. I'm alone."

"Why do you have Jubal with you? Why's he tied up?"

"We heard some shots and then we saw Gail's body near the caves when we came to investigate. Then we found Jubal in the area. After what happened to Razan, we weren't taking any chances."

"You? It was you?" Denise lunged forward and raised her rifle to club Jubal across the head. If he was the killer, if he was the one who killed Gail, she'd smash his head in like a melon if she had to. Creighton stepped forward and held her back.

"Whoa. Wait. What the hell? I don't know what's going on either. I heard some shots too, and then the next thing you know, the Red Coats here were telling me to put my hands on my head and get down on my knees. What the hell is happening here?"

No one bothered to answer Jubal. "Denise, what happened? Where is everyone else?" Silas asked.

"They're dead."

"How? Who?"

"Harrison and Dr. Marlow were both attacked by creatures. That bastard shot Gail right in front of us."

"My God. I'm so sorry," Silas said. He looked back at Jubal and then patted Denise on the shoulder.

"Have you seen van Rensburg?" Creighton asked.

"No, I haven't seen him since Shinzo was killed."

"Assuming he's still alive, that's only five of us left." Silas looked at Creighton, who grimaced.

"Did you kill Gail?" Denise asked Jubal.

"No. As a matter of fact, hell no. I was hunkered down in the base I originally set up the first night, then I hear shooting, and then these two ass-clowns show up."

"He was in the area," Silas said. "After hearing what we heard, we didn't want to just leave him where he was. We thought he might come after us next."

"Lies," Jubal spat.

"What are you doing out here?" Denise asked.

"There was some sort of, I don't know what to say, crab migration. It forced us out of the spot we were staying in," Silas said.

"The buggers swept across the beach in a big wave. We had to move inland to stay clear," Creighton added.

Denise nodded.

"We decided to angle toward this end of the island as best we could because we knew a few people had set up their base camps in this direction, yourself included. We wanted to huddle up with any other survivors we could. Then we heard gunfire and met Mr. Hayes here."

"Why are you trusting her? She said everyone she worked with is dead. She came from that direction, too. She's probably the killer. Tie her up, too. I didn't do shit," Jubal said.

"Shut your trap." Creighton waved his rifle in Jubal's general direction.

"Hobhouse is coming on the *Shield of Mithridates*," Denise said. "We were hoping he would be able to pick us up before dawn."

"We saw the lights out on the water," Silas said.

"Where were you planning to go?"

"Originally, we thought we might try to find your camp. We figured we'd be fairly safe with you and your friends. Numbers are good in a situation like this. However, given what you told us, we'll probably try to find Balthazar aboard the *Hookstadt* now. It's closer to us than your base at the moment anyway. I'd like it if you would come with us."

"I...yes...sure. Absolutely. I don't know where else I would go either at this point, and I'd rather stick with you two. What are you going to do with him?" Denise thrust her rifle in Jubal's direction.

"He's coming with us. If Balthazar is at the *Hookstadt*, it means Jubal was most likely the one behind the shootings."

"I will punch you in the dick if you keep accusing me of things I didn't do," Jubal protested. Neither Silas nor Creighton seemed particularly alarmed by this new threat.

"But I mean, what are we going to *do* with him?"

"Oh. I think I see now. We'll keep him tied up, and I imagine Mr. Hobhouse will turn him over to the Dutch colonial authorities after this is all over."

Behind them, the booming noises were getting closer. One of the Komodo dragons was approaching. Denise could hear trees being bent and pushed aside. Some of the smaller ones snapped and crashed to the ground in a racket.

"We should find Balthazar," Silas said. The *Hookstadt* wasn't far ahead. Denise could see its prow jutting onto the beach from here.

"Yeah," Denise agreed.

"I want to check Razan's pack first," Creighton said. "There could be something useful in there. Maybe water. I could do with some water. It's been a long night." He got down on his knees and opened up the hefty pack, tossing its contents out onto the sand.

The pack contained a lot of the same things Denise brought with her. Dry clothes, extra ammunition. Maps. A book for down time.

Just below Creighton, the sand shifted slightly. Denise looked down, wondering what she had just seen. "Did you guys see—?"

A pale, sand-covered hand shot out of the beach and latched onto Creighton's leg. He yelped in surprise. It was Razan.

What in the world? Was he still alive? No, he couldn't be. Denise had seen his body. The human form wasn't meant to survive that sort of trauma. Razan had been as dead as dead gets. Most of the top of his head had been missing. People didn't just wake up from that.

Then Denise realized what had happened. A worm, thick around as a sink pipe, chewed its way out of the pallid flesh on Razan's arm. Dozens of smaller worms tumbled out as the giant worm burrowed back into Razan's corpse.

The worms were affected by the moonlight just like everything else on Malheur Island. If this really was caused by moon dust leaking into the earth and making its way into the ecosystem, of course the worms would be affected.

They were busy tucking into Razan's corpse when the full moon rose. Now they were wrapped up in his body, using their own contortions to act like puppeteers. By working together, they'd turned Razan's corpse into a flesh marionette.

Creighton kicked at the arm with his free leg, but it was an awkward position. His boots only grazed off the knuckles. He shifted around, shifting into more of a push-up position to try to knock the corpse hand away.

Instead, Razan's other arm shot out of the sand and plunged straight into Creighton's stomach. Creighton had just enough time to make a little sick noise in the back of his throat before the arm ripped back out, a knot of his intestines locked in its grip.

Creighton tried to back away, but his guts were still caught in the corpse's fist. He jerked backwards, but that only caused more of his insides to spool out of him like a magician's never-ending handkerchief trick. Only in this case, the handkerchiefs were all red.

Denise raised her Savage 99 and fired. The arm holding a clump of Creighton's innards disintegrated like a long blade of grass before a lawn mower. Bone and pulped worms flew across the sand, taking shreds of Creighton's intestines with them.

Sitting on the sand, Creighton was breathing on short, sharp little gasps. He was going immediately into shock. Denise knew first aid. Maybe she could wipe the sand off Creighton's guts and stuff them back inside, but she wasn't sure he'd live long enough to be transferred to the *Shield of Mithridates*.

More sand exploded outward, and what was left of Razan emerged from his shallow grave. No, Denise corrected herself. This wasn't Razan. This wasn't like one of those voodoo tales in the pulp magazines where someone came back from the dead as a zombie slave to some occult master. It was Razan, but every last scrap of him was dead. There was no more Razan left in there. This was just a collection of worms using his body as a mobile feeding ground.

Worms poked out of Razan's pale flesh in a writhing mass. His mouth hung open, and a knot of worms slithered where his tongue should have been. His eye sockets were filled with constant wriggling motion. Bigger worms pulsed and throbbed under his skin, feeding on the very muscles they were replacing. Soon, Razan's body would be no more than a skeleton encased in hundreds of oversized worms, all of them working together to move his limbs and help feed the whole.

Razan's remaining arm reached over and grabbed some of the offal torn from Creighton's body. The arm jittered and shook as the worms tried to coordinate by feel. A second later, Razan's dead claw hands grabbed up the red mass and brought it back. The hand stuffed it directly into the gaping gunshot wound in Razan's torso, feeding it to the worms inside there. They didn't seem the least bit concerned that Denise had blown off Razan's other arm.

Firing again, Denise blew Razan's head off. The heavy caliber bullets disintegrated what remained of Razan's head and launched the resulting debris into the jungle.

Razan simply kept coming, though. His corpse pulled itself the rest of the way out of the grave, despite missing an arm and a head. The body kept coming toward them, flopping out of the grave and clawing its way forward with its remaining arm.

Denise fired again, this time straight into the corpse's center of mass. Whereas the shots to the head and arm merely tore those peripheral extensions off, a shot directly to Razan's chest from close range distributed the impact throughout his whole body.

In a split second, Razan all but flew apart. Rotting meat and stinking worm shreds sprayed across the beach. The incredible impact all but liquefied Razan's already-decaying flesh. A pair of legs twitched and scissored wildly inside the grave, but the rest of Razan was simply gone.

The worms that had survived burrowed back under the beach as quickly as they could. In other places, worms that had been chopped in half by the blast flailed across the sand.

Breathing hard, Denise turned her attention back to Creighton. He didn't look good. His eyes had gone glassy, and his skin was pale and clammy-looking. Blood continued to gush out of the hole in the middle of his belly, though the flow had dwindled. That wasn't a good sign, though. It simply meant there wasn't a lot of blood left in his body by that point, and what was left was rapidly leaking out onto the once white sand. Now the beach was a dozen different shades of crimson.

"Silas, I need help lifting Creighton up. We're going to have to drag him to the *Hookstadt*." Denise was looking over Creighton's injuries. Moving him was a bad option, but their other choice was to leave him here on the beach out in the open, where he was all but guaranteed to die before they could get back, either due to blood loss or because something found him. She didn't have any supplies to take care of him here.

"Silas?" She turned around to see why he wasn't rushing to his friend's side and helping her.

He and Jubal were both facing the opposite way. She followed their gaze across to the edge of the jungle, and then she followed it up...and up. The booming footsteps they'd heard earlier had been getting closer, and her rifle blasts were enough to give their position away.

One of the Komodo dragons was staring down at them, raised to its full fifty feet of height. At the ragged edge of the jungle, it towered over the scrubby trees and bushes that clung to the sparse, rocky soil.

It stood only a few feet away from a large, white statue that looked like a screaming beast head. When she first saw those sculptures, Denise thought they might be a panoply of strange gods or idols. But they weren't; they were warnings to everyone who ventured onto the island. Here be dragons.

The massive Komodo dragon took a step forward, clearing the jungle in a single bound. Its foot pressed into the sand, leaving a footprint that Denise could lay in with her arms and legs outstretched and probably still not touch the sides. The dragon was a walking apocalypse. A prehistoric biological catastrophe. A throwback to times of gods and monsters.

Silas turned to her. "Run." He pulled out a pistol, aimed it, and shot Creighton in the head in a single movement. Creighton's head whipsawed back in a puff of red, and he collapsed on the sand.

Denise couldn't tell if what she'd just seen was admirable or horrifying or both. There was no way to save Creighton. Perhaps he was better off like this.

She ran anyway. Silas and Jubal took off after her.

Behind them, the dragon roared, a noise like a volcano erupting. It took another yawning step forward, its foot coming down squarely on Creighton. The massive weight caused bits of Creighton to go squirting across the sand. When the dragon took another step, he was stuck to the underside of its foot like a candy wrapper, reduced to a gummy ruin.

The *Hookstadt* lay ahead on the beach. A single lantern light burned in the bridge. Maybe they could make it. Maybe. The dragon's footsteps were drawing steadily closer, its every stride covering an amazing distance.

Denise willed herself to lift her legs higher, to pump her arms harder, to squeeze every ounce of speed from her battered body that she could. Each step sent twinges into her muscles like they were being prodded with hot irons. Everything hurt.

But the alternative was to feel a lot more pain very suddenly and then never feel anything again. Her lungs were like bellows, drawing in great gasps of air and pushing them back out. Her legs were like pistons. She tried to clear her mind of everything except taking the next step, moving incrementally closer to the beached ship each time. Even if they could just crawl inside one of the rents in the armor near the prow, they'd be safe. The Komodo dragon was much too big to follow them inside.

Suddenly, a new noise caught her attention even above the sound of the dragon's footsteps, a sound she would always remember and dread. The howl came from behind them, quickly picked up by a matching call and then another.

Some of the villagers had broken loose from behind the wall. Denise didn't know if they finally managed to climb the wall or if they ripped Harrison's gun away from the door and scrambled out into the night from there, but it ultimately didn't matter. They were loose now, and they had her scent.

She risked a glance backward, and she saw shapes running on the beach behind the Komodo dragon. They were gaining rapidly, running on all fours like wolves. Their eyes were sickly yellow searchlights in the darkness, bobbing along as they gained on their quarry.

The Komodo dragon was only a hundred feet behind her now, covering twenty feet for every ten she managed. However, the *SMS Rear Admiral Hermann Hookstadt* lay just ahead in all its rusting glory.

This was their only chance at safety. Everything else was simply too far away. Denise reached the edge of the hull, Silas and Jubal right behind her. The metal at the prow of the ship was crinkled up like melted chocolate where it had smashed directly into the beach and ridden up onto the sand. There were plenty of places where the rivets shot loose and the welds gave way and the carefully laid steel rolled back like taffy.

Denise dove through a hole about eight feet wide and four feet high and found herself in what had probably been the ship's forward magazine. Artillery shells the size of infants lay scattered on the floor, their casings slowly corroding and accumulating a thick patina of grime. Toppled, damaged machinery that was probably built to load the shells up into the guns lay strew about in heaps of rusted junk. She looked around.

There was no way out. Only a single, thick blast door led out of the room, and it was dogged shut. However, there was no going back now to try to reach a different part of the ship.

Behind them, the Komodo dragon had reached the ship. The beast raked its huge claws against the hull, trying to peel the metal back further. Rusted and old, the hull groaned and squealed, but it didn't give very far. Not even a monster that size could do much against naval armor.

Denise wasn't worried about the Komodo dragon, though. She was more worried about the escaped villagers. Unlike the dragon, they could fit through the same hole she, Silas, and Jubal had come through.

"You've led us right into a corner, you bitch," Jubal said.

Rather than respond to him, Denise simply body checked him into the wall on the way to the blast door. She took the butt of her Savage 99 and banged it against the hatch. "Balthazar! We're in the forward magazine. Let us in," she hollered.

Hopefully, Balthazar was actually in the *Hookstadt* as opposed to dead in a ravine somewhere. Hopefully, he noticed them running toward the ship from his camp on the bridge. Hopefully, he not only noticed them but ran down so he could let them in. Hopefully, he wouldn't just let them all die down here. Denise had to rely on hope. She didn't have much of anything else left at this point.

"We're about to have company," Silas said, holding his own rifle. Outside, the villager things had reached the outer edge of the ship. Denise could only see their glowing eyes from where she was standing.

The Komodo dragon noticed them, too. It swung around and tried to scoop one up its massive claws. The villagers danced away, yapping and snarling. They were much more nimble than the huge reptile.

"Balthazar! Open up!" Denise kept banging on the door.

"Untie me. Give me a gun," Jubal said. "We'll shoot the sumbitches."

Silas already had his gun raised, but the villagers were moving too rapidly outside the entrance scampering around the Komodo dragon's feet as it tried to snatch them up. The dragon snarled in frustration as it shot its claws forward and came up empty again.

Silas pulled the trigger, and a roar filled the whole room. The blast was cataclysmic inside the confined space. Denise could feel the sound resonate through her whole body. An explosion of sand sprayed up outside, scouring the exterior of the ship.

"No, you'll kill them," Denise shouted.

"That's the point," Jubal said.

"But they're people," Denise said.

"Not anymore." Silas reloaded his gun.

The first of the villagers darted straight between the Komodo dragon's feet and pulled itself into the interior of the ship with them. A second creature scampered around the dragon and also scrambled through the opening into the ship's forward magazine. They approached together, claws raised. Drool dripped from their fangs.

Denise swallowed. Now it really was down to them or her. Denise didn't want to shoot them. They didn't have any control over what they were doing. The moon had driven everything on Malheur Island into an unnatural bloodlust. She didn't know if the human parts of their brain were still alert but powerless to stop any of this or if the islanders would all wake up in the morning with no memory of what happened the night before.

Either way, they had friends and family. Killing one of the monsters would mean killing the person, too. Denise didn't want to do that. They weren't to blame for what had happened here tonight.

She raised her rifle anyway. No matter how much she didn't want to kill them, she wanted to be torn limb from limb even less. Her mind conjured up Harrison's screams as he was ripped apart and eaten alive. The people they'd once been might not want to harm her, but the monsters they'd become sure did. Denise had reached the last resort. She looked down the rifle's sight and planted them squarely on the chest of the first villager.

TWENTY-TWO
THE SECOND BOER WAR

With a sound like a bayonet crunching into a tin can, the blast door behind them slid open. Balthazar stood in the narrow space opening and looked out at the scene unfolding inside. He saw Denise and Silas, armed and facing off against two of the creatures, as well as Jubal, still with his hands tied behind his back.

"Get inside," he said.

Jubal scrambled backward and leaped through the narrow gap first. "Balthazar! Quick, untie me. These two have gone crazy. I need a gun, too."

Balthazar shoved Jubal aside. Denise was closer to the door, and she hopped through next, Silas hard on her heels. Realizing that their prey was escaping, the villagers lunged forward, howls erupting from their throats.

Shoving his weight against the heavy blast door, Balthazar tried to push it closed before the monsters could reach it. But the door was made from heavy, extra thick steel meant to limit damage from an explosion inside. There was no way to open or close it quickly.

A twisted claw shot through the opening before the door could close all the way, preventing it from shutting. A snarl rumbled through the hallway as the door clamped down on the hand near the wrist. The sound of claws scraping against the door from the other side, trying to push it open again, was loud in the hallway.

Denise spun her rifle around and smashed the butt down on top of the hand. Bones crunched like beetles under a boot. The hand writhed as if an electrical current had been run through it and withdrew. With a final heave, Balthazar heaved the door shut and dogged it closed, sealing the monsters out. They would need an artillery battery to get inside now.

Balthazar turned to his new company, looking them over. He stared long and hard at the ropes binding Jubal. He glanced at Denise and then frowned. He turned his attention to Silas instead. "Explain," he said, gesturing at Jubal.

"Creighton and I found him after hearing some gunshots. We think he's the one that killed Andris Razan and Gail Darrow."

"Gail was killed?" Balthazar shook his head. He finally looked back at Denise. "I know you two were friends. I'm sorry."

"I...thank you." She'd spent the entire trip avoiding Balthazar. Accepting niceties from him felt strange.

"Who all is left?" Balthazar asked.

"We're the only ones," Denise said. She briefly recapped the deaths of Dr. Marlow, Gail, and Harrison. She had to speak with a knot in her throat as she mentioned what happened to both her friends. Silas covered how Creighton died and how they'd discovered Jubal in the area shortly after Gail was shot.

"I didn't do anything. Lies, all of it. Balthazar, you know me. Do I seem like a madman to you? I think she killed her friends and is trying to pin it on me. Untie me and we can throw her out there with those things. We're not safe with her in here."

"Come up to the bridge with me. The *Shield of Mithridates* is getting close," Balthazar said.

They followed the large man down the narrow corridors of the *Hookstadt*. Without regular maintenance, the ship was slowly crumbling to rust. The thick, grey paint covering the interior was peeling off in sheets, giving the walls an unpleasant, scabby look. Their feet sent echoing footsteps down the long, dark hallways. Denise had to sling the Savage 99 over her shoulder in order to walk through the tight spaces.

In a few places, Balthazar had laid lamps down, but most of the ship was dark. They passed rooms filled with overturned bunks or soldering supplies, but Denise could only see the vaguest outlines. Distantly, she could hear the wash of the ocean sloshing against the hull. Denise stopped dead as a long, wavering roar sounded from somewhere below them.

"I sealed off the parts of the ship I was using," Balthazar said. "But there's so many holes in the hull that those things can go pretty much wherever they want on a couple of the decks. Don't open any doors unless I tell you to."

They came to a staircase so encased in rust that Denise thought her eyeballs might get tetanus just from looking at it too hard. A skeleton occupied the space beneath the stairs. The body was still wrapped in the ragged remains of a German Imperial Navy uniform. Most of the corpse's skull had been caved in, apparently smashed against the wall. Denise realized that not all the stains on the stairs were rust.

Balthazar noticed where they were all looking. "There's more skeletons elsewhere, too. Not a full crew's worth, though. I don't know if they were attacked by ahools, and they accidentally ran aground fighting them or if they beached themselves by accident and then died during the next full moon. I tried to get to the village to ask them about it yesterday, but they turned me back at their gates. I guess they didn't want to talk to somebody they thought would be dead soon anyway."

They moved up the staircase, taking each step carefully. The stairs groaned like stepping on them hurt terribly. A few flights up, Balthazar opened another door, and they found themselves on the ship's bridge. Levers and bedraggled charts and broken glass greeted them.

Balthazar had set up a cozy little arrangement with a sleeping bag and gas cooker in the back. Netting covered the windows at the front of the bridge to keep out flying intruders. At over fifty feet above the ground, he had an excellent view of this part of the island.

At the moment, a large portion of that view was the back of a Komodo dragon. The behemoth had finally given up at peeling back the hull and was making its way toward the jungle.

A chair and rifle sat near one of the windows.

The radio crackled to life. Denise nearly shot it. She hadn't had a chance to communicate with the *Shield of Mithridates* in so long she nearly forgot about the radios entirely.

"Hello? Are you still there? What's happening?" the radio asked. Denise recognized Hobhouse's voice.

Balthazar walked over and picked up the mouthpiece. "I saw some of the other hunters running toward the ship. I went down to let them in."

"There are other survivors? We haven't heard from anyone else in a long time."

"Denise, Silas, and Jubal are here. Everyone else is dead."

"Denise, Silas, and Jubal." Hobhouse seemed to consider that for a moment.

"Put Denise on for a moment," Hobhouse said.

Balthazar handed her the mouthpiece without looking at her. "Hello?"

"Denise? Glad to hear that you're still with us. Do you know if that ahool you captured is still sedated?"

She looked down at the radio. Hobhouse just found out that sixty percent of his expedition had been killed, and he wanted to know about the ahools.

"We think Jubal killed Razan and also Gail. Silas and Creighton tied him up. We'll be turning him over to you once you come pick us up," she said, choosing to address the most important things first.

"We've put together an armed landing party to come pick you up. We'll be there soon. Until then, just leave him tied up. We'll deal with that once we have you. Do you know if the ahool is still sedated, though?"

Denise ground her teeth together. "The tranquilizers should last a bit longer. The things on this island don't go by the natural order of things, but I suspect it's still down."

"Well thank God for that, at least."

"Listen, there are people dead here. Six of us died in just over a day. My friends are dead. There's things a lot more important than Yersinia's research and development at stake here. This whole project went straight to hell, and I want to make sure you know that." Denise was breathing hard. Her grip was tight enough around the radio's mouthpiece that it was starting to flex slightly, in danger of breaking in half.

"Right. I don't want to undermine the seriousness of what's happened here. However, when the landing party collects you, they're also going to be picking up the ahool for further study. I just want to ensure the safety of my own people here, too. I'm sorry if I came off as callous. Believe me, nothing could be further from the truth. I just want to make sure we all know what to expect."

Denise's grip on the radio loosened. She took a couple of deep breaths. "Alright, I understand. I'm not sure it's a good idea to go specimen hunting, though. The island is too dangerous." She pictured the ship's crew traipsing along the beach with pistols and shotguns. They'd be torn to shreds.

Suddenly, she remembered something. She pulled the broken watch out of her pocket and looked at the inscription on the back.

"Let me talk to Balthazar again. I want to ask him something about the ship you're on," Hobhouse said.

"Is this the first expedition Yersinia has sent to Malheur Island?"

"What?"

"Is this the first expedition Yersinia has sent here? Has the company ever sent another team here for any reason?"

"No. Absolutely not. This is the first time we've ever tried to study the place."

Denise handed the mouthpiece back to Balthazar, a queasy feeling in her stomach. Hobhouse was coming to rescue them. Soon, they'd be safe aboard the *Shield of Mithridates*.

But something wasn't right. Hobhouse wasn't telling them something. She didn't know what other cards he could possibly have in his pocket at this point, but she didn't like that he was keeping things from them. Balthazar and Hobhouse talked for another few minutes, coordinating their locations, and then they signed off.

"Balthazar, let me ask you something," Denise said.

Balthazar simply nodded.

"Do you trust Hobhouse?"

"No. I heard what he said, but you showed us that watch earlier. Yersinia isn't telling us everything."

"That was my thought."

"I'm inclined to agree," Silas said. "There's something very much not on the table here."

"Things might go wrong here. We're all going to have to work together here, and that means we're going to need some degree of trust in one another."

"What about me?" Jubal asks.

"We're not trusting you with anything more dangerous than a set of Lincoln logs," Silas said. Jubal scowled at him.

"So here's the deal, Balthazar. I know you hate me. You always have, but I have to know I can trust you."

"I don't hate you," Balthazar said. "I just try to keep you away from me."

"That does sound rather like you're splitting hairs, my friend," Silas said.

"Alright then, why are you so determined to keep me away from you? You've done a pretty good job in the past. I want to know what your problem is. We may have to watch each other's backs."

"You mean your father really never told you?" Balthazar asked.

"Told me what? Did you two have some sort of sportsman's disagreement?"

"I always assumed you knew what you father did during the Second Boer War."

"He was with the British military before he became a hunter. During the Second Boer War, he administered a refugee camp."

"That's one way of looking at it."

"What is that supposed to mean."

"Let me take you back to 1899. The Boer Republics hadn't been incorporated into South Africa yet. The Boer territories had recently discovered enormous mineral wealth within their borders, but they didn't have nearly enough people to mine it all. The British wanted to annex the territories, they always had, and the influx of thousands upon thousands of *uitlanders* who came in to prospect and work provided them their chance.

"Most of the new arrivals were from the British parts of South Africa, so the Crown demanded that the Boer Republics allow them to vote there. Given that the populations in the Boer areas had become upwards of fifty percent British in a couple of years, allowing the *uitlanders* to vote would be tantamount to handing the Transvaal over to Britain. Instead, the Boers demanded that the British remove their troops from the border areas. When they didn't, the Transvaal declared war on Britain."

"I was just a young man at the time, and I fell for the same lie that has probably killed more young men than any other statement in the history of the world. The war will be short but glorious, they said. Transvaal troops had already defeated the British a generation ago, and we could do it again. This time, people seemed to think we could keep the *uitlanders* away from our lands for good.

"Like most of the men in my town, I mustered out with the veldt commandos. I said goodbye to my wife and two daughters and promised I would be back in time for their birthdays. The war did, in fact, proceed just like they said it would at first. The British marched into the African interior, overextended their supply lines, and were swiftly kicked in the nose every time. We laid siege to British holdings. We surrounded Ladysmith, Kimberley, and other towns close to our borders. It was all terribly exciting.

"First, I missed my older daughter's birthday. I wrote to apologize. The war was taking just a little longer than anticipated, but I'd be home soon. The British kept marching columns up to our positions, and we kept knocking them down. Even after they were reduced to eating horses and rats, the British towns didn't surrender, though. I missed my wife's birthday next. Then Christmas.

"Then the Prime Minister and his lords seemed to decide we were more than just pests, and we discovered why the British had managed to colonize so much of the world. They had many more men waiting in reserve, waiting to be shipped out and deployed to the southern tip of the world. Your father was one of them.

"They poured thousands more troops at us. The Transvaal didn't have very many men to begin with. There weren't really any reinforcements we could call on. Eventually, they shoved us back from the towns we'd surrounded, forcing the end to one siege and then the others. By June of 1900, they'd marched their way into Pretoria, our capital. It was the end of the Boer Republics. They're simply part of the Crown's South African colony today.

"I was young and hotheaded, though. A lot of us were. I didn't take well to losing. A lot of us could see the writing on the wall early and knew we couldn't stand up to the full might of the British military. Even before Pretoria was captured, the Boer armies more or less dissolved into guerilla units.

"We burned down warehouses full of supplies, chopped down telegraph lines, ambushed troops as they moved from town to town. Basically, we made life hell for any of the troops sent out to try to pin us down. They couldn't control every inch of the countryside at once, so we would simply go wherever they weren't and then give them a good jab when they weren't expecting it.

"I don't know what we thought we were doing at that point. I guess we were all just too incensed to see *uitlander* boots trampling the sacred Transvaal soil or some such rot that we forgot we lost the war already. I suppose we just thought that if we were obnoxious enough, maybe the British would just leave us alone. Maybe if the bees just stung the bear enough times, it would abandon the honey.

"It didn't work, though. The British caught on pretty quick that a lot of the countryside was perfectly happy to feed us, clothes us, and hide us on their land. The British army was large, but there was no way for them to cover every square inch of the countryside or station troops at every Boer farm. So they came up with a plan we never expected.

"They brought the countryside to them. Troops would block off a section of the Transvaal and round up everyone inside who wasn't British. Women. Children. African tribesmen. Basically, anyone who didn't have the right accent was suspect, so they were thrown on the back of a freight car and taken elsewhere. The abandoned farms left behind were usually burned, so that there was nothing for the guerillas to scavenge, and no new crops to gather.

"Honestly, it was a good strategy. It was like something out of General Sherman's march through Georgia during the American Civil War. The British troops would come in, and another section of the countryside would go up in flames. Men in the guerilla units would find out that their families had been moved to the camps and their livelihoods turned to ash. It took the fighting spirit out of a lot of men, though it just made some even angrier.

"My wife and daughters were taken early, and I was wounded and captured shortly after that. I was put in one camp for prisoners of war. They were put in another for civilians, a camp run by your father. They weren't refugees. They were taken there by the British government."

Denise interrupted Balthazar. "And you're still mad about that today, and now you're taking it out on me because of my father."

"No. I'm afraid not. It's more complicated than that. I was never mad at your father. It's my understanding that he did the best he could under the circumstances. However, the British never properly allocated resources for the internment camps they set up. There were many problems. Disease spread rapidly, and malnourishment was a constant problem. My wife and oldest daughter were among the twenty thousand or so Afrikaner civilians that died in those camps."

"Oh," Denise said, not sure what else to say. "I'm sorry." The apology sounded incredibly lame, even to her ears.

"I didn't find out until the conflict had been completely snuffed out. That's when I was released from my own imprisonment. For a long time, I was genuinely mad at your father. I viewed him as responsible for what had happened. With time, the anger faded, though. There was nothing he could do from his position. There was only so much food, so much medicine to go around. I was lucky that my younger daughter survived. Some of the men had their entire families wiped out."

"Where's your daughter today?"

"I don't know."

"What?"

"When I was captured, some of the paperwork was filled out incorrectly. My family was told I was dead, not merely wounded. It took years after the war to prove that I was actually alive because somebody checked the wrong box on a form. However, my family thought I was gone that whole time. When first my wife died, another family took my daughters in. The camp didn't keep track of that sort of thing. There was no paperwork to find out who had my daughter, no formal adoption system to look her up.

"Once the war was over, I tracked your father down. Part of me wanted to murder him, but I was ultimately more interested in getting my daughter back. He'd stayed in South Africa and opened up a hunting shop in Cape Town after the war. I went there and demanded he help me.

"In the end, there wasn't much I could do. Your father didn't have any of the paperwork from the camp, and the British government had probably destroyed everything right after the end of the war and the public relations fiasco over the camps. There was nothing he could do to help me.

"I might have stood there and badgered him all week just out of spite, except he had a young daughter of his own. She was a bit older than mine, but she still reminded me of the daughter I had lost. She had the same inquisitive eyes. I left that day because it was too heartbreaking seeing you standing there like my own daughter's ghost. It was heartbreaking then, and it's heartbreaking today. I can't look at you without seeing her, so I do everything in my power to keep you away.

"After this, I was planning to use my ten thousand dollars from Yersinia to take out newspaper ads in every rag in South Africa to help me try to find her. She'd be in her early twenties by now, a bit younger than you. Most likely, she doesn't even remember me that well, but I'd do anything to be a part of her life again."

Denise sat in surprised silence. Her father had always told her he administered a refugee camp during the war. She realized he'd been ashamed of the truth.

He'd given her the sanitized version of everything. When she was younger and asked why Balthazar seemed to dislike them, he'd merely told her that some people had their own issues they needed to work through. For that matter, he'd probably though that Balthazar hated him, too.

The large man was looking down at his feet. Denise put a hand on his elbow. "Balthazar, I'm so sorry about what happened. I didn't know there was more to the story than that. I was planning to retire from hunting after this expedition. If you want, I could help you draft ads to send into newspapers when we get back to South Africa."

"That's very kind of you. I will have to consider that. Why are you planning to stop hunting? You're the best hunter in Cape Town."

"*Was*. I was the best hunter in Cape Town. I don't do that anymore, though. The only reason I agreed to come along on this trip is because they said it wouldn't be a true hunt."

"But why?"

Denise gave him a shortened version of the tale of the elephants and the Belgian dentists. Balthazar nodded grimly as she told him about the baby elephant nuzzling its dead mother.

"I have seen this sort of thing before. There are people who simply enjoy the killing for the sake of the killing. They don't do it for the sport."

"Yeah. Watching that sort of ruined the sporting part of it for me. In a weird sort of way, I think this trip helped me figure out what I wanted to do with myself afterward, though."

"Oh?"

"I don't think I could sit around in an office all day or spend all my time cooking dinners. The veldt is where I belong. For the past few months, it was like life pulled the rug out from under me. The thing I loved most, something I always assumed I was put on this earth to do, had become abhorrent to me. It all but made me physically sick to try to go out there and hunt more because I knew I was destroying something beautiful.

"However, I managed to shoot one of the ahools with a tranquilizer dart earlier tonight. It attacked our camp, and I managed to stop it thanks to a heavy dose of sedatives. I realized something, though. There's plenty of zoos that need live specimens. Research teams sometimes need to capture live creatures. Game preserves have been slowly springing up, and they often need animals to be sedated and tagged. I could do that for a living.

"I could still spend most of my time outside and tracking animals, but it would serve a better purpose. At this point, I don't think I would do anything else for Yersinia, though, regardless of the pay."

"I wouldn't either after this," Balthazar said.

The radio crackled to life. "Anybody copy?" Hobhouse asked.

Denise looked out the windows and was surprised to see the sky was less dark than before. Dawn was still several long hours away, but they'd passed through the darkest part of the night.

Balthazar picked up the radio. "We're still here."

"The *Shield of Mithridates* is in position. We're sending a group out to pick you up. Get down to the beach. I'll meet you there myself. You're coming home."

TWENTY-THREE
PET HYENAS

Denise stood in a gap in the ship's armor, watching the dinghies approach. Their motors whined over the sound of the wind. She could see people sitting in the dinghies with rifles. At least it looked like Hobhouse had come prepared.

A few minutes later, the dinghies skidded ashore on the beach. Denise, Balthazar, Silas, and Jubal emerged from the shadows under the ship and dashed toward the boats.

The men piling off the dinghies were oddly dressed. They all wore matching, puffed out clothes. No, not clothes. Armor.

The material looked a little like medieval padded armor meant to protect troops from archers and light projectiles. Unlike the chainmail and plate metal knights wore, the padded armor wasn't so much meant to deflect blows as to absorb them with a minimum impact for the wearer. They were stuffed with wool, sawdust, or anything else that could be packed in tightly while still maintaining a modicum of maneuverability and still being light enough to wear in battle.

Today, soldiers obviously didn't wear padded armor. A bullet could punch right through it where an arrow couldn't. However, animal trainers sometimes wore a variant, especially people training attack dogs. Claws and fangs couldn't penetrate the ultra-thick padding.

For a moment as she rushed forward, Denise thought it was odd that Hobhouse had so much of the armor on hand. He'd expected to pick up some large animal specimens from Malheur Island, though. Maybe he'd prepared well ahead.

The crew also all had tranquilizer rifles. Denise wanted to shout at them to just hop back on the boats and take her to the ship, not try to mount any further thrusts into the island interior for specimens. They also wore big, black, greasy-looking machine pistols on their sides.

Hobhouse stepped forward and offered a hand as Denise and the other survivors came to a halt in front of the boats. He offered them a big smile like he was meeting them in his office after an important meeting to hammer out some last minute business strategy and needed to crank up the charm.

Denise batted his hand away. "Let's go," she said.

"Now hold on just a minute here," Hobhouse said. "I realize you've been through a lot, but I've brought in my team now. We can still learn a lot from this island if we can capture some specimens. We'll collect that sedated ahool, too."

"That's not a good idea," Balthazar said.

Denise stared at the men Hobhouse had brought ashore with him. She recognized a lot of them from the ship ride out to Malheur Island. Whereas she'd expected grim looks and worry, but they were all looking at her and the others with something resembling eagerness.

"Not to worry," Hobhouse said. "The crew of the *Shield of Mithridates* are all trained in basic combat techniques. A lot of former Navy special warfare-types. Ah, I see we have company. Gentlemen, would you offer a demonstration?"

Denise turned around. A pair of glowing eyes lurked in the shadows at the edge of the jungle. As Denise watched, a claw reached out and brushed some fronds aside, revealing one of the things the villagers had become.

"Get on the boats. We need to get out of here," Denise said.

Several of the crew pulled out their machine pistols. They checked the guns and grinned.

"Wait, you shouldn't do that. That thing is actually—"

Denise didn't get to finish her sentence before the crewmen fired off a stream of bullets. The arcs of light from the muzzle flashes sent staccato flashes across the beach, lighting up the sand with flashbulb brightness. She was as much concerned for the crew as she was for the creature. She'd seen these things shrug off small arms fire like it was little more than a nuisance. Their flesh healed over too quickly in the moonlight.

Instead of weathering the hail of bullets, the creature fell to the ground, nearly chopped in half. More bullets slammed into the body as it lay prone on the ground, reducing it to red mulch in the span of a couple of seconds.

"That...that was a person," Denise said.

"Not anymore it ain't," one of the crew muttered in response.

"Hell yeah," Jubal shouted.

"How did you do that?" Balthazar asked.

"*Why* did you do that?" Denise demanded.

Hobhouse looked at them. "I'll answer in order. Raul, hand me your gun." He took the machine pistol from one of the ship's crew. Snapping out the magazine, he showed it to them.

Denise stared at the bullets lined up inside. There was something different about them, but it took her a second to figure out if it was the moonlight playing tricks on her eyes or not. But no. The heads of the bullets were all a different color from the usual brass.

"Silver bullets," Hobhouse said, slapping the magazine in and handing the weapon back to his henchman. "Very effective. As to why we did that, I'll tell you. I lied to you a little earlier. Yersinia has sent a research team to this island. How did you know, out of curiosity?"

Denise pulled out the watch she'd found and threw it to Hobhouse. He looked at it for a moment before noticing the inscription on the back.

"Ah, very nice. For thirty years of service. Yersinia does like to reward loyalty. You see, the last group we sent here was simply a research team. They weren't armed like you were. We didn't realize what we were dealing with at the time, although we gained some idea when we recovered their research notes later. That's when we knew we had something really special.

"I told you I'm with Yersinia's research and development division, and that's completely true. Yersinia makes medicines and does research. We also produce a limited number of biological weapons, which we sell through government contracts. Mostly government contracts, anyway. That's the department I'm in charge of.

"This island represents a really great opportunity for Yersinia. Absolutely fantastic. Imagine if the military could wait until a week before any full moon and release creatures pumped full of moon minerals behind enemy lines. It can be anything. A fly. A house cat. Anything at all. A week later, that section of the front is absolutely devastated when the full moon comes out. It's completely untraceable and amazingly effective. First, we needed to test it out against armed subjects, though. Being trained to deal with wild animals, big game hunters from a variety of disciplines were our first choice. You and Mr. van Rensburg here specialize in African big game. Your friends Ms. Darrow and Mr. Quint had experience with American game. We thought it would be good if there was some variety."

"Wait a minute. You knew this island was infested with…with monsters, and you didn't tell us at all beforehand? You knew this was going to happen?"

"More or less. I expected a few more of you to survive, actually."

"Did you know about the maniac who's been shooting at us this whole time, too?" Denise pointed to Jubal. "Two of us weren't killed by the creatures here. Razan and Gail were both shot."

"I did know some members on your team had certain proclivities. The issue was deemed more useful than not when I discussed it with the other people in my research and development section."

"More useful than not? You realize that we're not going to just stand idly by about this, don't you? My friends are dead, and you knew exactly what we were walking into? You sent a serial killer here with us. No amount of money you could offer us would convince me to keep quiet about this," Denise said.

"Yes, well I figured about as much. But really now. Did you really think we were going to pay you ten thousand dollars for a single hunt? Or a hundred thousand dollars for one single specimen? Don't you know that some things are too good to be true?"

"You mean we're not getting paid?" Jubal asked.

"No, I'm afraid not. Your contracts specify that you only get paid if you survive. I put some measures in place to assure myself that the cost of this excursion wouldn't be too exorbitant. That's where those proclivities I mentioned come in handy. Silas, would you please?"

"Did I ever tell you three what Creighton and I specialized in hunting?" Silas asked. "People." He grinned, and then he pulled out his pistol and shot Jubal in the head.

Denise was already running, Balthazar close behind her, before Jubal even collapsed onto the beach. She leaped over the bloodied remains of the villager and fled into the jungle.

"You can run, but I'll find you. It's a long time until dawn," Silas called after them.

Suddenly, a lot of things made far too much sense to Denise. Creighton and Silas had killed Razan and Gail. Hobhouse had hired a pair of killers to ensure that no one got off the island alive. Not only would he not have to pay anyone, but they would take their secrets about the island with them to the grave.

Maybe they'd just killed Razan for sport. Maybe he'd found some scrap of information that implicated Yersinia's plans, something like the watch Denise found, and he made the mistake of sharing it with Creighton and Silas first. She'd never know now.

Most likely, the dishwasher who had disappeared on the *Shield of Mithridates* was their doing as well, murdered and then thrown overboard in the dead of night. They were Hobhouse's pet hyenas.

Silas and Creighton had pulled a masterful coup. By blaming Jubal for the murders and using each other to deflect suspicion, they'd divided and conquered. They'd collected the remaining survivors, knowing full well that Hobhouse was on his way, so he could get whatever information he wanted, and then they would conveniently have everyone in one location for the final culling.

"We're going to find you," Silas called after them. Then he laughed.

She tore into the jungle at full speed, more afraid of the inhuman things behind her than the inhuman things that might be in front of her. Balthazar ran behind her.

They'd been betrayed. Betrayed from the very beginning. Hobhouse already knew about the island's horrors. He knew, the bastard. She and Balthazar were just guinea pigs to test out the ferocity and deadliness of Malheur Island's creatures. By bringing in his own team, Hobhouse could dispose of all the witnesses and save a whole pile of money in the process. His crew would probably receive a nice bonus for this, but it wouldn't cost anything like the ten thousand dollars paid out to ten different hunters.

"Wait," Balthazar said. He pointed to a crevice beneath a rotting log. "We need to talk for a minute. We should be safe if we hide here briefly."

Denise nodded. "Alright. We won't last long if we just rush blindly along like animals being flushed into a trap." She took a few deep breaths. She couldn't hear anything following behind them, but that didn't necessarily mean there wasn't something or someone back there. They vaulted behind the log and crouched there.

"We're being hunted," he said. "We need to be smart about our next moves. What we need is some sort of plan."

"Okay, the way I figure it, our ultimate goal needs to be to get off this island. Even if we avoid Silas and Hobhouse's hunters for the night, they'll just sail off and maroon us, and then we're in no better a position than before."

"Got any ideas?"

"There's only one way off this island. We've got to hijack one of the dinghies on the *Shield of Mithridates*. I don't think we can operate the ship itself with just two people. We'll probably have to disable the *Shield of Mithridates* too, or they'll just follow us. We can motor a dinghy to safety by ourselves, though."

"That ship is anchored out off the coast and manned by dozens of Hobhouse's people. How are we going to manage to disable it and steal a dinghy?"

"We kill everyone who gets in our way."

"I can deal with that. What happened to the woman who couldn't go hunting anymore, though? I thought you basically renounced killing anything."

"It's one thing to kill an animal that's just minding its own business, trying to survive out there in the world just like us. I couldn't do that anymore. There's no point to it. It's another thing to shoot a lion that's about to tear your throat out. I wouldn't be happy about it. The lion's either hungry or feels threatened. I like living a lot more than I like being a pacifist, though. I'd shoot it without hesitation."

"This situation is more like the lion, then."

"Oh no. This is a whole different category. These people set us up to die. They sent us in knowing we'd be torn to shreds. They sent a pair of killers to take us out one by one in case the island didn't kill us all on its own. They murdered one of my friends and allowed the other to die. Now they're trying to kill us so we keep quiet and don't cost them any extra money. I may have given up on hunting, but I have no problem killing every single one of them to get off this godforsaken island."

"Good," Balthazar said. "So where do we start?"

"I have an idea," Denise said.

TWENTY-FOUR
CRUNCH TIME

They angled through the jungle, staying close to the beach when they could but veering away whenever they heard anything that sounded like human activity. Hobhouse hadn't just landed dinghies near the *Hookstadt*. He'd set his crew loose on this entire side of the island.

Occasionally, she could hear the chatter of their machine pistols and the furious animal shriek of whatever they'd wounded. She grimaced at those noises.

What she was really listening for was the sound of Silas approaching, though. Most of the crew seemed to be here to collect specimens. Their priority wasn't to deal with Denise and Balthazar. Silas, on the other hand, was presumably actively seeking them out. Denise wondered just where Hobhouse had found Silas and Creighton. Had he sprung them from some backwater prison? Did he have enough contacts with the underworld that he could simply keep a serial killer on retainer for whenever he needed people eliminated? Did Silas even work for money, or did he just like the killing?

She brushed those questions off. Directly ahead of them, a pair of Yersinia workers stood over a sedated bird. The creature was over nine feet tall, with a serrated beak that looked like it could crush a human skull without much effort. A blood-red crest flopped to one side on its head. Denise thought it might have originally been a chicken from the village, but now it looked like a prehistoric terror bird.

One of Hobhouse's men pulled some sort of gun off his belt, and for a second, Denise thought they were going to kill the captured animal for some reason. Then the man raised the gun over his head, and a bright red flare shot up into the sky and burst in a fireball.

A few minutes later, a larger transport boat sped off from the *Shield of Mithridates* and bounced across the waves toward the shore. The transport boat had a small crane attached, and after a few minutes of huffing and puffing, the Yersinia men managed to roll the bird onto a tarp and cinch it up with the crane. The crane lifted the bird onto the boat, and then the vessel sped back to the *Shield of Mithridates*. Elsewhere on the island, another flare shot up into the air, indicating another live capture.

Hobhouse had obviously put a lot of thought and preparation into this endeavor. There was a distinct and orderly system to transport things to the ship where they could be loaded up.

Perfect.

"Where are we going?" Balthazar asked.

"Toward my old base camp. Hobhouse will have sent a team there to pick up the ahool I tranquilized earlier. I think I can hitch us a ride to the *Shield of Mithridates* from there."

A few minutes later, Denise carefully peeled back the fronds of a large fern to reveal exactly what she was looking for. The coastal cliff with her base camp wedged in the base lay just ahead. A dinghy sat near the surf line. There were no signs of the crabs that had invaded the beach earlier. They had moved on to some other part of the island.

However, there were two of Hobhouse's men in their place. The pair of crew members stood near the downed ahool, pointing their tranquilizer rifles at the net draped form. At some point, the ahool had awoken from its stupor, but it was still too groggy to disentangle itself from the net. It lurched toward the Yersinia men before flopping back down in the sand.

One of the crew members approached, taking short, careful steps as he inched forward. The ahool swiveled its head around and tried to bite the man through the net, but he jumped back with time to spare. As it raised its head to snap at him again, he shot a dart into the soft flesh of its throat.

The ahool coughed and gagged. It tried to swivel its head around to chew the dart out of its skin, but it couldn't angle its head that far down. After another minute, it wobbled and collapsed back onto the sand, still but for its breathing.

Putting his rifle aside, the man who shot the ahool gave his partner a big thumbs up. Denise chose that moment to shoot him with the Savage 99. The man's upper half separated from his legs as the blast tore him in half. His torso flew a few feet and landed on the sand nearby. The man's legs collapsed where they stood, dropping down to their knees as if in prayer. For a moment, the man looked around as if he couldn't figure out quite how he had gotten down on the ground.

Even though the Yersinia men were wearing padded armor, it was never meant to stand up to gunfire, and it was certainly not meant to keep the wearer safe from big game rifles. The huge rounds from the Savage 99 ripped through the padding like it wasn't even there.

The other man stood in stunned surprise for a second, as if his brain wasn't sure it had really just seen his buddy torn in half. He adjusted quickly though, grabbing his machine pistol and looking around to figure out where the shot had come from.

He didn't adjust quickly enough. The Savage 99's rotary magazine clicked another round into place before the man could even duck for cover. Denise's next round caught him in the ribs, a little under his armpit. The impact was like having a truck full of sledgehammers fall off a cliff and land directly on top of him. Every bone in his chest shattered, and the bullet ripped his ribcage and arms off his body. For a second, he continued to stand there, trying to shoot at her. His body took a second to realize that his arms were now a good ten feet away and that he was dead. The man collapsed, jerking a couple of times on the sand before going completely still.

Denise and Balthazar stepped forward. She picked the machine pistol out of the second man's severed arms. She pulled the clip out and examined the contents. Silver bullets, just like in Harrison's pulp magazines. Very useful on Malheur Island, but they would kill anyone who got in her way just as well. Hobhouse in particular deserved a nice, expensive bullet straight through the teeth. He'd paid for them after all. It would only be fair if he got to keep one as a special memento.

She unzipped the man's pack. Most of the contents weren't immediately useful. Some basic first aid supplies. Water. Canned rations.

A couple things caught her eye, though. She scooped up the extra magazines for the machine pistol. There was also a dark, metallic-looking tube that puzzled her for a moment. Then she realized it was a silencer for the machine pistol. She'd never had cause to use one before; she didn't do wetwork for a living. It might come in handy, though.

"Don't mind if I do," she said to herself, picking the silencer up.

"These gentlemen came prepared," Balthazar said, eyeing the other man's hardware. With some reluctance, he picked up the other machine pistol.

"That they did. Does your friend over there have a flare gun?"

"Yes. I assume we're going to call in their collection boat and hijack it?" He picked up the flare gun and handed it to Denise.

"I had something a little different in mind. The crew on the *Shield of Mithridates* will notice pretty quick if it's us steering the collection boat back rather than their guys. However, if we—"

Denise was cut off as a game rifle bullet shot past her face. The wind in its wake blew her hair around as if she'd been standing too close to a train. If the bullet had hit her, it would be a lot messier than getting hit by a train.

"It's Silas," she said. "Into the jungle. Quick!" For all the chaos he'd caused, Silas was only a mediocre shot. It took two bullets to kill Razan rather than a single, quick kill shot. They'd probably only been able to hit Gail earlier because she was standing still. So far, they hadn't been able to hit a target moving low through the jungle.

Denise didn't know where Silas was, so she sprayed the dead Yersinia man's machine pistol into the jungle in a wide arc as she moved. If nothing else, it would force Silas to duck down long enough for them to get into the dense cover the foliage provided.

Silas's laughter followed them into the brush. She couldn't tell exactly where he was. The thick layer of greenery seemed to muffle and dampen sound. Hopefully, that would limit his ability to find them as well.

She pointed a direction ahead to Balthazar. They couldn't run forever. Silas would track them down eventually, and even if they somehow managed to avoid him until dawn, Hobhouse would still pack up and leave without them. Right now, they needed a way to force Silas's hand so they could take him out. Denise thought she might know a way to flip the tables.

Hopefully.

Maybe.

"Oh, Denise." Silas's voice came from nowhere and everywhere. He was somewhere behind them, probably following a trail of footprints and thrashed vegetation. He stretched out the S in her name until it became a long hiss. "Balthazar. Where are you two going? Come back."

Denise picked up a rock and threw it behind them. It crashed through the foliage and landed in a pile of leaves somewhere with a crackle. A rip of machine pistol fire answered the noise. Silas had switched to one of the smaller weapons for close-up work.

"You know, I'm going to miss my good friend, Creighton. He will be sorely missed indeed. We never had much in common really, except we were both what you might call scholars of Jack the Ripper. The both of us were both just young boys when he haunted the streets of Whitechapel, but it was an enormously exciting time to be a young man in London. Creighton and I met when we decided to do some, I suppose you might say, research into the killings years later. It was lovely. We always had someone to provide an alibi for the other. Yes. Of course. He was with me the whole night for dinner. No, I wouldn't know anything about such things, officers. It was splendid."

Silas was trying to herd them forward, to keep them moving. By talking, he was letting them know he was constantly approaching. He didn't want them stopping and setting up an ambush. Even though they didn't know exactly where he was, being outnumbered two-to-one still put him at a disadvantage.

His tactic was working, too. Denise and Balthazar forged ahead through the jungle. He was following their trail. Surprising him would be very difficult.

She spotted a creek she recognized and started following it. What Silas didn't know was that they weren't just running blind. They still had a few plays of their own to run.

"Of course, both being upper-class lads, we were expected to have an interest in fox hunting. We certainly enjoyed it, but the real fun was traveling to some distant corner of the country, to yet another sleepy village where the locals were all so kind and didn't bother to lock their doors at night. Expeditions abroad were even better. Why, when Mr. Hobhouse told us he had a special task just for us, a unique hunting opportunity on a tropical island, we all but jumped at the chance. A chance to hunt our very favorite prey completely unencumbered by restrictions. Marvelous, don't you think so?"

Denise followed the stream and burst into a grassy clearing. She'd been here once before. It had been less than a day before, but it felt like years ago. The long grass came up to her hips.

She purposely squelched through the mud near the creek, leaving a very good set of footprints. Then she and Balthazar diverted into the high grass. The reeds of greenery sprang back up after they stepped through them, leaving minimal signs of where they'd gone.

"Down," Denise said. She and Balthazar both went prone on their stomachs. The grass tickled her face, but her main concern was the rotting orangutan carcass a few feet in front of them. The smell from the corpse wafted up and slapped her across the face each time she tried to breathe.

Silas barely made a sound as he moved. She only caught a brief glimpse of him as he slid off the path they'd taken and noticed the field of long grass. He immediately went into a low crouch and started moving forward just below the height of the grass. He'd stopped talking too, sensing something amiss. Before, he knew roughly where they were as he flushed them forward. Now they were all in the thick of it together. Aside from the occasional rustle of grass, Denise quickly lost track of Silas's exact position.

She could spray down the grass with her own machine pistol, but there was no guarantee she'd hit Silas. If she didn't, the burst of fire would only give away her position and make her an easy target. Instead, she had something a little different in mind.

Reaching down to her belt, she pulled the flare gun out. She didn't need to be accurate with the gun. She just needed to know vaguely which part of the field Silas was moving through. The rustle of grass and periodic snapped twig told her that. He was maybe one hundred feet ahead, moving through the clearing toward the opposite side. Most likely, with no one firing at him, he thought they'd cut through and he could pick up their fleeing tracks again on the other side of the clearing.

Wrong. Denise stood up and leveled the flare gun about where Silas was creeping along. She squeezed the trigger, and a bright red flare shot out, streamers of dazzling light exploding off the central flare.

Silas looked up above the grass just a split second before the flare struck the ground near his feet and burst like a giant firework. Red light exploded all around him, and Silas jumped and twisted in midair, trying to shield his face from the small explosion.

He whipped around and fired off an entire clip off his machine pistol in Denise's general direction, but the blast had temporarily blinded him. Denise had been standing much further away, but there was a big, angry red blotch of afterimage dancing across her eyes. Silas wouldn't have his night vision back for a long time.

The grass in front of Silas started burning as the smoldering flare sputtered burning pieces off into the reeds. Silas backed up, reloading as he moved. He swatted his hand in front of his face, trying to brush aside the smoke already billowing in front of him. Slapping a fresh magazine of silver bullets into the machine pistol, Silas fired that one off into the darkness, too.

Even though he had experience hunting, experience killing, Denise had managed to surprise him with the flare, breaking his discipline. Half blind and probably a bit burned, Silas retreated from the growing fire. He wasn't thinking tactically anymore, he was just trying to get away and keep her and Balthazar at bay. They'd put him back on his heels.

That was probably why he didn't hear the rumbling footsteps behind him. He apparently didn't notice the overwhelming smell of decay that began to overpower even the scent of smoke.

While Denise had been to this field before, Silas hadn't. This was where she first discovered that Malheur Island had its own subspecies of Komodo dragons.

The flames, explosions, and gunfire had drawn the nest's attention. Silas was busy digging out a fresh magazine from his belt when a tree crashed down directly beside him. He stiffened and went stock still as he suddenly realized there was something behind him at the other end of the clearing.

Slowly, very slowly, he turned around to see what was behind him. Then he looked up…and up…and up. Three Komodo dragons stood behind him, eyeing the tiny human at their feet. Ropes of drool hung from their jaws.

Silas bolted. He took off running, speeding blindly through the tall grass. The growing inferno prevented him from bolting straight across the field, so he had to run at an angle toward the jungle. He tried to reload his machine pistol with silver bullets as he ran.

The largest dragon took a single step forward and scooped Silas up in its claws. His machine pistol tumbled forty feet to the ground and landed in the reeds. Silas screamed and tried to break free from the creature's grip, but there was nowhere for him to go except tumbling to the ground in a bone crunching heap.

For a moment, the dragon stared at Silas, as if its reptile brain was processing whether anything so small was even worth eating. A second later, it completed its ponderings, and its van-sized jaws cracked open to reveal fangs as long as a big man's boot.

Silas had just enough time to scream before the dragon thrust its head forward and gobbled him down. Denise heard a loud crunching noise, and then the scream cut off. A single severed leg thumped to the ground, and then the Komodo dragons turned around and retreated back into the jungle, away from the fire consuming more and more of the clearing.

Denise stood up as the fire grew closer and the dragons retreated further into the jungle. Balthazar gazed out at the billowing flames.

"Those flames will be visible from the shore soon. Hobhouse will know something is happening."

"I guess it's time to deal with him, then."

TWENTY-FIVE
STOWAWAYS

Denise and Balthazar picked their way back through the jungle until they had reached Denise's abandoned camp again. The ahool remained still under the netting, and the two dead Yersinia men remained spread across the sand.

"Help me clean these two up," Denise said, gesturing to the shattered dead men. A few minutes later, she threw the last piece of offal into the jungle where they'd hidden the bodies. She kicked clean sand over the blood on the beach, and then she moved down to the surf and scrubbed the blood off her hands.

"Now on to the *Shield of Mithridates*," Balthazar said. "How exactly were you planning to do that?"

Pulling the flare gun out again, Denise loaded in another flare. She pointed the gun skyward and shot the flare off with a *pflunck*. The flare rocketed skyward and exploded into a crimson flower. The remnants drifted down in a brief glow before disappearing in the night sky.

"I'll show you. They're going to send a boat out from the *Shield of Mithridates* to collect this ahool now, right?" She walked over to the giant bat and started to unwrap the net from around it.

"Correct. But you already said we weren't going to hijack the boat."

"Yeah, we aren't. They'd spot us in a minute when we started to get close to the ship. We can't just steal the boat and ride off into the night. They would figure out what happened and track us down pretty quick." She threw the top of the net away from the ahool. If it was awake, it could escape now.

Balthazar realized what she was planning. "I do not want to be that close to this creature."

Denise lifted one of the ahool's wings up and laid down, wriggling under it like she was tucking herself in. The wing was surprisingly light, and the skin was warm and leathery, like a recently occupied saddle. As she snuggled in next to the huge, hairy bat, its musky scent almost made her gag.

"It's completely sedated. There's no risk of it waking up." She started to rearrange the net around the bat so it still looked like it was captured with no interference. Looking up, she spotted the collection boat moving toward them in the distance. "C'mon, there's not much time left."

Glancing out at the sea, Balthazar swore in Afrikaans and then moved over to the bat himself. A minute later, he was tucked under the other wing. The membranous wings were thick enough, that their bodies barely created any noticeable lumps.

Denise lay in the net, trying to fit her body between knots and wrinkles in the thick rope mesh. The heavy-duty fiber was rough and scratchy, but she held still as best as she could. Nestled beside the huge bat, she could feel its chest rise and fall as it took long, slow breaths. Each exhalation produced an odor that was reminiscent of dog breath, but it came at her in a hot, wet monsoon.

Next to her, the bat's body radiated a massive amount of heat. She was sweating, but she couldn't tell if that was primarily due to her own anxiousness about the approaching Yersinia boat or the fact that she was basically wedged into a monster's armpit.

For a moment, the same sense nauseous, creeping guilt she became so familiar with after her failed hunt with the Belgian dentists seized her chest and squeezed. She'd killed people in the last half hour. She'd committed premeditated murder by intentionally ending their lives. That was something she could never take back. If everything went according to plan over the next few minutes, she'd kill a lot more people before the end of the night, too.

The steady whine of an approaching boat engine steeled her. If the men aboard that boat discovered her here, they would have no compunctions against shooting her down. The deaths already on her hands were unfortunate, but she would have put down a rabid dog if it approached her. She didn't have to like it, but it was for the good of everyone involved. Only the dog would probably disagree.

Well, as her father liked to say, if you're going to drain the swamp, don't bother asking the frogs for their opinion. This was a swamp that needed to be drained. She reached down into one of her vest pockets and found the silencer for the machine pistol. If she had to use the weapon in the next few minutes, her plan would be shot, but she'd rather come up with a new plan than end up dead.

Finally, the big skiff motored down and cruised up to the sand. Denise heard it glide to a halt on the beach, and then two pairs of boots splashed into the water. She couldn't see anything at all aside from some fur.

"Oy! Saul! Garret? Where the hell are you pricks? You're supposed to help us haul this thing on board," a voice called.

"Forget it. They ditched us so they wouldn't have to do more work. Let them hang. They'll just have to hitch a ride with another boat later. I'd rather help with the lifting than get stranded on this damn island."

"You think something could have happened to them?"

"Nah. They got silver bullets, just the same as us. That'll kill anything here deader than McKinley. They're just being dicks. What are you? Their mother?"

"Alright, alright. Let's just get this done quick. Hobhouse wants everything loaded, and I don't want to be the one who gets blamed for gumming things up. Man, this is one ugly son of a bitch. You want to hook that end up to the crane while I get this end?"

"The toothy end? No thanks."

"Too bad. Just hook it up. Hobhouse said the poor saps on this island sedated this one themselves, and he wanted a bat especially. The weapons division wants something that can fly."

"Fine. Just keep me covered while I hook this big bastard up. I don't want it waking up, and I don't want any of its friends to swoop down and get me while I'm working here."

"That's what Saul and Garret are supposed to be here for."

A pair of boots worked their way across the sand and stopped a couple of feet away from Denise's head. The net jerked and bobbed for a couple of seconds as the man worked a rope through the mesh.

"Well, if they don't show up soon, I'm going to tell Hobhouse that they wandered off and left his prize bat all by itself over here. He'll probably leave them on the island to fend for themselves."

"Eh, they'll show up. There's a fire going somewhere back in the jungle there. Silas probably drafted them into helping him hunt the last couple of losers the monsters didn't eat."

A winch started to drag the ahool across the beach, taking Denise and Balthazar with it. She suddenly realized that she'd been holding her breath while feet crunched in the sand all around them. She exhaled as quietly as she could and then tried not to make any unpleasant noises as she inhaled a big lungful of bat fumes.

After the winch pulled them up next to the collection boat, it lifted them up and onto the low deck, putting them down on a large pallet waiting there for them. The Yersinia men hopped on and snapped some heavy straps over the ahool and attached them to the pallet so their prize wouldn't slide off into the sea.

Tension flowed out of Denise as the boat's motor started up again and they reversed away from the shore. The first step of her plan had gone off without any major problems. They were headed toward the *Shield of Mithridates*. She wanted to reach over and give Balthazar a thumbs up, but that would give her away. Instead, she stayed as still as she could, remaining nothing more than a slight bulge in the ahool's wing.

Within minutes, they sped away from the choppy surf near the coast and were out into the open water. The two Yersinia men continued to chat amongst themselves, unaware of the stowaways hidden on their boat. After a short skim across the water, the little collection boat pulled up to its big sister.

A hook lowered down from the deck of the *Shield of Mithridates*, and the two Yersinia men attached it to the straps on the pallet. Then, the hook pulled the entire pallet up and brought them up onto the deck, lowering them onto a large dolly. Almost immediately, someone wheeled the dolly around and took it to the cargo elevator at the center of the deck. Hobhouse had a precision operation moving along, trying to capture as many specimens as possible before daylight.

Even though she couldn't see anything, she could hear the elevator's whine as it descended. Powerful arc lights burned in the ship's hold, illuminating everything in glaring detail. As soon as the elevator reached the bottom, the dolly started moving again.

"Got another one for you, Stanley," the man pushing the dolly said.

"Ooh. So they were able to capture an ahool. I'd heard the hunters managed to snag one, but I'm impressed nonetheless. I have just the place for this one. Just the place. Over there in the corner. The enclosure with the extra netting. Yes, perfect."

The pallet was unstrapped from the dolly and shoved off. A moment later, she heard footsteps moving away and the cargo elevator grinding its way back upward.

Denise risked peeking out from under the bat's wing. They were in an enormous cage of some kind. The bars were inches thick and looked like they could keep a dinosaur contained. However, the large cage was actually inside a larger but less sturdy enclosure that was simply covered in a thin cloth screen.

It made sense. While the ahool was still under the effects of the full moon, a massive security apparatus was required to keep it from escaping. The rest of the time, it was merely a normal bat, with a wingspan less than a yard. Once it transformed back to its usual size, it could fit right through the normal bars.

All around her stood more cages, most of them just composed of the heavy metal bars. About half of them were filled with huge, slumbering forms. She saw something that had once been a Sumatran tiger but was now the size of a cheap New York apartment. The beast barely fit inside the enclosure. A pair of massive fangs poked out of its maw like a prehistoric saber-toothed cat. It was also snoring like a power saw.

Another part of the cargo hold was just heaped with carved moon rocks. They ranged in size from the diameter of a beach ball to the size of a healthy cow. They were all carved into a variety of intricate designs, all of them shaped like angry animal faces. Obviously, Hobhouse wanted the source of what made Malheur Island special, not just a few stray specimens. Most likely, the animals he was collecting now would be studied and then disposed of in the process of making his own monstrosities.

Balthazar stuck his head out from under the bat's other wing. Denise looked around. As far as she could tell, the only other person inside the cargo hold was a man in a lab coat with his back turned to them. He was busy at a workstation, working furiously at something tiny with a scalpel. Based on the squealing noises, whatever he was vivisecting was still very much alive.

Right now, they needed to get out of this cage. If they were still stuck in there when the ahool woke up, it wouldn't be pretty.

Denise stepped up to the bars and examined the lock. A massive padlock kept the door shut. She had been hoping for a lever that she could reach and operate from the inside. No such luck. Without a key, she couldn't open it.

She pulled out the silenced machine pistol and held the barrel up to the lock. Nearby, the huge tiger-thing continued to snore. Denise waited until the massive cat reached the apex of another loud snort, and then she pulled the trigger.

The silencer didn't work as well as she'd hoped. She thought the piece of equipment muffled the noise down to no more than a whisper. It certainly cut down on the noise, but it was closer to the volume of someone shutting a heavy door too hard.

Thirty feet away, the man in the lab coat stiffened. He grabbed a pistol of his own off his workbench and spun around as the lock dropped off the ahool cage.

Denise shot him in the head. The machine pistol coughed out another round, which caught Hobhouse's field researcher just above the left eye. He collapsed midway through the process of raising his pistol, falling backwards and slamming his head against the work table. The impact left a big smear of blood down the edge of the cabinets built into the table.

"We're not going to have a lot of time before somebody else comes down here with another catch from the island. I don't think we can clean up before then," she said, eyeing the growing pool of red spreading across the floor.

"If we're going to disable the *Shield of Mithridates*, we need to do it quick. Hobhouse still has a lot of personnel on this ship, and they could chew us apart in a couple of minutes if we get cornered down here."

"We need some sort of distraction so they don't realize we're down here right away." They looked around the cargo hold for a couple of seconds.

"I have an idea," Balthazar said.

"So do I."

She looked over to see what Balthazar had in mind. He picked something up off the worktable and showed it to her. It was a bottle of liquid animal stimulant. He held a syringe in the other hand.

"Let's open up some of these cages and wake the cargo up."

"I like the way you think."

"What do you have planned?"

Denise pointed to a canister of gasoline against the far wall, next to a small generator. The generator sat directly beneath a sign pointing toward the engine room. "Let's blow their engines. The fire will draw their attention and ruin the equipment at the same time. While they're trying to extinguish the flames, we can make a break for it on a dinghy."

"Why not both methods at once?"

"I like the way you think, too."

Balthazar took the bottle of animal stimulant, an oversized syringe that looked like an industrial turkey baster, and a ring of keys off the dead scientist. A few minutes later, all the cage doors were unlocked, and Balthazar was administering the first dose.

He only took little squirts of the stimulant. They didn't want the monsters all waking up instantly. The two of them wouldn't last long if everything down here came out of its stupor all at once. For another thing, giving them too big a dose while they were already sedated might cause their hearts to all but explode as the stimulant and sedative duked it out inside their bodies.

When he was done, Denise shot all the locks off the cages. Even if Hobhouse managed to somehow regain control of the ship after the creatures woke up, he couldn't just lock them back up.

The cargo elevator above started to whir and grind its way down again just as Balthazar set the syringe down. Already, the first creature was starting to stir. The tiger opened one bleary eye and gazed out at them. Its eye wasn't focused yet, but it tried to push itself up into a sitting position.

"Time to go," Denise said. She looked at the ahool and saw it was already starting to twitch.

TWENTY-SIX
ENGINE TROUBLE

They scrambled down a hallway toward the engine room. The rumble of the engines quickly overtook the squeak and grind on the cargo elevator. A loud, steady thrum filled their ears, almost loud enough to drown out the shout of alarm from behind them. A few seconds later, the shout was replaced by a scream.

Denise and Balthazar hopped through the last door in the hallway and closed the water tight seal behind them. Now, the men aboard the *Shield of Mithridates* would have one major issue to deal with, so it was time to give them another.

The jerry can of gasoline bounced and sloshed at her side as she moved. As they drew closer to the engine room, the noise became overwhelming, like they'd fallen into the lungs of some giant beast.

Only a couple of men were in the engine room. Almost everyone was on Malheur Island, leaving only essential crew behind to run the *Shield of Mithridates*. One of them glanced over at them and then did a double take as he realized that they weren't part of the regular crew. Denise shot him in the head as he fumbled for his own weapon, and Balthazar gunned down the second man. The noise from Balthazar's unsilenced machine pistol was all but swallowed up by the omnipresent engine noise.

An intercom started squawking overhead, but Denise could barely hear the words. "All personnel should report immediately. There has been a containment breach in the cargo hold. I repeat, there are subjects loose in the cargo hold. Possible rogue agents aboard the *Shield of Mithridates*. Use extreme caution."

She thought that was Hobhouse's voice. He must have come back to the ship after greeting them on the beach. He could better oversee all the operations from his command center here.

Upturning the jerry can, Denise started splashing gasoline over the equipment and controls. She made sure there was a thin layer across most of the floor and leading toward the coal storage. Once this area went up, they would have to get off the ship fast. Lighting the coal supplies on fire would quickly lead to the boilers overheating and exploding, which would take out everything and everyone on this end of the ship.

The moved toward the closest staircase leading to the upper decks. With everyone distracted by the creatures loose in the cargo hold, the next step was to steal a dinghy and head for land.

Actually, there was something she had to do before they found their ride out of here. Denise turned around and fired a bullet into the engine room. The silver round struck a piece of the metal shaft and created a spark.

With a *FOOMPH*, the engine room came alive with fire. Flames crawled across the floor in every direction. The gasoline was too spread out to create an explosion of any significant size, but Denise could feel the air start to move as the huge fire gobbled up oxygen. The fire crawled right up the walls and licked across the engine shafts. The control consoles, with their levers and buttons, went up like funeral pyres.

A smell reached her nose. It was the scent of burning paint and overheated metal, and roasting human corpses. Some of the ammo on the two dead bodies started to cook off like giant popcorn kernels, adding pops and bangs to the sound of the crackling flames.

Even as Denise watched, rubberized hoses and the insulation around wires started to melt and drip. The heat reached out and bit at her face, trying to scorch her, even from a distance.

She turned around and dashed up the stairs as the thrum of the engines started to rise in intensity, growing to an angry howl. There wouldn't be much time at all now.

A klaxon started to blare even as Denise and Balthazar moved up the stairs. They took the stairs in leaping strides, vaulting two and three at a time. Red lights must be flashing all across the ship's bridge. Soon, they'd lose the systems down here completely, and that would be absolute hell to repair out here. Hobhouse would have to wait for a passing freighter, radio out, and then get towed to a port somewhere. Denise and Balthazar would definitely be to shore somewhere by then, and there wouldn't be a damn thing Hobhouse or Yersinia could do about it.

As they reached the main deck, Denise could hear screams and hoarse shouts. A few errant bursts of gunfire rattled away.

The ship's intercom system buzzed to life again. Now Denise could definitely recognize Hobhouse's voice. "We're recalling Teams Six and Seven from the island. Keep the cargo hold contained. Team Two, find the firefighting equipment immediately and get to the engine room."

Balthazar was about to open the door in front of them when it flew open from the other side. A man with a fire extinguisher in one hand and a machine pistol in the other charged inside. He made it about three steps before he registered who Denise and Balthazar were, and he tried to scramble back behind the door for cover.

Denise raised her weapon and pulled the trigger. A line of red dots stitched its way up the man's chest, the final round tearing his throat out in a great crimson gout. He fell to the ground in a tangle of limbs. The noise from Denise's gun was barely audible above the wailing siren, the shouting, and the other sporadic bursts of gunfire.

She poked her head out of the doorway. To her left, she could see a group of Yersinia men firing down into the cargo hold. Furious animal shrieks answered them as they poured silver bullets down the elevator shaft.

Suddenly, a huge shape swooped out of the opening and grabbed one of the men in its massive talons. The ahool didn't even slow down as it sped upward into the night. A high-pitched scream dopplered away from them only to cut off suddenly.

"They're moving into the forward part of the ship," one of the men shouted.

"Oh Jesus, that whole hallway is on fire," another said.

"Should we abandon ship?" a third man asked his comrades.

"No," a commanding voice said. "Do not abandon ship. Even if we have to kill all our captured specimens, we need those lunar rock samples down in the hold. Team Two will deal with the fire. You need to go below decks and deal with those specimens." Hobhouse appeared behind the men and gave orders with sweeping hand gestures.

The men looked around, uncertain among themselves, but they moved out. They disappeared through the big glassed-in dining room that Denise remembered. There was a way down into the lower hold from in there. Hobhouse disappeared, probably retreating back to the bridge where he could monitor the situation.

A furious orange glow was emanating out of the cargo hold now. Denise could feel the metal around her growing warm, too. Short of flooding the engine room with seawater, Denise didn't think the Yersinia teams were going to be able to save the *Shield of Mithridates*. It might not be as luxurious as the *Titanic*, but it was going down nonetheless.

So long as the fire disabled the ship, Denise didn't really care if it stayed afloat or not. She just needed to make sure that the big ship couldn't follow them as they were gunning away toward the coast of Sumatra.

There was one other thing she wanted to do before she abandoned the ship, though. She looked at Balthazar. "Do you think you can get one of the dinghies ready to launch without being seen?"

"Probably. I think I can sabotage the others while I'm at it, too. It looks like everyone is pretty distracted at the moment."

"Good thinking. We can't do anything about the dinghies they've already dispatched to the island, but we don't need them launching their lifeboats and then using those to pursue us."

"Where are you going to be while I'm doing all this?"

"There's something I should do for Gail and Harrison. For everyone, really. They weren't all my friends, but none of them deserved what happened on that island. I'm going to go air some disagreements about how he ran this expedition with Mr. Hobhouse."

"Air them right between his eyes." They shook hands.

"If I'm not back in a few minutes, launch the boat without me."

"I'm sorry for the way I've behaved over the years. There were some feelings that were simply too raw to deal with, and I only made the matter worse by behaving the way I did."

"And I'm sorry for the way some things worked out. If we make it out of this alive, I want to help you find your daughter."

Their handshake turned into a brief hug, and then Balthazar split off. He went through the door and disappeared around a corner.

TWENTY-SEVEN
NOT BAD FOR AN EVENING'S WORK

Denise took a deep breath. *What are you doing? Go back and get in the damn boat with Balthazar. Get as far away from here as possible*, the voice of reason demanded. This wasn't a matter for reason, though. This wasn't even a matter of survival.

Her friends were dead because Herschel Hobhouse lied to them. He lied to them all, and she'd fallen for every word of it. Not only had he lied to them about the nature of what they were facing, but he'd sent a pair of killers to make sure everything went according to his plans, and there were no loose ends to tie up. They'd come to this island expecting one thing, and they'd walked into a buzz saw when they got another thing entirely.

It was like those German sailors from the Far East Fleet who expected to patrol a few colonies but ended up trapped on the opposite side of safety as the world burned around them. Sometimes, the world handed you a big bucket of crap, and you just had to do what you could to clean it up.

Now, it was time to clean this mess up for good. Denise Demarco, the world-class hunter who could no longer bear to even set her sights on a bunny rabbit, was going on one last hunt.

She slid around the edge of the doorway and moved across the deck. Crates and equipment, abandoned when the crew learned their specimens were loose, littered the surface of the deck, making it easy to stay hidden. She moved from cover to cover.

Somewhere down below, she heard gunfire promptly followed by terrified screams. A bone-rattling roar followed.

A moment later, a huge shape leaped out of the cargo hold. The Sumatran tiger had blood and shreds of padded armor stuck to its claws. Most of a man's body was clamped firmly between its massive jaws. Faint wisps of smoke wafted off its fur.

Denise ducked low as the cat looked in her direction, but there was no problem. The cat wasn't interested in her. Trotting across the deck, it launched itself over the railing and splashed into the water below, leaving nothing behind but the faint smell of singed fur and bloody paw prints the size of hubcaps. A second later, Denise saw it paddling back toward the island.

Good. Denise didn't want it dying on this ship. Once dawn arrived, it would just be another magnificent creature doing what came naturally. If it ate some more Yersinia crew members in the meantime, that was fine, too.

The ship's bridge was directly on the other side of the cargo elevator, above the dining room. She looked up at the windows enclosing the bridge. There were figures moving around up there, bouncing from one set of controls to the next, trying to maintain some sort of grip on the situation.

For a brief moment, she saw Hobhouse. He stood near one of the windows and grabbed a radio. He shouted something into it, listened for a second, and then shouted something else. Then he slammed the mouthpiece back onto its cradle and disappeared from the window.

"All teams aboard the *Shield of Mithridates*," his voice came over the intercoms. "Your priority is now to extinguish the fires in the cargo hold and engine room. Every team is being recalled from the island to help. We cannot lose those meteorite samples. Deal with the fires."

More gunfire erupted from below. Hobhouse must have heard it, too. "The fires, you idiots. Deal with the fires. Ignore the specimens."

Denise suspected that order would be difficult to follow, especially if the specimens didn't want to ignore the Yersinia men scrambling about below decks.

She scuttled up to the dining room and ducked inside. The oak tables were still here, as was the piano. With the heat and smoke, the room no longer looked elegant and luxurious. Now, it looked like the personal hell of a washed-up lounge act playing in one of Satan's crummy casinos.

The staircase to the bridge lay just ahead. Denise ran up it as quietly as she could. Directly ahead lay a closed door. Closed but not locked.

Flexing her fingers around the grip of the machine pistol, Denise took the final step up and laid her hand on the door's handle. With a final pause, Denise tried to swallow, but her mouth was completely dry.

She shoved the door open as hard as she could with just one hand. Her other hand was already squeezing the trigger of the machine pistol.

The ship's captain and his immediate subordinates in the bridge weren't wearing any padded armor, not that it would have done them any good. There was one guard standing in the middle of the room, a massive bruiser carrying a Maxim machine gun in his muscular arms. A belt of silver bullets hung from the side of the weapon, ready to use against any creature that tried to break into the ship's control center.

Denise's first blast from the machine pistol tore the guard apart. He dropped the huge machine gun, where it clattered to the floor. The men running the ship turned in horror to look at the intruder. There were four of them, each with a machine pistol of his own.

Two of them never even had a chance to draw their weapons. Denise's gun chewed through them and threw them against the walls. Blood flashed in the muzzle blasts. The third man managed to claw his weapon free before Denise swiveled her machine pistol onto him. He went down, his chest a gaping mass of red mush and protruding bone.

A bullet crashed into the wall next to Denise, smashing a hole through the map hung there. Denise turned to the last man and speared him through the forehead with a final shot. He flopped to the ground like a bird blasted out of the sky by a lightning bolt, dead as the Roman Empire but bearing an almost comically surprised expression.

None of the men were Herschel Hobhouse. Denise looked again, kicking one corpse so it was face up. Her eyes hadn't deceived her the first time, though. Everyone here was simply part of the crew, not the head of Yersinia's bioweapons division. Another staircase on the opposite side of the bridge led back down onto the deck. After making his announcement, Hobhouse must have gone down below.

Dammit! Denise fired the last of her current magazine into the radio equipment. Now at least, even if the crew somehow got the fire below decks under control, they wouldn't be able to radio out for help. She grabbed another couple of magazines off the corpses at her feet.

She glanced up and saw a group of Yersinia men running from a stairwell near the prow of the boat. They didn't look like they were fleeing. The man in front gave a series of hand signals, and they fanned out and started moving toward the bridge. Presumably, they heard the gunfire from behind them and realized they must have found the source of all their problems.

Denise debated running back down the stairs and joining Balthazar at the ship's stern. If she ran, she could probably make it before the Yersinia team made it to her position and gunned her down.

Then she noticed the Maxim machine gun sitting on the ground. The belt of silver bullets lay spooled on the ground, sparkling in the moonlight. An alternative to running occurred to her.

Grabbing the Maxim, she hefted it up. "Urrgh," she said. The thing was heavy. With a heave, she dropped it on top of a desk next to the window. Adjusting the aim on the massive weapon, she aimed it at the man giving hand signals.

A second later, he all but ceased to exist. The Maxim frappéd him into a pile of dog food. She tilted the weapon back and forth, sweeping the deck.

Some of the Yersinia men tried to find cover behind wooden crates, but the machine gun chewed the planks apart and tore the crew members apart. There was precious little cover on that part of the deck to begin with, and soon there was a scattering of severed limbs and shattered bodies littering the ground. The last couple of Yersinia men scampered back to the door and plunged down the stairs, deciding to take their chances amid the flames and monsters rather than deal with Denise anymore.

Alright, time to go. There wasn't anything else she could do. Hobhouse was God only knew where on the ship, and the boilers were ticking time bombs by this point. This party was all but officially over. Hobhouse would either go down with the ship, or he'd make it back to the island and live to regret not going down with the ship.

She scampered back down the stairs, leaving the big machine gun where it sat. Foul smoke drifted upward and stung her eyes.

Moving through the dining room, she kept her machine pistol raised, ready for anything that might come running in at her.

Balthazar and the dinghy were just a short jog away. All she had to do was get to the other side of the ship. She put some more hustle into her step as she crossed the dining room.

From what she could see, the cargo hold was a pit of flame now. The raging inferno spat streamers of flame upward against the night sky, illuminating the deck. Embers shot toward the stars, drifting toward the hateful moon as it slid toward the horizon.

For a moment, the glow of the flames prevented her from realizing just how close to dawn they really were. In addition to the glow all around her from the fire, the horizon was starting to turn a shade of faded pink. It wasn't exactly a sunrise yet, but in half an hour or so, the sun would sneak into view and banish the nightmares on Malheur Island for another month.

She stepped out of the dining room, and then Hobhouse shot her. The bullet tore into her upper arm and took a hunk of flesh with it. For a second, Denise didn't even feel a thing except for a strange tug at her arm, but there was a surge of hot wetness followed by a howling red wave of pain.

Hobhouse stood pressed up next to the door, a revolver in his hands. He'd heard what happened above and laid out an ambush for her. She swung her own weapon around, but Hobhouse swatted it away. Her arm hung at her side, leaking blood down her elbow. It felt like someone had filled her arm with fire ants and then told them their favorite soccer team had lost.

Raising his revolver again, Hobhouse readied the kill shot. Denise swung her good arm back around and backhanded him with the machine pistol. The gun crashed into his face and tore a chunk out of his cheek.

Reeling backwards, Hobhouse tried to level the revolver again, but Denise closed in on him. She shoved his gun away and tried to maneuver her own weapon into his gut. He squirmed and twisted away. They were both dancing inside the other's range, trying to stay out of the others sights by ensuring their opponent never had a chance to get off a proper shot. Whoever made a misstep first would take a bullet from point-blank range.

Denise gritted her teeth. The pain in her arm was ferocious, demanding her attention. But she couldn't check the wound. She couldn't take her focus off Hobhouse for a second. If she did, she'd get something a lot worse than the wound on her arm.

Hobhouse tried to kick her, and she countered by stepping inside his range again. They were practically chest-to-chest. Their eyes glared at each other from no more than a few inches away as they tangoed through a dance of death.

But Hobhouse had the advantage. He had full use of both his arms. Denise needed to finish the Yersinia executive off quick if she had any hope of surviving. She looked around and figured out her best option.

"You bitch," Hobhouse spat. "You've ruined everything. *Everything!* The research we pulled from this project would have guaranteed us government projects until I was old enough to retire. Hell, with the bonuses, I could retire tomorrow if you hadn't stepped in. You should be dead."

Denise expressed her counterpoint to his argument by head-butting Hobhouse in the face. He lurched backwards, hands clutching at his face. It was the same mistake Jubal Hayes made earlier. She charged forward and augured her shoulder of her good arm into Hobhouse's chest. Even though she'd used her other shoulder, the impact sent a wave of pain down her other arm that made her want to curl up on the deck and puke.

Hobhouse tumbled backwards, falling on his butt and rolling backward, right to the very edge of the open cargo elevator shaft. Denise kicked him in the ribs as he tried to reach for his revolver. Denise's boot lifted him clear off the ground, knocking him to the very rim of the shaft.

"No, you've ruined everything. Because of you, Gail is dead. Because of you, Harrison is dead." She punctuated her statements with more kicks. Hobhouse used his arms to try to deflect the blows, but her boots still landed punishing blows to his chest. "Shinzo and Razan and Marlow and even Jubal. You helped kill them, all for your little test here. There's a lot of horrific creatures on this island, but you're the only one who's a monster."

She delivered one last kick, rolling Hobhouse over the edge of the precipice. Before he fell, though, he lashed out with one hand

and clamped down around Denise's ankle. He plunged over the edge, but he only fell a few feet before Denise became his anchor. The sudden force of arresting Hobhouse's fall caused Denise's leg to jerk out from under her. She landed on her tailbone with a tooth-rattling impact. Her arm sent a blaze of howling white noise up to her brain like a swarm of enraged hornets. For a second, the pain took her breath away and dulled the entire world. It was like the sensation overwhelmed the operating capacity of her brain, and she couldn't process anything else for a moment.

Shaking her head, the next sensation she felt was the realization that she was sliding across the deck toward the fiery pit below. Hobhouse was trying to climb up her legs, and in the process, he was pulling her down into the ruined cargo hold.

She threw out her good arm and used it as a break against the pulling force of Hobhouse. The machine pistol clattered out of her hands and skittered across the deck, well out of reach. Denise cursed and tried to kick Hobhouse free, but his grip was like iron.

As he pulled himself up her legs, he kicked and thrashed. The soles of his feet were probably burning. Even though only her feet and lower legs were directly over the flames, the heat was enough to make the sweat dry on Denise's face even as it sprang out of her pores. Dangling directly over the flames, Hobhouse would no doubt be sizzling like a hunk of fat left on a barbecue.

A moment later, Hobhouse reached up and clamped a hand onto her knees. She looked around. There was no way she could reach the machine pistol, and she couldn't seem to knock Hobhouse loose. She needed another option to get rid of him.

Hobhouse's other hand appeared at the rim of the elevator shaft, his revolver still gripped tight in his soot-blackened fingers. He hauled himself up until his face was above the level of the elevator shaft. A triumphant smile was on his face as he started to angle the revolver toward Denise.

The smile disappeared off his face a split second later as he realized what was pointed at him. The barrel of Denise's Savage 99 elephant gun came to rest against the skin of his wrist, just below the hand attached to Denise's leg.

The muzzle flash froze everything in time for a single second, as if a giant strobe light had gone off. One moment, Hobhouse was there, his revolver pointed at her chest; the next moment, there was only a severed hand attached to Denise's knee. The only other signs Hobhouse had been there were a splash of blood and a burn mark on her pants from the muzzle.

All around her, the elephant gun blast seemed to fill the entire world. But Hobhouse's scream rose even above the blast of the huge gun. The scream went on and on, as loud as any or the roars from the creatures on Malheur Island.

She'd fired the gun with only one hand, not wanting to risk further damage to her injured arm. The recoil flipped the Savage 99 out of her grip and sent it sailing backward. Denise nearly lost a finger in the trigger guard as it launched away from her, twisting her whole body off balance. Rattling across the deck, the gun slid under the railing and fell off the side of the boat down to the sea below.

Denise pulled her legs back over the edge and plucked off the hand still clutching her knee. The severed hand flopped to the deck, and Denise pushed it over the edge of the elevator shaft with the tip of her boots. The flames roared below.

She checked her bleeding arm. It hurt like all hell, but she could move it a little. Hobhouse's bullet had taken a chunk of flesh and a little muscle with it. In time, it would heal. Her other arm had nearly been wrench out of its socket by the Savage 99, but she could still use it. Frankly, her whole body felt like a second-hand piñata. Once she actually stopped moving for a few hours, she'd probably stiffen up and all but fossilize.

That was a worry for later, though. Right now, she had to get off the *Shield of Mithridates*. She looked up and saw more dinghies from the island buzzing in to help their stricken mother ship. Denise had no interest in being aboard when they got here, not that they'd be able to help by this point.

Most of the crew still aboard were probably dead already, either eaten alive, burned to cinders, or shot dead by herself. Not bad for an evening's work.

She took off toward the ship's stern, angling back toward where Balthazar should have a dinghy of their own at the ready. The rest of the *Shield of Mithridates* was already a wreck.

Flames were starting to spread up to the ship's dining room now, and soon they'd devour the bridge, too. No one would be able to contain this, let alone get the ship into working condition.

As Denise half-ran, half-limped away, she noticed that the ship was listing to one side ever so slightly. Somewhere down below, part of the hull had given way, buckling under concentrated heat. Seawater was already moving inside the ship. Now, it was a race between the flames and the sea to see which one could gobble up the luxury freighter first.

Denise reached the rear of the ship. Balthazar was already standing in one of the dinghies, starting to lower it into the sea. He saw her and took his hands off the ropes. A pair of dead Yersinia men lay nearby, their efforts to abandon the ship in vain.

"You look like hell," he said.

"Nice to see you, too. Ready to go?"

"Absolutely. I snatched some extra food and gas from the other lifeboats before kicking their motors off. We can go for a long time, and nobody can follow us."

"Good. I don't think the rest of Hobhouse's men have enough fuel to make it anywhere on their boats. They can either stay on the island or go adrift in the Indian Ocean. I don't think they'll survive either way."

"Fine by me," Balthazar said. "Let's get out of here. I didn't think you were going to make it."

"For a minute, I didn't think I was going to make it, either," Denise said.

"You aren't going to," a voice said from directly behind her just as a red hot revolver barrel pressed up to the back of her neck.

TWENTY-EIGHT
I WANNA WATCH YOUR FACE AS YOU DIE

"Turn around real slow," the voice gurgled. The gun barrel pressed up against her neck burned like it had just come out of an oven. She hissed as her skin blistered. "I wanna watch your face as you die," Herschel Hobhouse growled.

Denise turned around and came face to skull with the Yersinia bioweapons executive. He must have dashed through the flames and up to a staircase. She didn't know how he was still alive.

Hobhouse reached out and grabbed her arm as she turned. His grip was as hot and greasy as a newly cooked burger. The skin on his palm sloughed off in an oleaginous film on her arm, leaving little behind but a claw of red flesh and blackened bone.

His face had all but melted. Almost every last flap of skin had been singed off, and his head was now nothing but weeping pus and angry connective tissue. Hobhouse's eyelids were mostly gone, and his eyeballs were almost as red as the rest of him. The veins inside his eyes must have burst, filling them with blood.

Nothing at all was left of his lips and cheeks except for some seared tatters. Denise could see all Hobhouse's teeth, even with his mouth closed. All the hair had burned from his head, leaving nothing but bright red scalp that gave way to exposed bone. On the rest of his body, his clothes had either melted or burned away entirely. There was almost nothing left of the man except for a vengeful skeleton.

"You two are going down with me," Hobhouse said. His tongue was a swollen mass, flapping against the ruins of his lips as he spoke. Denise had to struggle to understand his words.

He had to know he was dying. Not even Yersinia's best doctors could do much for him at this point aside from slather him in lotion so he wouldn't die screaming. That wasn't going to stop him from committing one final act, though.

Denise didn't have her machine pistol. She didn't have her Savage 99. Her personal sidearm was still holstered at her side, but Hobhouse had his revolver pointed two inches away from her forehead, and there was no way for her to reach it before he could pull the trigger. Balthazar was still armed, but her body blocked any shot he had at Hobhouse's ghoulish frame.

Hobhouse pulled back the hammer on his revolver, leaving a gob of hot flesh on the gun. This was it. This was the end of the line. Denise stared right down the cold black eye of the revolver barrel.

A shriek suddenly filled the night, and a gust of wind hit Denise.

Was she dead? Was that her own scream and the sensation of her soul being ripped from her earthly form by a silver bullet through the brain?

No, it was something else entirely. The shriek was the cry of an ahool tearing through the night, and the gust of wind came from a flap of its massive wings as it alighted upon Hobhouse.

The man screamed as the ahool's talons sank into his gooey, cooked flesh. He was jerked off his feet as the ahool flew past, barely slowing down to grab its prey. Shrieking in triumph, the ahool flapped up high into the night and wheeled toward its roost on Malheur Island.

Denise blinked. The revolver that had been squarely in front of her face a second before was gone. Hobhouse was gone. The spot on the back of her neck burned in the night breeze.

The flames had reached the bridge of the *Shield of Mithridates* now, turning the structure into a great pillar of flame. Below her feet, the ship was tilting at an even steeper angle as it took on more and more water. In the distance, the dinghies of the Yersinia men were turning around, realizing that the situation was hopeless. Nothing could save their ship.

"Let's go," Denise said. She hopped into the lifeboat, and Balthazar lowered them the rest of the way down to the sea. They uncoupled the ropes tethering them to the ship, and Denise started the motor.

They steered toward the rising sun together, leaving the island behind.

THE END

CHECK OUT OTHER GREAT KAIJU NOVELS

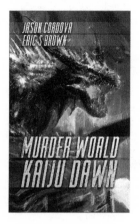

MURDER WORLD I KAIJU DAWN
by Jason Cordova
& Eric S Brown

Captain Vincente Huerta and the crew of the Fancy have been hired to retrieve a valuable item from a downed research vessel at the edge of the enemy's space.
It was going to be an easy payday.
But what Captain Huerta and the men, women and alien under his command didn't know was that they were being sent to the most dangerous planet in the galaxy.
Something large, ancient and most assuredly evil resides on the planet of Gorgon IV. Something so terrifying that man could barely fathom it with his puny mind. Captain Huerta must use every trick in the book, and possibly write an entirely new one, if he wants to escape Murder World.

KAIJU ARMAGEDDON
by Eric S. Brown

The attacks began without warning. Civilian and Military vessels alike simply vanished upon the waves. Crypto-zoologist Jerry Bryson found himself swept up into the chaos as the world discovered that the legendary beasts known as Kaiju are very real. Armies of the great beasts arose from the oceans and burrowed their way free of the Earth to declare war upon mankind. Now Dr. Bryson may be the human race's last hope in stopping the Kaiju from bringing civilization to its knees.
This is not some far distant future. This is not some alien world. This is the Earth, here and now, as we know it today, faced with the greatest threat its ever known. The Kaiju Armageddon has begun.

CHECK OUT OTHER GREAT KAIJU NOVELS

KAIJU WINTER
by Jake Bible

The Yellowstone super volcano has begun to erupt, sending North America into chaos and the rest of the world into panic. People are dangerous and desperate to escape the oncoming mega-eruption, knowing it will plunge the continent, and the world, into a perpetual ashen winter. But no matter how ready humanity is, nothing can prepare them for what comes out of the ash: Kaiju!

RAIJU
by K.H. Koehler

His home destroyed by a rampaging kaiju, Kevin Takahashi and his father relocate to New York City where Kevin hopes the nightmare is over. Soon after his arrival in the Big Apple, a new kaiju emerges. Qilin is so powerful that even the U.S. Military may be unable to contain or destroy the monster. But Kevin is more than a ragged refugee from the now defunct city of San Francisco. He's also a Keeper who can summon ancient, demonic god-beasts to do battle for him, and his creature to call is Raiju, the oldest of the ancient Kami. Kevin has only a short time to save the city of New York. Because Raiju and Qilin are about to clash, and after the dust settles, there may be no home left for any of them!

CHECK OUT OTHER GREAT KAIJU NOVELS

KAIJU SPAWN
by David Robbins
& Eric S Brown

Wally didn't believe it was really the end of the world until he saw the Kaiju with his own eyes. The great beasts rose from the Earth's oceans, laying waste to civilization. Now Wally must fight his way across the Kaiju ravaged wasteland of modern day America in search of his daughter. He is the only hope she has left . . . and the clock is ticking.

From authors David Robbins (Endworld) and Eric S Brown (Kaiju Apocalypse), Kaiju Spawn is an action packed, horror tale of desperate determination and the battle to overcome impossible odds.

KUA MAU
by Mark Onspaugh

The Spider Islands. A mysterious ship has completed a treacherous journey to this hidden island chain. Their mission: to capture the legendary monster, Kua'Mau. Thinking they are successful, they sail back to the United States, where the terrifying creature will be displayed at a new luxury casino in Las Vegas. But the crew has made a horrible mistake - they did not trap Kua'Mau, they took her offspring. Now hot on their heels comes a living nightmare, a two hundred foot, one hundred ton tentacled horror, Kua'Mau, Kaiju Mother of Wrath, who will stop at nothing to safeguard her young. As she tears across California heading towards Vegas, she leaves a monumental body-count in her wake, and not even the U. S. military or private black ops can stop this city-crushing, havoc wreaking monstrous mother of all Kaiju as she seeks her revenge.

CHECK OUT OTHER GREAT
KAIJU NOVELS

ATOMIC REX
by Matthew Dennion

The war is over, humanity has lost, and the Kaiju rule the earth.

Three years have passed since the US government attempted to use giant mechs to fight off an incursion of kaiju. The eight most powerful kaiju have carved up North America into their respective territories and their mutant offspring also roam the continent. The remnants of humanity are gathered in a remote settlement with Steel Samurai, the last of the remaining mechs, as their only protection. The mech is piloted by Captain Chris Myers who realizes that humanity will not survive if they stay at the settlement. In order to preserve the human race, he leaves the settlement unprotected as he engages on a desperate plan to draw the eight kaiju into each other's territories. His hope is that the kaiju will destroy each other. Chris will encounter horrors including the amorphous Amebos, Tortiraus the Giant turtle , and the nuclear powered mutant dinosaur Atomic Rex!

KAIJU DEADFALL
by JE Gurley

Death from space. The first meteor landed in the Pacific Ocean near San Francisco, causing an earthquake and a tsunami. The second wiped out a small Indiana city. The third struck the deserts of Nevada. When gigantic monsters- Ishom, Girra, and Nusku- emerge from the impact craters, the world faces a threat unlike any it had ever known - Kaiju . NASA catastrophist Gate Rutherford and Special Ops Captain Aiden Walker must find a way to stop the creatures before they destroy every major city in America..

Made in the USA
San Bernardino, CA
26 January 2017